THE VIRGIN RULE BOOK

LAUREN BLAKELY

LITTLE DOG PRESS

ALSO BY LAUREN BLAKELY

Big Rock Series

Big Rock

Mister O

Well Hung

Full Package

Joy Ride

Hard Wood

Rules Of Love Series

The Rules of Friends with Benefits (A Prequel Novella)

The Virgin Rule Book

The Virgin Game Plan

The Virgin Replay

The Guys Who Got Away Series

Dear Sexy Ex-Boyfriend

The What If Guy

Thanks for Last Night

The Men of Summer Series

Scoring With Him

Winning With Him

The Gift Series

The Engagement Gift

The Virgin Gift

The Decadent Gift

The Extravagant Duet

One Night Only

One Exquisite Touch

MM Standalone Novels

A Guy Walks Into My Bar

One Time Only

The Heartbreakers Series

Once Upon a Real Good Time

Once Upon a Sure Thing

Once Upon a Wild Fling

Boyfriend Material

Asking For a Friend

Sex and Other Shiny Objects

One Night Stand-In

Lucky In Love Series

Best Laid Plans

The Feel Good Factor

Nobody Does It Better

Unzipped

Always Satisfied Series

The V Card

The Real Deal

Unbreak My Heart

The Break-Up Album

21 Stolen Kisses

Out of Bounds

My One Week Husband

The Caught Up in Love Series

The Pretending Plot (previously called *Pretending He's Mine*)

The Dating Proposal

The Second Chance Plan (previously called *Caught Up In Us*)

The Private Rehearsal (previously called *Playing With Her Heart*)

Seductive Nights Series

Night After Night

After This Night

One More Night

A Wildly Seductive Night

ABOUT

A sexy, brother's best friend sports romance from #1 *New York Times* bestseller Lauren Blakely!

Let me make a few things clear. I didn't go to the wedding intending to dance with the best man, to dare him to show me a very sexy pic on his phone, or to accidentally kiss him in the hotel elevator after the reception ended.

But you know how it goes. Things just happen at weddings...

The next day, Crosby and I agree to put all those shenanigans behind us. The fun-loving, stupidly gorgeous, all-star baseball player might be my brother's best friend, but he's my friend too and has been for years, so it's easy to move on, especially because I have a high-profile business to run.

But since he's newly single and I'm *always* single, it turns out we both desperately need *plus ones*. We agree to "publicly date" over the next two weeks of galas, parties and events before his baseball season begins.

The only trouble is the more time I spend with Crosby, the more I keep imagining how much I want him to take my V-card.

And when I broach the possibility with Crosby, his answer surprises the hell out of me.

THE VIRGIN RULE BOOK

By Lauren Blakely

Want to be the first to learn of sales, new releases, preorders and special freebies? Sign up for my VIP mailing list here!

PROLOGUE

Nadia

A woman needs three things in her purse when she's out with her friends for the night: tissues, lipstick, and a Leatherman multi-tool.

Just the thing for picking the lock on a bathroom door if, say, your bestie gets stuck in the ladies' room at The Extravagant hotel right before the sold-out concert you're there to see.

Who only needed forty-five seconds and that Swiss Army knife for lumberjacks to spring Scarlett in time for the opening song?

This girl.

But when morning rolls around, it's time to change out the handbag arsenal.

Because by day, every badass businesswoman must have three weapons at her disposal when she marches into the boardroom.

Not lipstick. Please, gloss works just fine for nine to five.

Definitely not tissues, because I don't ever let a business associate see me cry.

And save the Leatherman, because wits matter more in the bright light of day.

What's in my purse when I meet with the guys is this: my ovaries of steel, my ultimate poker face, and one hell of a mantra to navigate any conference room or sports arena where I'm the only one who doesn't pee standing up.

Don't be afraid to speak up.

I'm not one bit hesitant to use my voice.

My father instilled sky-high confidence in me, whether it comes to school, to life, or to running the football team he gave me before he died a year ago.

He prepped me to fill his big shoes since I could walk, since I could talk, since I could fly down the street on my bike like the wild child I was. *Look, Ma, no hands!* That was me.

He taught me to be a squeaky wheel, and I aim to get the grease.

I'll tell you when your fly is down, when you've ticked me off, and when you have made my day with your awesomeness.

I'll be your biggest champion, and I'll *also* be the one to let you know when you've stepped in mud.

That's how I am in business and in friendship.

But there's another side to every woman.

The secret side.

I have mine. Oh hell, do I ever. I have a drawerful of classified intel on *moi*.

And when it comes to dating and mating and other forms of associating, I rarely share any hush-hush info. First date, second date—I can't remember when I last had a third—I've never been one to spill the insider scoop on the heart, mind, and body of Nadia Harlowe.

And that's how it's been. Until my brother's wedding, when I asked to see the best man's dick pic.

With that, my secret starts to unravel, and once it does, there's no reeling it back in.

1

CROSBY

It's official.

I'm radioactive.

My relationship fiascos have gotten so bad that they belong on a BuzzFeed Top Five list. Actually, I'm lucky no wiseass has made one.

Confronted with the final bill from my lawyer, I take a hard look at the results of my latest belly flop into the dating pool. My cousin Rachel introduced me to Daria, a motivational speaker who was highly motivated to sell a racy shot of my favorite body part to a sleazy publication.

Fine, fine. I shouldn't have sent Daria the dirty pic in the first place, but you should have seen the one she sent me.

Along with a dare: *Ball's in your court.*

And my balls very nearly wound up in court as evidence of her malfeasance.

That was fun.

And costly. From my comfy couch, I hit send on the payment to Bentley & Cohen Partners and heave a sigh.

"Good riddance, Daria," I mutter. I ended that fling months ago, but the wreckage took this long to clean up.

Rachel blames herself for the Daria debacle, and she's been texting daily to ask how I am or to send a picture of her kittens chasing their tails, or to forward me a particularly witty column from my favorite political satire site.

But she thinks a new woman will make up for the last one being a rotten egg.

How about Rosemary the schoolteacher? What about Marisa the boutique owner?

And this latest one that just arrived:

Rachel: Can I set you up with my fabulous friend Sasha? She's a nurse! She loves baseball, rescue animals, and hiking in Muir Woods, just like you do. Plus, she's a sweetheart.

She's included a picture of her friend—a gorgeous redhead smiling at the top of a mountain she just climbed—but I'm not even tempted.

Okay, I'm a *little* tempted. I'm not made of iron, and Rachel's hiking pal is smoking hot.

But I'm turning over a new leaf.

I stand, grab my keys, and tap out a reply as I leave my pad in Pacific Heights.

Crosby: Love ya, Rach, but I'm benching myself. I am out of the running for dates, setups, hookups, situationships, or more.

Rachel: Really? Are you just saying that? I swear, she's nothing like Daria. I still feel terrible.

Crosby: We're all good. And yes, really. If I kept hitting into double plays or striking out looking, my manager would bench me. So I'm doing the same to myself.

Rachel: Has there ever been a time when you couldn't use a baseball analogy?

Crosby: Life is baseball.

Rachel: Ah. So, what if you miss a shot at a home run with this woman while you're benched?

Crosby: That's a chance I'll take. Gotta run—tux fitting with Eric in ten minutes.

Rachel: You'll meet someone soon who's a sweetheart. I just know it! Keep the faith.

I respond with a noncommittal smiley face. Rachel's a good one, but she's dead wrong. I don't meet sweethearts. I meet bad girls.

I *like* bad girls. And bad girls like me.

But they haven't been *good* for me. Hence, it's time for a change.

Tucking my phone into my jeans pocket, I zip up my fleece—San Francisco is fuck-all cold in February—and make my way up Fillmore Street to Gabriel's Tuxedos, feeling solid with my dating game plan.

The *zero*-date plan.

In baseball, a player sometimes needs to sit out a few innings to reset. And I figure if that works in baseball, it must work for anything else, including dating.

I meet my longtime bud outside the tuxedo shop, knock fists, then head for the changing rooms in the back, where Gabriel shows us the wedding duds.

He's my regular supplier, and he takes care of the guys on my team too. I've got my own tuxes—every pro athlete does—but Eric's bride loves the color blue, so I needed a new one for his nuptials.

I change into a navy-blue tux, then step out to check my dapper reflection in the three-way mirror. "Can't help it. I was born to make tuxes look good."

Eric smooths a hand over his lapel. "Need Gabriel to find a bigger door for your ego when we leave?"

"The loading doors are in the back," the shop owner says, straight-faced.

"Double-wide for my pal's head, I hope," Eric says.

"On it." A new customer walks in, and Gabriel

excuses himself to take care of them. "Let me know if you need anything."

"Will do." I turn to Eric as Gabriel moves off. "You didn't give me a chance to share the love. I was going to say you look like a cool cat too. We both look good."

"Thanks, that was heartfelt," Eric says dryly.

"That's what the best man is for. Moral support and the occasional compliment."

"Everything I could ever want."

I adjust my cuff links in the mirror, catching Eric's gaze more seriously. I need to tell him I've decided to hand over the keys to the dating car for the next stretch of road. That I need a designated driver because I can't be trusted behind the wheel.

"Speaking of moral support . . ." I clear my throat. "Remember that time in eleventh grade when I vowed not to send Avery Forrester a bouquet of flowers from a secret admirer, aka me?"

Eric laughs, shaking his head as he fiddles with his sleeves. "Knew she was bad news when she claimed you copied her F. Scott Fitzgerald essay to cover for copying yours. And yet you still wanted to bone her."

I narrow my eyes as he serves up my teenage woes. But, fact is, I need the reminder. "So you do remember."

"You've been the king of bad judgment for ages when it comes to women." Eric knots his bow tie. "Just like I remember that time last fall when you told me to take your phone away for the day so you'd abstain from calling Camille Hawthorne."

I wince at the cruel memory. "She stole my best

socks. The ones with the giraffes. Those were my lucky socks. I needed them back."

"Dude, all your socks are lucky. At least that's what you tell me." Eric adopts a lower tone, imitating me. *"I wore the hedgehog socks when I won the ESPY. I wore the wolf socks when I won MVP. I wore the penguin socks when I hit my fortieth homer of the season."*

I smile, cocky bastard that I am, as he rattles off my accomplishments. "Thank you, Almanac of Crosby Cash."

"I'm the protector of your socks too. If I hadn't kept you from caving and calling Camille, surely she would have stolen the penguin ones next."

I bring a hand to my heart. "And I love you for looking out for my weak ass when it comes to the ladies." I tug up the hem of my blue tux pants, showing him my footwear. "By the way, I got the giraffes back. Wearing them today as my Eric-is-getting-hitched good luck socks."

He peers at the long-necked animals on my feet. "How did you retrieve them?" He holds up a stop-sign hand. "Wait. Do I want to know? Does it involve you and Holden breaking into Camille's apartment for an elaborate heist?"

"Ha." Holden is also a good friend, despite the fact that he was just traded from Los Angeles to San Francisco to play second base for the city's *other* major league team. The enemy team, so to speak. But rivals can be buds. "O ye of little faith." I wiggle a brow at Eric. "It involves your sister."

He hums doubtfully. "How did Nadia get involved? She's not here in San Francisco yet."

"Got 'em back right before Christmas. Camille was in Vegas then, and she loves magic, so I arranged for a trade. And Nadia had a good laugh when I asked her to score a pair of tickets for a new magic act in the city for Camille—the ransom price for my favorite socks."

Eric shakes his head, laughing. "Two tickets to a magic show for the woman who held your socks hostage? You could have bought another pair, you know. There's this thing called the internet—you say, 'Google, find me purple socks with giraffes on them.'"

I scoff. "I wore these when we went to the playoffs two years ago. Don't you remember my walk-off homer in game two? These are irreplaceable."

Eric rolls his eyes. "You are a special kind of super-stitious. Also, you're aware that you have the worst taste in women?"

"Well aware. That's my point, man. I can't risk losing my lucky socks—or worse, my sanity—by getting involved with the wrong woman again. Camille was bad news. Daria was worse. They are all bad news, and I am drawn to bad-news ladies." I punch his arm. "So, just like you asked me to stand up for you and be your best man, I need you to be my best bud and keep me far away from women. *All women.*"

He strokes his chin, nodding thoughtfully. "So you need an accountability partner again? This is bigger than holding your phone for the day. You need me to be your sponsor?"

A reel of images flickers before my eyes—my

personal BuzzFeed list of my top dating woes. The stolen socks, the contraband dick pic, the missing car, the disappearing dough, and the Cabo vacation that nearly got me tossed into a Mexican jail.

It's the easiest answer I've ever given. "I do, man. I really do. I'm swearing off women for the next several weeks. Through spring training."

Eric lets out a loud, barking laugh. "Oh, that's rich."

I square my shoulders. "I can do it."

"I doubt it," Eric says.

"I have to do something. Women are my kryptonite, man."

He nods. "And you're toxic right now." His dark eyes hold my gaze, like he's weighing whether I'm serious. "No take backs? No excuses?"

I hold up my right hand and avow, "I am nuclear, and I need to change."

"Then I'll be the rubber band on your wrist, and I'll snap like a son of a bitch if you get near anyone."

"So I'm entering Ladies' Men Anonymous through spring training," I announce grandly.

Staring in the mirror, I consider that challenge. I do like women.

Scratch that. I *love* women.

Serial monogamy is kind of my thing. I dig dating when I'm in town and when I'm out of town, dating during the season and during the off-season. I relish the company of women, and I'm a people person who loves getting to know someone.

Can I seriously go a whole two months without a date?

I draw a fortifying breath, staring at my reflection like I'm staring at the pitcher's mound.

Patience.

I am the king of patience at the plate, and I know how to wait for my pitch.

Fuck yes, I can do this.

I'm a goddamn athlete. I've spent my whole life as a devotee of self-discipline—early morning workouts, diet regimens, training, training, and more training.

If I can resist an outside pitch, I can resist women.

"I can do it," I tell Eric emphatically as Gabriel heads our way. "From now through spring training. I can't risk losing another pair of socks, or someone snapping a shot of my prized baseball bat," I say, gesturing to my crotch.

"I'm holding you to it, bro." Eric holds up a palm for me to smack, and I do.

The shop owner reaches us, his lips twitching like he's holding in a laugh, then he clears his throat. "Everything good?"

I give him a suspicious stare. "You were laughing at me too," I accuse, wagging a finger at him. "You don't think I can do it either."

Gabriel adopts an expression as serious as a priest's. "Every man has his Achilles' heel."

Eric's eyes twinkle with mischief as he chimes in, "Crosby, even Gabriel knows of your weakness."

"Seriously? How do you know this is my Achilles' heel?" I ask Gabriel, indignant.

Gabriel smiles sympathetically. "Remember when

you and Holden were here in December buying tuxes for the New Year's Eve gala?"

"Yes," I mutter. "One of my former Tinder dates called while we were here."

"And she said she'd lost her diamond earrings in your apartment," Gabriel continues, even-keeled. "Said she needed them to pay for a medical procedure for her sister. Asked if you had seen them or could replace them."

Can I just grab a paper bag to cover my face? Chagrin, thy name is Crosby.

"Dude," Eric says, chiding me.

"I didn't fall for it," I insist.

Gabriel pats my shoulder. "You didn't. Because Holden and I told you it was a known scam."

"You *almost* fell for that?" Eric asks incredulously.

"Fine," I grumble. "I have a soft spot. I wanted to help her."

"And we want to help you," Eric says. "You need it, man. Not only are you a magnet for trouble, your heart is too squishy."

"That's not a bad thing," I say, but combined with my terrible taste, maybe it is.

I toss up my hands in defeat. I've got nothing left in the protest tank because they're both right. Time to man up. "Fine. I'm doing this. Whole-hog, cold-turkey, full-on woman ban through spring training. Hell, better make it until Opening Day."

The shop owner whistles.

Eric claps.

I take a bow.

"You heard it here first," Gabriel quips. "Would you like me to let Holden know when he stops by to pick up his tux later today?"

I roll my eyes. "Spread the word, why don't you? Hire a skywriter. Hoist a banner."

"We'll all be your no-date sponsors, Crosby," Eric says with a grin.

That's what I need.

Backup.

Accountability.

My guys to have my back.

"Fair enough. You can all call me out if I slip."

Eric stares at me. "No slipping."

"It's for your own good," Gabriel adds, then snickers under his breath, "Diamond earrings."

Eric shakes his head, amused. "Did you even sleep with the diamond earrings chick?"

"No," I practically shout.

Eric holds out his arms in a wide *there you have it* shrug. I could caption this pic, *I told you so.*

"I get it. She was never even in my apartment. But I felt bad for her."

"You're a good one. That's why you're going to need a team of men to back you up. I want daily reports."

"And when he's on his honeymoon, you can report in here," Gabriel puts in.

"Fair enough." I've got a trainer for fitness, one who whips me into tip-top shape with ruthless sprints, squats, and crunches. I'll enlist these guys as my no-love trainers. "Also, Gabriel, I'll be sure to give your store a shout-out on my social media." I run a finger along the suit jacket. "Because this tux is dope."

"Thanks again for finding these blue ones," Eric adds, taking off his jacket to hang it up. "Mariana will be thrilled."

"Happy wife, happy life," Gabriel says with a smile. "I'll meet you at the register when you're ready."

I shuck off my own jacket and undo my shirt buttons, turning to Eric. "Speaking of your nuptials, I don't need to bring anyone, do I? Since obviously, with the detox, I'd rather go solo."

"I hear ya, but fair warning—Mariana does have a ton of single friends." Eric taps his chin, lost in thought for a moment. "That might be like serving cupcakes at a meeting of the cupcake resistance. What do we need to do so you can just say no?"

It's a valid question. I take a deep breath and noodle on the dilemma. Then the answer arrives in a flash.

I have a genius idea to avoid the cupcake temptation. But to pull it off, I'm going to need the help of Eric's sister once again.

2

NADIA

Who authorized all this stuff?

We're talking boxes, shelves, drawers, racks, and hangers upon hangers of clothes. Stacks upon stacks of sweaters.

"My sweaters have been self-propagating. That's the only explanation," I declare from the middle of my walk-in closet.

Scarlett studies the scene, humming thoughtfully before she answers, "It's hard to argue with that." She meets my gaze, her green eyes flashing question marks. "But how do you know your sweaters are replicating themselves and not just mating with each other when you're not looking?"

Snapping my fingers, I point at her. "Maybe it's both," I say, gesturing wildly to the clothes. All the clothes. "I can't possibly have *bought* so many things. It's impossible that I purchased so many shoes."

Though the evidence suggests otherwise—floor to ceiling shelves full of heels, sandals, flats, boots.

My heart thumps harder as I gaze at my pretties. Is there anything better than shoes?

But before I get lost in the beauty of all those pairs, I've got to get to the bottom of this bedeviling closet.

I tap my chin. "I heard a podcast recently about possible scientific developments in nanotechnology involving machines and tubes and rays and *stuff* that would enable DNA and RNA to self-replicate. What if that happened to my clothes?" I run my hand along a fire-engine-red cashmere V-neck that I wore to a December meeting last year. It's folded on top of a cherry-red twinset, on top of a cranberry turtleneck, perched on a burgundy crewneck. "Evidence, clearly evidence. What if my clothes are on the frontier of experimentation?"

"Yes, that could very well explain your closet," my friend says, then purses her lips together like she's trying to rein in a laugh.

"Right? But that's not all." I march out of the closet, ushering Scarlett with me. I point to the pile of silk, wool, and fleece ascending into a Mount Kilimanjaro of scarves on my bed—scarves I tossed there earlier while packing. I stab my finger in the direction of the offending mound, winding myself up even more, because, oh mama, I am wound tight right now. "I have *sixty-seven* scarves. It's simply not possible that I purchased sixty-seven scarves. Either they're replicating, or someone has been sneaking scarves in here to make me look like a shopaholic."

Scarlett doesn't even try to stifle a laugh this time. "Would that person be you?"

Aghast, I shirk back. Indignant. Utterly indignant. For . . . *reasons.* "No. Of course not. I would never do that. Because I can't possibly own that many scarves."

"How do you know there are sixty-seven? Did you actually count the number of scarves?"

"Yes! And I was annoyed that it wasn't sixty-nine."

"Understandable." She fingers the thin emerald-green silk number tossed jauntily around her neck. "I'd contribute to your pile, but alas, that would only get you to sixty-eight."

"Sixty-eight is a sad number, and an embarrassing one," I say, flopping onto the bed, moaning like I'm a balloon running out of air.

Petering out.

Because of that word.

Embarrassing.

It cuts me to the core.

I'm coated in embarrassment courtesy of one stinking email.

An email that's the sour cherry on top of my ice-cream sundae of worry.

"But are you actually stressed about the number of scarves and shoes and sweaters you have?" Scarlett asks gently, setting a hand on my knee. "Or maybe, possibly, is something else going on?"

There she goes, seeing through me like I'm made of Saran Wrap. Or maybe she knows me that well.

Releasing a long, sad sigh, I pick up a scarf, dropping it listlessly around my neck. "I'm moaning in embarrassment. I have too much stuff. I simply can't move all this from Las Vegas to San Francisco, and I'm gross for having bought so much. Just gross."

This minimalism fail is a fraction of the swirl of emotions tangling me up as I prepare to move back to my hometown to run the football team I own.

Home, where I want to be.

Home, with all its complications.

A mother who wants me to find Mr. Right.

An older sister who wants every damn person in a three-hundred-mile radius to love the team.

A brother who worries I work too much, just like our dad.

And a football team that I've moved back to its original city. A city full of angry fans who detest the franchise for moving to Vegas in the first place, and adoring fans with sky-high expectations because we're finally coming home.

Scarlett offers a hand and tugs me up. "Let's tackle this one at a time. Let's donate some of your clothes. That's easy enough. I'll help you sort it all."

"But you're leaving soon. Let's not waste our time sorting clothes and stuff." I make a feeble protest, though I would love some help. "You're going back to Paris soon. This will take a year."

"We can sort everything in a few hours. I'm highly efficient, and I want to help. This is how I want to spend my time with you. Moving is a big deal."

I try to inhale some of her steadiness, slightly more relaxed now that Scarlett has to-do-listed my clothes. "Winnowing down my wardrobe is a good idea."

"Yes. But is that going to settle your . . ." She lowers

her voice, shifts her gaze from side to side, then whispers, "Nerves?"

Ugh.

Nerves.

I hate them.

Scarlett is my best friend, and though I don't see her often, since she lives in another country, she knows my heart and I know hers. But she doesn't know what I've been up to for the last year.

She doesn't know one of the secrets in my drawer of them.

And this one aches a little bit today.

I blurt it out. "I failed."

She rubs my shoulder in soothing circles. "What on earth are you talking about?"

I head to the living room, waving her along. From the coffee table, I grab my phone. Cheeks burning, I click on my email and find the offending message from Samantha Valentine, otherwise known as the most successful matchmaker for discerning men and women in this city.

I show her note to Scarlett.

"Read it out loud," I grit out. "Hearing the words again will remind me that I'm better off alone."

Scarlett sighs sympathetically then reads the note.

Dear Nadia,

Thank you again for your business. You've been a pleasure to work with, and I'm delighted to have had the opportunity to seek a match for you. You're a wonderful, intelligent, viva-cious woman, and I know you'll find just the right man some-day. However, your situation is simply too vexing, and I find that I'm going to have to bow out of playing your Cupid. You're quite particular (as you should be!), but I also simply can't seem to find a man who meets your criteria.

You're a wee bit direct, you like to tell it like it is, and you have, as it turns out, more money than most men I represent. That tends to scare men away. Perhaps consider donating your riches to charity? It might be easier to find a suitable mate then.

Wishing you all the best,

Samantha

Scarlett flares her nostrils. Her eyebrows shoot to the stratosphere. "Seriously? A matchmaker just broke up with you, told you to donate your money, and then settle for a man who's not man enough to handle you the way you are?"

In a nutshell. "Yes! Can you believe it?"

"Who the hell does she think she is? Are we still in the twenty-first century or have I traveled back in time? This is ridiculous and insulting, and I refuse to believe so many men are intimidated by successful women."

"I'd like to believe that too," I say, gesturing broadly to encompass Vegas and everyone in it. "Only this city's men chewed me up and spit me out like so much gristle." And I'm annoyed to the bone about it, but also resigned. "I'm afraid she's right though. Most men don't want a woman who owns a football team. And it's all mine now too." I recently bought out my co-owner, Eliza. She wanted the funds to purchase a basketball team, so we did a deal, and now I'm the sole owner. "Samantha secured me six dates in a year. Six measly dates, and none of them resulted in a second or third. I am one hundred percent undatable."

"That's crazy. What kind of man is intimidated by a successful woman?"

"Let me share a few gems." I count off on my fingers. "*One*, a well-known hedge fund owner said thanks but no thanks to a second date because he prefers to have the biggest wallet in the room. *Two*, a land developer said he had no interest in seeing me again as long as my title remained CEO. *Three*, a personal injury attorney, who has a gazillion dollars because he sues everyone and wins, said one date with me was enough to remind him he wants to wear the pants in his house. And this after I wore a skirt on our date too. My cute red pencil skirt with white polka dots. It was fashionable and adorable."

Her nose crinkles. "And he didn't deserve it. Any man meeting *you* while you're wearing *that* should thank the goddesses of luck for even giving him a shot at a brilliant, bold babe."

"Three Bs? Whoa."

She gives an approving nod. "You're B cubed, and some man someday will recognize your exponential awesomeness. Then you can bestow upon him your red-and-white polka dots and he'll fall to his knees in gratitude."

I crack up at the image she paints. But soon my laughter fades and my shoulders slump again. "Maybe someday."

I'm back to latent frustration, topped with a dollop of where-did-I-go-wrong. Samantha's note was like a shot of *un-confidence*. "And look, I know this is a mega first world problem. Don't cry for me, Argentina, and all that. But it seems men don't want to date a woman who makes more than they do, or who is used to ordering men around. I have fifty-three guys on my active roster, but sheesh, it's not like I'm a dominatrix." I screw up the corner of my lips in a rueful half smile. "At least, I don't think so. You probably need to have sex to be a dominatrix. But even so, I'm pretty sure I'm not."

"Nothing wrong with it if you are," Scarlett says. "But I don't think you're one either."

"Exactly. I'm a virgin." It's not a secret with Scarlett. This isn't my woe-is-my-lonely-hymen speech. My friend knows me, knows why I've waited. My virginity isn't an albatross, simply a choice that I made. "But I wasn't using a matchmaker to ditch my V card. I was using one because I wanted some companionship. But alas, I'll be heading to the West Coast virginity intact, and that's fine."

"Of course it's fine. You'll be ready when you're ready."

Since it seems to be my confessional hour, I sweep my hand out to indicate the scarves in the bedroom and the shoes beyond. "So that's why I have all this stuff. I went a little shopping crazy in the last year. Every time I was dateless, every time a date flopped, every time Samantha emailed to say she was 'still working on it,' I bought shoes. Or scarves. Or sweaters." I dip my head, frowning. "I'm the worst."

Scarlett wraps her arms around me. "You're not the worst. But I think you're particularly stressed out today over everything going on—the move, your dad's legacy, and your expensive, elite matchmaker being a useless twit."

She's right. Moving is stressful in itself, but add in my belief that this was my dad's dying wish and my dating woes, and I'm extra twisted and tangled up.

I don't expect anyone to feel sorry for me. I'm an heiress after all. I have wealth and material riches, and I'm very grateful for that. But I want to do right by my dad.

I want to do right by the fans.

And someday, yes, I want what my parents had—love, happiness, respect, partnership.

The trouble is, all those desires are slamming together like carnival bumper cars.

And that was before Samantha's smackdown made me a woman on edge.

I'm uprooting my life from Las Vegas. Not only do I feel it's what my father would have wanted, it's what I want. My father's biggest regret was moving the team away from his hometown. He missed the San Francisco fans, and he wanted his wife—my mom—to be happy. Her entire family is from the Bay Area, so he vowed to return the team there so she could be near her brother and sisters again.

Then, he fell ill so I'm finishing the job for him. The job of bringing the Hawks home. After he died, I wasn't sure if I was ready to move it back, so I kept the team in Vegas. But when I saw my mom at my brother's engagement party, everything clicked. And I knew it was time to get out the U-Haul.

I worked my ass off campaigning to move the team, to win approval from the NFL and the city. Plus, it makes business sense. Attendance has been dipping here because Vegas is the land of endless entertaining distractions.

I pulled it off, and now I'm bringing the Hawks to a city where the team is both hated and loved.

But at least I can see my mother, sister, and brother more regularly.

That is, when I'm not working. I have a ton of events already lined up in San Francisco, back-to-back meetings with the city regarding tax breaks, appointments with legal counsel over business operations, and interviews with a slew of candidates for the position of general manager.

Can you say *busy*?

I want to do my father proud. When he died, he split his businesses down the middle, leaving them to his three kids—Eric runs the private equity firm, Brooke oversees the real estate holdings, and I've got the team.

I need to go to San Francisco ready to tackle the job and that's all. I don't need sixty-seven scarves to pull that off.

Or countless shoes.

I need to shed the reminders of my datelessness.

Decisively, I snap, "You know what? Screw Samantha Valentine. I don't need a man. My job is to bring the Lombardi Trophy to the Hawks."

Scarlett waves imaginary pom-poms. "Two, four, six, eight, who do we appreciate? Nadia!"

I thrust a hand in the air like an orator. "I'm going to San Francisco embracing singlehood. I've tried dating for the past year, but I'm moving on. I have bigger fish to fry," I declare. "And it shall begin with a culling of the clothes."

"Brava," Scarlett says, clapping.

Emboldened by her friendship and by my newfound determination, I saunter into my bedroom, tossing my phone on the edge of the bed then heading for the closet, where I grab a pair of black heels. "Shoes are only a sublimation. Shoes are better than necklaces, better than earrings, better than sex, or so I've heard, but it's time to say goodbye."

Scarlett clucks her tongue. "Hmm. I'm going to have to disagree on that last one. But regardless, let's donate that pair of heels." She motions to a pair of silver heels with a slim strap. "How about those too? They look brand-new, but I was with you when you bought them a year ago. Have they even been worn?"

I square my shoulders, owning it. "I bought those as solace after Samantha told me the land developer also didn't care for me having—*gasp!*—opinions."

"Opinions are sooo dangerous," she says, her voice dripping with mockery. "Just keep them to yourself, you pretty little thing." She tucks the silver shoes under her arm and points to a pair of red stilettos that look fresh out of the box. "What's their story?"

"If memory serves, I purchased those shoes after my fifty-ninth dateless night in a row. That was the lull between the *quit your job* guy and an off-the-Strip casino owner who wanted to know if I would use a sperm donor if I didn't find a man soon."

My friend's jaw crashes to the floor, then the one below it, maybe even to the underground parking garage of my skyscraper. "Please tell me you put him in his place. Please, please, please."

My lips curve up in a grin. "I said, 'If I do, I'll be asking for a man with a high IQ and a big heart. Basically, the opposite of you,'" I say with fiendish glee. "I came up with that on the spot."

"You zinged a deserving target. Nice." She frowns in disgust, shaking her head as she adds the red heels to the donation collection. "And these are a definite donation. We're getting rid of all the pity shoes, because there is no pity needed in your life."

When we're done, the pile on my bed has grown ceiling-high, a mountain of donatable goods.

"This is good," Scarlett says. "You're cleaning house. Starting fresh."

Buoyed by her support, I nod enthusiastically. "I'm going to San Francisco ready to conquer the world of football and franchises and getting back to the Super Bowl. I don't care about dating. I don't care about anything but a few pairs of shoes for the events I need to go to. I will take the city by storm, bring home the Lombardi Trophy, and do my father proud."

She grabs her phone, clicks on her music app, and belts out the first anthemic notes of Beyoncé's "Run the World" as it blasts through my penthouse.

We rock out to the woman-power anthem as we scoop up my clothes, shoes, scarves, and purses, folding them neatly, then tucking them into shopping bags to take to Dress for Success, a fantastic non-profit that helps women get back on their feet with the right clothes for job hunting.

When the tune ends, I'm ready to state my intention with Scarlett as witness. "From now on, no more matchmaking, no more shoe sublimating. There's just the team."

"I'm rooting for you," she says. "You can do anything you set your mind to."

Maybe, but there's one thing I need to sort through still.

"Do I have to get rid of my large family of vibrators?"

"Hate to break it to you, but no one takes those for donation," she says in a stage whisper.

I roll my eyes. "I know that. I'm simply wondering if I should cull them as part of this house cleaning?" But I dismiss that crazy thought stat. "Pretend I didn't say that. I would never do such a terrible thing. Let's go sort the little darlings."

Scarlett gives me a look that says *oh no you didn't*.

"News flash. I wasn't asking you to touch them," I say.

"News flash. I wasn't going to touch the vibrators," she retorts.

I slide open the nightstand then pack up my friends. "I have a feeling I'm going to be needing these the day I arrive." I raise my favorite pink rabbit in my right hand, and pledge, "I hereby declare my allegiance to vibrators and only vibrators. All of them. We have a polyamory thing going on."

"A little reverse harem with your battery-operated friends?" Scarlett asks with a quirk of her brow.

"I am their queen, and they live to serve me." As I pack the pink one, my phone beeps from the bed. "Can you grab that?"

She does and scans the screen. "Crosby. It's a text."

My lips curve up in a grin at the mention of my brother's best friend. "Read it to me, please."

She adopts a masculine tone. *"Hey, Wild Girl, want to buddy up at your bro's wedding?"*

I laugh at her imitation. Crosby called in a favor a few months ago, and I was happy to help. He's Eric's friend, but I've always had a good time with him.

Her eyes twinkle as she meets my gaze. "Wild Girl? He calls you Wild Girl?"

I wave a hand dismissively. "He called me that when I was younger. He means nothing by it," I say, even as my cheeks flush, even as my skin heats. "I've known him for years."

"And he wants to 'buddy up'?" She sketches air quotes.

I roll my eyes. "It's not code for sex. I've known Crosby since he and Eric were ten and built dams in the stream behind our house in San Rafael. Since they were twelve, filming themselves with lightsabers doing *Star Wars* moves in the garage. That's why it says 'buddy up.' I'm his buddy too."

"Why are your cheeks flushing, then?" she asks, amused. No, utterly delighted.

I raise a hand to my cheek as if to hide the heat.

But it's spreading.

"It's just . . . hot in here," I mutter.

Her eyebrows wiggle. Her lips twitch. "Is that so? Or is this Crosby a McHottie? I just can't remember from the last time you mentioned him," she says, egging me on. "Let me refresh my recollection of the man you've known for so long." She taps around on my phone for a moment, then gasps. "Aha! He is!"

She shows me Crosby's team headshot as if she's never seen his image before either, but obviously I know what he looks like too. Heck, there are photos of him and Eric in our family home. Pics of Crosby, Eric, Brooke, and me. He's a feature in our lives.

But damn, does he ever look good in his team headshot, with his ball cap on and his uniform snug across his broad chest, the short sleeves showing off those hard-won biceps and those pants hugging his muscular thighs.

My God, baseball uniforms are just delish.

Of all the sports uniforms, those are my favorite.

But the best part is he's cracking a hint of a smile, his jaw is lined with his trademark stubble, and his blue eyes are sparkling with the promise of naughty secrets.

He's got the whole sexy-athlete vibe working overtime.

And Scarlett knows it. "Have fun *buddying up* with the hottest player in Major League Baseball at your brother's wedding."

Buddies.

We're just buddies.

That's all.

As soon as she leaves, I pounce on my phone and call him back so fast.

"Hey, Wild Girl," he says in a voice that makes me feel like he can deliver on the promise of those blue eyes.

3

CROSBY

Wild Girl.

It's hard for me to call her anything but the nick-name I gave her when we were kids.

Ever since I met her when we were in grade school, Nadia Harlowe's been a Tasmanian devil. A whirling dervish of energy, spark, and all kinds of sass.

Two years younger than I am, she was the definition of the word *spitfire*. She was always joining Eric and me for sports in the park, swinging a bat or playing running back in a flag football game. At home, she loved to blast her music loud in her bedroom, pretend she was singing into a hairbrush, and challenge us to sing-offs, usually Kelly Clarkson, Gwen Stefani, or Lifehouse. Full of confidence and smarts, Nadia was never quiet at the dinner table. Over chicken and rice, she'd rattle off questions about the electoral college, equal pay, or famous female scientists.

She made every meal at the Harlowe house an

engaging debate, and that fiery spirit traveled with her out of the house too.

One weekend when I was seventeen and she was fifteen, her family took me skiing with them in Tahoe. Fearless to the max, Nadia raced down the trails at Sugar Bowl on her snowboard, schussing over moguls, cruising around bends, and tackling every kind of terrain.

Always ready to do it again.

That's why she's the Wild Girl, the name I gave her in my phone.

While walking down Fillmore, passing a boutique with scarves and wrap thingamajigs in the window, my phone rings and a picture of her flashes across the screen.

It's a shot of her from the LGO Excellence in Sports Awards Gala last year. We both attended—her for the football awards, me for baseball. When I saw her at the gala, I marched up to her, wrapped her in my arms, kissed her cheek, and said, "Please tell me you saved a spot on your dance card for me."

She laughed, hugged me back, and said, "If they ever have dancing at these awards, I'm outta here."

We grabbed a drink instead, caught up, and toasted to next year, since neither of us had won that night.

But damn, did she look good. And I'm glad I took that shot of her decked out in a ruby-red dress that worshipped her curves, her dark hair pinned up in one of those fancy buns and her eyes looking all smoky.

I smile when smokey-eyed, red-dress-wearing Nadia appears on my screen.

"Wild Girl," I say, nice and easy when I answer.

"Wannabe All-Star," she tosses back, using her nickname for me when we were younger and I was all hopes, dreams, and bright-eyed bravado.

"You do know you can just call me All-Star now? You can drop the 'wannabe' part," I say as I adjust the phone against my ear.

"Hmm. But I do like keeping you on your toes. If I don't, who will?"

Considering what just went down at Gabriel's, a whole damn menagerie of dudes will. But I don't want to think about the guys while talking to a woman who makes red dresses look like they throw themselves at her feet and beg for the chance to grace her curves. "You're the only one, Nadia. So keep it up."

"Speaking of your toes, how are your lucky socks faring?"

Stopping at the corner, I wiggle them in my shoes. "Happy as clams to be home and safe with their keeper. I even have on my purple ones today."

"And is it your lucky day?"

With a grin that she can't see but I bet she can hear, I say, "I'm on the phone with you. How could I be anything but the luckiest?"

"Perfect answer, Mr. Purple Socks," she says, her laughter floating across the phone line.

"Tell me stuff," I say as the light changes and I cross the street. "Are you stoked to come back to San Francisco?"

"I am counting down the days," she says, but her tone is mixed—a little too cheery, and a little bit melancholy.

"Bullshit," I say as I stride down the hill, making my way to the gym a few blocks away. "I hear a little reticence in your voice."

"And why do you think that is?"

"Because you're a Vegas woman," I say as my gaze catches on the window display in the lingerie shop I'm passing—red lacy bras and white teddies and all sorts of itty-bitty numbers that would look fabulous on—

Whoa.

Stop, brain. Stop thinking about women. I force my amphibian mind away from pretty underthings and lovely curves, from soft skin and the scent of a woman.

"You're going to miss Vegas, Nadia. You love to gamble. You love the neon and the billboards. You love to clean up at the poker table."

"That is true. I do kill it at poker. Maybe I'll just have to start my own game in San Francisco, open a casino, bring the high rollers there."

I can see that perfectly, can picture her doing precisely that. "I've got all sorts of teammates who would love a high stakes game of poker."

"Fantastic. Molly's Game will be my next gig," she says, then she sighs, but it sounds contented. "And truth be told, I'll miss my friends here, but I'm excited to return to the Bay Area. It's been a while, but it's always good to be home, even though I have a ton on my plate when I arrive."

"Let me know if you need anything when you get here, okay?"

"I will. I promise."

"I'm holding you to it. And it'll be good to have you here. It's been way too long," I say.

"That's why I did a crazy thing. I called as a reply to your text. Isn't that wild?"

"Among the many reasons you're the Wild Girl," I say. "I mean, hell. Who does that? Calling in response to a text? You're all about shaking things up."

"That's me," she says lightly, then shifts her tone to a bit more serious. "But tell me something about this 'buddy up' request. Last time we talked when I was in Paris for business, you said you weren't sure if you were bringing anyone to Eric's wedding. Did something change?"

Do I tell her or not? Do I let her know I've sworn off women? "I'm not bringing anyone," I say, not entirely answering, since I'm not entirely sure what to tell her. Instead, I seize the chance to needle her. "You just had to drop that you were in Paris for business."

She laughs. "I'm not just dropping it in. I *was* actually there. I'm trying to expand the NFL into Europe more, and I had meetings with marketers."

I hum appreciatively as I reach the next block. "It is so sexy when you talk about marketing and expanding sports to other places. Can you please do that for baseball too?"

"If I owned a baseball team, I damn well would," she says.

Does she have any idea how hot it is that she owns a team? That is equator-level heat. A powerful woman. A confident woman. A brilliant woman. Nadia Harlowe has got it going on.

Wait.

Don't do that either, brain. Do not think about your buddy's sister like that. Hell, do not think about any woman like that right now. You're in time-out with the ladies.

"Then buy a baseball team," I say, sticking to the conversation rather than the director's track of innuendo running through my mind.

She laughs. "Rules. The NFL has them. If I buy a baseball team, it has to be in San Francisco, so do you want me to buy your team or the Dragons?"

I wince. "Ouch. Don't talk about buying my local rival."

"How about I just move back to San Francisco and run the football team?"

"Fine, be that way. But you know you love baseball more."

"I love both sports, and I love interesting stories. So what's the story with you suddenly wanting to buddy up? And are you enlisting me as a fill-in date? Is this like the start of a romantic comedy where we agree to plus-one each other? Ooh, can we call our story *Plus-Oneing with the Best Man?*"

"Let's sell the movie rights and make a mint," I quip. Then I answer truthfully. "Yes, I was hoping you can plus-one the best man, since I'm not bringing anyone. In fact, I am taking a break from dating. I am officially off the market from now through spring training. Probably beyond too."

She laughs as I head down the next block. "I'm sure there's a fabulous story behind that. But I'm going to wait to hear it in person."

"You're already ordering up the entertainment you want from me at the wedding table? I hope I can deliver."

"I sure hope you can too, Crosby."

"I'll be prepping all of my best jokes for you. All of my best stories. I'm going to be thoroughly entertaining in my blue tux. Did you know Mariana has a thing for blue?"

"Hello? Bridesmaid here. Yes, I knew that. And I have a blue dress ready for the event. Mariana has great taste in bridesmaids' dresses, and this one is quite pretty."

"So is my blue tux. It's got some badass ruffles on it and bell-bottoms."

She makes a husky growling sound low in her throat. "Mmm. Hold me back."

I blink, processing that sound. Did Nadia always sound this . . . sexy? Maybe? Possibly. Hell, she looks sexy, so it stands to reason she sounds that way too.

"It'll be hard to hold anyone back once you see me in my wedding ruffles," I tease. "Consider this your fair warning, because I look pretty damn handsome in it."

"So you think I won't be able to keep my hands off you? Because I don't think that's going to be a problem," she says, a little flirtier than usual.

But perhaps I'm reading into her tone, hearing things that shouldn't be there. She and I have always had fun together. Have always indulged in a flirty, friendly vibe.

That's just who we are. Nothing more, nothing less.

"I guess we'll just have to see about that. Maybe I

won't be able to keep my hands off of you," I toss back, and then I want to smack myself as I near the gym.

She chuckles lightly, in a sort of challenging tone, as if her laugh is saying *just try me*. "We'll just have to see when it comes to the big day," she says.

"I guess we'll see who's best at hands-off."

"We will indeed."

Why am I talking to her like this? Like I'm going to be touching her? I'm not. We are friends. She's my buddy's sister. I've known her forever. I'm not going to touch her. Ever. She's my plus-one at her brother's wedding. That's what I need her for.

I reach Total Body Fitness, a little reluctant to end this conversation. It's so easy to talk to her. Always has been. "Hey," I say, gentler.

"Hey to you."

"I'm glad you're coming back to town," I say, speaking from my heart, not my need to serve up sarcasm. "It's been a while."

"It has been. Too long, Crosby," she says, her voice warm and tender.

And there we go. We're us again. Like we've always been. Two good friends. A man and a woman who've known each other forever.

"And I appreciate you being my plus-one. It'll be good to see you," I say.

"And it'll be good for me to keep you from dating," she says.

"True. That is true," I say with a smile. I'm about to push open the door to the gym when an idea flashes before me. "Do I get to see this blue dress beforehand? You know, if I need to get you a corsage."

"It's a wedding. It's not prom. But a corsage and boutonniere do sound kind of fun." She takes a beat, humming. "Actually, Mariana is big on flowers. She always wants people to have the flowers they like best. And I'm pretty sure my mom said the other bridesmaids were going to have them and they were picking out their own, so yes, let's do it."

"I'm on it. Let's do it up. You better send me a picture of your dress so I know exactly what color to get when I go to the florist's shop," I say.

"Consider it done."

We say goodbye, and I head into the gym, more excited than I expected to be to go to my best friend's wedding.

And not simply because I'm happy as hell to see my best friend get hitched.

There's a spring in my step as I imagine his sister in a blue dress.

How it might dip between her breasts. How it might swing on her hips. Land on her knees.

But that's dangerous. I shouldn't think of her like that.

Even so, when a picture lands on my phone as I'm working my quads, my breath hitches.

The air rushes from my lungs.

And it's not from the extra weight. It's not from the workout.

It's from this goddamn dress and the way she looks in it.

She didn't merely send me a shot of her dress, artfully laid out on the bed.

She sent me a picture of her in a boutique somewhere in Vegas, trying on the dress. It's a mirror selfie, and it is smoking.

Nadia's all done up, her lips pursed like she's about to blow a kiss, and she is wearing the fuck out of a sapphire-blue dress that clings to her trim, toned body.

This dress defies any notion of hideous bridesmaid's attire.

This dress is all sex appeal and secrets.

It looks like exactly the type of dress that's going to make it hard for me to sit next to Nadia Harlowe.

But that's the kind of thinking I can't entertain.

Instead, I entertain the triceps machine and do my best to push the forbidden thoughts of this woman out of my head.

4

NADIA

One week later, Eric picks me up at the airport.

"It's the blushing groom," I say as I sail past security into a big-brother hug.

"Yes, that's me," he says, wrapping his arm around me, then letting go. "I'm all nervous and atwitter before the wedding."

"Aww." I pat his shoulder. "Do you want me to make sure you get a foot rub and a massage before the big day? So you can relax?" I ask, hoisting my purse onto my shoulder as he takes my carry-on and we weave through the crowds.

"That sounds perfect. Why don't you and I spend a day at the spa? Get our hair done." He slides a hand through his dark-brown hair, the same shade as mine. "We'll relax and get hot stone treatments or something."

"Perfect. I want to make sure you're totally relaxed before you walk down the aisle," I say, squeezing his arm playfully as we make our way through the SFO airport.

He shakes his head, amused. "You do know that Mariana is actually walking down the aisle toward me?"

"Oh my God, I had no idea. Thanks for clarifying," I add.

Eric raises his gaze ceilingward, then says, over-the-top aggrieved, "My fiancée, my older sister, and my younger sister give me a hard time every single day."

"Of course we do. And you wouldn't want it any other way," I say, bopping his nose.

"Speaking of walking down the aisle, Mariana wants you and Crosby to walk together."

That piques my interest.

Makes my skin tingle a little bit.

Just from the mention of his name.

Exactly the reaction I can't have.

"Why's that?" I ask, focusing on the wedding plan, not the tingles plan. "Crosby is the best man, and Mariana's sister is the maid of honor."

Eric holds up a making-a-point finger. "But Mariana's sister's husband is a groomsman, and Mariana thought they'd enjoy walking together, so she put you and Crosby together."

I smile widely. "What Mariana wants, Mariana shall have."

"I'm pretty sure that's the secret to a happy marriage. But," he says, his tone downshifting to serious as we reach the exit, "no dating him."

A cough bursts from me. "Did you seriously just warn me not to date your best friend? Doesn't it usually go the other way around?"

Eric shakes his head, his dark-brown eyes intense.

"Crosby is in time-out right now. I'm personally in charge of making sure all women stay far, far away from him."

I scoff. "I have no interest in dating Crosby or anyone."

That's the truth, the whole truth, and nothing but.

"Good. Because it's my duty to keep him on the wagon. No dating, no women, no nothing."

"Trust me, not dating Crosby will be just like . . . how it's always been. Crosby and I are friends."

"Good. Then you'll do your part to keep him woman-free too," he says.

"Of course," I say quickly, because he's definitely a friend, so I'm definitely down with the program.

As we slide into the town car, I tell myself that heeding Eric's warning will be as easy as a quarterback lobbing a pass to a wide-open receiver.

And the receiver running it in for a touchdown.

Except there will be no scoring with Crosby.

Mark my words.

* * *

At the night-before-the wedding dinner the next Friday, I walk into the private room at one of San Francisco's swankiest celebrity chef restaurants, my eyes scanning the place for all the people I love—my mom, my sister, my brother, his bride, and all my extended family.

Warmth spreads through me at the sight of all this family. I say hi to my mom, sister, brother, and Mariana, looking gorgeous with her waves of brown hair, and her olive skin.

There's no sign of Crosby, until a hand clasps my shoulder.

And the faint scent of pine mixed with soap wafts past my nose.

For a sliver of a second, I close my eyes.

Then I open them, turn around, and ignore the hell out of the swoopy sensations in my stomach.

Crosby's here, looking as handsome as he did at the LGO Excellence in Sports Awards Gala.

But he's always been handsome, and I've always handled it just fine.

Because we're just friends.

"A hundred bucks says your brother's teary-eyed by the end of the night when he gives his toast," he says in that gravelly, sexy voice that sends a dangerous zing down my spine.

Zero in on the way we are.

"You're already throwing down bets? The dinner hasn't even started."

He lifts a shoulder, all casual and confident. "I know your brother well."

"As do I. So why would I bet against him?"

Crosby's blue eyes gleam with mischief. "How about we lay down a bet on how long into his speech it takes for him to tear up?"

"You're so cruel," I say with mischievous delight, then lower my voice. "But I love it."

I look at my watch, a slim platinum band that my father gave me when he asked me to take over the team.

My heart clenches as I hear the echo of his voice, the somber intensity in his request, and the inscription I read daily. *It's your turn.*

I wear a ruby ring he and my mom gave me too, a gift when I graduated from my master's program. They remind me of him, of them, of their love.

I wish he were here tonight.

But if he were, he'd want us all to have fun. To enjoy friends and family to the fullest.

That's what I vow to do.

I raise my chin, dig into the analytical portion of my brain, and lay down my bet. Bets are fun. Bets are friendly. "Twenty seconds."

Crosby's grin goes crooked. "You don't have a lot of hope in your big brother."

I narrow my eyes. "Who's to say that's not hopeful? Maybe I like his sweet and soft side."

"Fair enough. But I'm going with forty seconds," he whispers.

I offer him a hand to shake. He takes it, then he jerks me closer so I'm inches away. "How about a hug, Wild Girl?"

My breath catches. I'm nearly flush against a wall of muscle. His chest is so broad, so sturdy. I'm near enough for his scent to drift past my nose, and my nose likes the way he smells.

"So we're sealing our bet with a hug instead of a handshake?" I ask, evening my tone. I don't want to let on that this proximity is scrambling parts of my brain.

Parts I didn't expect to be scrambled so soon.

"Hell yeah. Best way to bet." Crosby wraps those

major league arms around me, bracketing me in. I steal another inhale of that fresh scent of wood and freshly showered man, and my traitorous body does a salsa dance.

I sternly lecture all those tingles trying to take over my mind.

It's nothing.

He simply smells good.

Intrinsically, objectively good, like a cologne ad in a magazine.

That's it. He's simply one of those eau de manliness spreads in GQ. You'd feel this way about any handsome man. It's only logical, considering how long it's been.

When he lets go, I punch him on the shoulder to keep us in the pals zone. "Then we're on. One hundred dollars. But for the record," I say, lifting my chin, "there's nothing wrong with a man getting a little emotional about getting married."

"Did I say there was?" he asks. Around us, guests mill about, lifting champagne flutes, catching up, snagging stuffed mushroom appetizers and avocado sushi from the waiters circling by.

"No. But you seem to be mocking him."

"That's literally my job as his best friend," he deadpans.

I point to my chest. "Hey, that's my job too, as his sister."

He leans in, his face near mine, his voice turning a bit . . . naughty. "Then, should we spend the night mocking him together?"

That rumble in his voice makes the little hairs on the

back of my neck rise, like they're sashaying closer to him.

What is up with my body's reaction to him? Settle down, hormones.

"I think we should definitely mock Eric," I whisper conspiratorially. Talking about my brother *has* to alleviate these Crosby-induced heat flutters.

So that's what we do during dinner—playfully mock my brother like we did when we were younger.

Trouble is, all this teasing—leaning close, whispering jokes, laughing together—brings back memories of growing up. Memories and emotions that I shelved, happy to ignore them.

Like the crush I had on him way back when.

Yes, that memory, which struts to the forefront of my mind and brings along with it little flutter kicks to join the tingles still ignoring my lectures.

These are the same flutters I felt for Crosby when he was my older brother's best friend in high school.

You're older now.

You're not the sophomore to his senior.

You're not the girl watching the prom king go to the dance with another girl.

I straighten my shoulders, letting all those old memories fall away. I don't have crushes. No matter how good the crushee smells.

At the end of the meal, my brother stands, taps his glass, and clears his throat. "Here we go," Crosby whispers in my ear, and I rein in the shiver.

"Thank you all for coming," Eric says, smiling as he surveys the table. "It means the world to me to see so many of our friends and family here. I look around this room and know that I'm a man who wants for nothing." He takes a beat though, licking his lips. "The only thing I'm missing is my dad."

Eric's voice cracks. I'm right on time, twenty seconds in, but I'm not enjoying victory. Too many hard emotions swell in me too.

My heart clenches, and grief tightens my throat. I cover my mouth, and Crosby reaches for my free hand under the table, squeezing it.

He's quiet, but that squeeze speaks volumes. *I know this is hard. I know you all miss him. I know you all wanted him to be here.*

Eric goes on, and when he's done, I turn to my seatmate and coconspirator, and say, "Thank you. And don't worry about the bet. I'm not planning to collect."

"You better," he says with a sharp stare.

I shake my head. "I can't. And you didn't win, so it's my call. Don't try to negotiate with me." I keep my tone soft but firm.

"Fine, then you'll have to let me take you out to dinner sometime," he says.

"Sounds like a deal."

But not a date. Not between us. It can't be.

As we make our way out of the rehearsal dinner, Crosby collects my jacket at the coat check then slides it onto my arms. "I'm picking up that corsage tomorrow, Nadia," he says. "You're going to look like a prom queen."

I laugh. Laughter is safer than all these other feelings. "And you'll look like the prom king you were."

He shoots me that cocky grin that charms his fans. That charms me. "And together we'll be wedding buddies."

Yes.

Buddies.

That's what we are. My teenage crush was just that, long forgotten.

Friendship is fine. Better than fine because friendship is all I have room for in my life, and I like having room for Crosby.

5

NADIA

Those tissues I tuck into my purse for a girls' night out? That's nothing compared to what I pack for a wedding.

Weddings make me cry.

Okay, *fine*. Blubber is more like it.

I can replenish vanishing seas at wedding ceremonies.

I cry when the music begins, when the groom sees the bride's face, when the vows are exchanged.

That is not entirely surprising, considering I cry over dog food commercials. One of the Hawks' biggest sponsors is an organic dog food company, and every time I see that sweet collie patiently wagging his tail while waiting to be adopted by his forever person, we're talking buckets of tears.

That's why I grab an extra packet the next day, snagging it from a drawer in the bathroom of my new penthouse in Cow Hollow, on top of a hill with a gorgeous view of the Golden Gate Bridge, the San Francisco Bay, and the glittering Pacific Ocean.

I've been here for a week now, and I'm fully moved in. I've been working hard, running back and forth to meetings with the city, interviewing general manager candidates.

This weekend, I'm off, focused solely on Eric's nuptials.

Wearing a sapphire-blue dress too, my sister, Brooke, reads *Percy Jackson* to her eight-year-old daughter, Audrey, who's convinced she wants to attend Camp Half-Blood, like the characters. They're smushed into the corner of my new dove-gray couch, surrounded by purple pillows.

After Brooke finishes a chapter and closes the book, she waggles a well-manicured finger in my direction. "I saw that you only packed two packets of tissues, Nadia. That's not going to be enough for you. Don't forget you needed a towel at my wedding."

Her daughter snickers. "A towel? Why did you need a towel?"

Brooke nuzzles her daughter. "Your Aunt Nadia cries at every single event. She cried at my high school graduation. I was soooo embarrassed," she says.

I sneer at my big sister. "Thank you for teasing me for *caring* about your rite of passage."

Brooke flings me an evil grin. She's particularly good at boomeranging those in my direction. "That was nothing compared to how much you cried at my wedding," she says.

"I was sixteen! I was hyperemotional. My big sister was getting married. Plus, you met your husband in China, and he moved to the US to be with you. That's amazing," I say, then arch a haughty brow. "Or maybe I was happy you were finally moving out of the house."

"Ouch," Brooke says, wincing in over-the-top pain. "I see you still have the zinger spirit, Nadia."

"And I see you still have the crushing spirit of an older sister," I tease.

My mom clicks across the floor, setting a hand on Brooke's shoulder, ever the peacemaker. "And I see you both have the spirit of totally loving each other."

I point at Brooke. "Yes, but I have a heart made of sponge cake and hers is carved from ice."

Brooke launches a saucy look at me. "Just call me Elsa."

Audrey and Brooke break into the famous song from *Frozen*, then they both laugh. "You know I love you. And all your cakey heart sponginess," Brooke says.

Audrey bounces up from the couch, her sleek black hair, thanks to her dad's genes, braided down her back. "I'm ready to see Mariana in her princess dress and then to eat all the cake."

"Me too," I say, offering a hand for high-fiving to my niece. She smacks back. "Cake is the best part of weddings. But vanilla wedding cake, not heart cake."

"And on that note, we agree." Brooke tips her forehead to the door. "I'll be downstairs in the limo with David. See you there in a few minutes."

She takes off with her kiddo to join her husband, and just to be safe, I grab one more packet of tissues, wielding it at my mom. "One more for the road for me."

"Grab an extra for me too, sweetheart," my mom says in a confessional whisper.

"You're not a crier," I say suspiciously. My mother isn't a cold woman, but she's more steely, steady.

Dad was always the crier. Tough as nails in business and a total marshmallow when it came to family.

He was the one with tears rolling down his cheeks when he walked Brooke down the aisle nine years ago.

He was the one with the trembling bottom lip when my mother received an award for all her philanthropic work in San Francisco.

He was the one whose voice broke when Eric told him two years ago that he'd just met the woman he was going to marry.

"Do you miss him?" I ask my mom.

She nods, her voice tight. "I do."

"You wanted him here today," I say, and it's a statement, not a question.

"So much. He'd be so proud of Eric. All he wanted for his son was for him to fall in love."

"He wanted Eric to have what the two of you had," I say, rubbing her arm.

Her eyes well with tears, and I draw her into a hug. "I miss him a lot too," I say when I let her go. "But I know it's harder for you. He was your one true love."

She pulls back, giving me a sad smile. "He was. But I also believe that we can have more than one true love."

I tilt my head, surprised. She's always seemed so *rah-rah soulmate-y*. "You do?"

"I'm not looking right now, but I loved love. I loved being in love. And I'm only sixty-five. I'd like to think some of my best years are still ahead of me. And I wouldn't mind being in love again."

My heart glows at that thought. At the idea that somebody who lost the man she was married to for more than thirty years has a heart that's open enough to love again.

It's an unexpected thought, but one that makes perfect sense now that she's voiced it. "I bet you'll find someone," I say.

She laughs dubiously. "You think it's easy at sixty-five?"

"Well, it's hard at twenty-five," I say.

She shakes her head. "Sweetheart, I'm winning this battle. There's nothing as hard as dating at sixty-five."

"Fine. You win, but then again, I wouldn't know what dating's like at twenty-five. Or twenty-four, or twenty-three."

"You've never really been in love, have you?"

I shrug, grabbing my silver clutch as we head to the door. "It felt like love a few times. But looking back, no. I liked my high school boyfriends, but it wasn't love. And being at an all-girls college, I never really met anybody there I fell for. I honestly don't think I've ever been serious enough with anyone to feel that way. Maybe that's why I cry at weddings. It all feels wonderful and magical and sort of far away."

She squeezes my hand. "It won't always be far away."

* * *

But it doesn't matter if my time is near or far away.

Today isn't about me. It's about my brother.

When we reach the Luxe Hotel atop Nob Hill, I find

Eric in the suite next to the ballroom, fiddling with his bow tie, the other groomsmen milling about in the hall.

"For a brother, you look fantastic," I say with a smile.

"For a sister, you look decent," he says.

As we leave and make our way toward the groomsmen, Eric lowers his voice and says, "Don't forget what I said the other day. About Crosby."

My brow knits. "Why are you reminding me right now?"

He gives me a look that says *you know why*. "You've kind of had a crush on him, haven't you?"

My jaw drops. I shake my head in adamant denial. Vociferous denial. "No. Of course not. Not at all. Not one bit."

A dubious brow lifts. "Nadia, I saw how you looked at him when you were younger."

I growl. "You must be confusing me with literally every other woman who crossed his path."

Eric shrugs, smoothing his lapels. "Maybe I'm remembering it wrong." He scrunches his brow, like he's trying to recall something. He tilts his head. "Or maybe he had a crush on you?"

I blink, stopping in my tracks, as the floor imitates a tilt-a-whirl. He did not say that. "What are you talking about?"

"Just seemed that way when we were younger," Eric says, like this yummy nugget is on the same level as remembering a test junior year that he earned an A on. Something mundane and ordinary, when it's actually the opposite. It's big and fascinating. "But what difference does it make now?" Eric asks philosophically. "He's off the market anyway, and I'm going to make sure he stays that way. I promised him I would."

"I'm off the market too," I say, since I need to remember that. I need to underline it, bold it, highlight it.

"Good. Just making sure. You both have way too much going on in your lives for anything to happen. But you're back in the same city now, and I know days like today make people do crazy things. I met Mariana at a wedding, so I know what happens at weddings."

I roll my eyes. Then I roll them once more all the way to the back of my head and around. "Nothing is going to happen at your wedding," I whisper.

I repeat that mantra as the ceremony begins.

I say it a few times as Eric walks down the aisle to the front of the ballroom.

I imprint it on my brain several times.

When the music begins for the bridal party, I clutch a few tissues strategically around my bouquet, ready to dab my eyes.

But it turns out, I don't feel like crying when I spot Crosby outside the ballroom.

The opposite occurs as he strides over to me, proffering a corsage, then the words, "For you."

Blue roses bloom brilliantly, and he slides it onto my wrist, next to my watch. My breath hitches as his fingers graze my skin.

Nothing is going to happen at the wedding.

My skin seems to feel otherwise though, all lit up and electric from the barest touch.

"Gorgeous," I whisper as I stare at the roses, then at

my ruby ring, which seems to catch their reflection. I tear my gaze away to take the matching boutonniere and affix it to his lapel. My fingers are steady, but my senses are frantic, out-of-whack radars that are going haywire as I slide the pin through the back of the boutonniere. A faint hint of his aftershave drifts past my nose, the scent woodsy and clean, and it scrambles my brain, sending those wild neurons into hyperdrive.

He smells so enticing.

And he looks like he belongs on a magazine cover beneath the headline "Rugged All-American Athlete."

The suit, the five-o' clock shadow, the twinkling eyes.

Everything.

Just everything.

I step back. "Excellent flower choice," I say, doing my best to sound friendly.

"Glad you approve."

He offers his arm, and I drink in the sight of him once more.

My libido roars, rises up, taps my shoulder, and whispers like the she-devil she is in my ear, *He looks crazy hot, doesn't he?*

Yes, Crosby Cash looks insanely yummy in that non-ruffled, non-bell-bottomed blue tux that hugs his muscles and shows off his flat stomach and makes me want to climb him like a tree.

He looks incredible with his dark hair that demands fingers be run through it, with his stubble that begs for hands to roam over it.

And those eyes . . .

Those eyes that simply say he's imagining a woman naked.

He gazes at me with those eyes right this second.

My skin heats everywhere.

Dear God, my rabbit is going to be working overtime tonight.

Especially when Crosby flashes his grin at me. That easygoing grin on his stupidly gorgeous face.

When he links arms with me, a hot shiver rushes over my skin, pulses between my legs.

He leans in closer and whispers, "That dress."

That's all he says.

Two words that if written down, if placed in the middle of a poster on a wall, wouldn't inherently seem like a lusty, sexy compliment.

But from his mouth, in this moment, with heat in his eyes, they feel like the sexiest thing anyone has ever said.

As we walk down the aisle arm in arm, I don't feel friendly.

I feel something else entirely. Something I haven't felt in ages.

Maybe ever.

A dangerous desire.

6

CROSBY

Two weeks.

My turn-off-the-nuclear-reactor-of-my-love-life experiment is fourteen days strong, and I haven't texted an ex or swiped right.

Hell, I killed my Tinder account.

I deleted all my exes' contact info from my phone.

Total reboot. Clean fucking sweep.

But now the real work begins.

No matter how good my best friend's sister looks, smells, or feels with her arm linked through mine, I won't move her from the friend zone to the I-am-dying-to-take-you-to-bed-tonight zone.

But standing next to her is an unexpected test of my Ladies' Men Anonymous resolve.

With each step down the aisle, my mind narrows to thoughts of her.

She smells like . . . a whispered moment, like the hint of a kiss.

And it's going to my head.

The faint scent of something tropical, a juicy mango or a lush flower, is tickling my nose, teasing my senses.

To make matters harder, she looks like a jewel. That sapphire dress hugs her lithe body in all the right places, while letting my overactive imagination do its favorite thing—picture what's underneath that material.

Halfway down the aisle, she steals a quick glance my way, her eyes flashing me a smile under her lashes, as she hooks her arm more tightly through mine.

My heart pounds a little harder.

How can one person look this good, smell this good, *feel* this good?

I have no answers.

We reach the justice of the peace, and I breathe a quiet sigh of relief as we fan to opposite sides—me with the groom, her with the bride.

Thank fuck for the ceremony.

The vows and promises will take my mind off the sensory overload in my body.

But that's easier said than done.

As the justice of the peace speaks, my mind wanders, tripping back in time, making a few quick stops along the way at the LGO Excellence in Sports Awards Gala last year, at the Sports Network Awards the year before, at a local hospital's big fundraiser for pediatric cancer a few years back. All these events where I've chatted with her, shared a joke or a drink.

The images of us laughing flicker before me.

As the justice of the peace talks about Eric and Mariana, my mind stretches further, reaches further into the past, landing on Nadia's senior prom.

I'd just come home from college at the end of my sophomore year to find her going to the dance with Charlie Duncan, a senior too, captain of the debate team and one of those guys who looked like he'd be cast as the best friend in a Netflix Christmas special.

Inoffensively handsome and completely forgettable.

Nadia was the opposite.

She'd practically floated down the stairs and through the living room in an emerald dress, with her chestnut hair in a twist, several strands framing her face in loose, curled tendrils.

Her lips were bright, slick with pink lip gloss.

But her eyes did me in. They knocked the breath straight from my lungs.

I couldn't get enough air.

Had her eyes always been so can't-look-away-from? So brown and warm? So big and open?

Or had I only just noticed?

I was parked on the couch, watching a ball game with Eric and his dad. The bases were loaded, and I didn't care.

She walked over to us on confident feet, the heels making her taller.

"Hey, Wild Girl," I'd said, my voice dry and husky.

I needed a bottle of water. I needed ten gallons. My throat was the Sahara.

"Hey, Wannabe All-Star," she'd said, then I stood and leaned in for a hug.

I was a thief, all right, stealing that embrace. As my arms wrapped around her, the force of my own crush—

it had come out of nowhere—hit me like a wild pitch slamming into my thigh.

She was stunning.

And some asshole was going to reap the rewards.

But then, nothing happened with Mr. Netflix, because she came home before midnight, made some popcorn, and invited Eric and me to join her in the kitchen.

Eric said he'd be right there after SportsCenter, but I was all too willing to leave the sports news behind.

"How was prom?" I asked, gritting my teeth, hoping her early return meant Charlie had been cast in the role of the too-boring-to-get-another-date role.

She rolled her eyes. "All he wanted to talk about was himself."

My shoulders relaxed. I had to fight off a smile. "I take it that's not on your list of favorite topics?"

She shook her head, tucking a loose strand of hair behind her ear as she kicked off her heels. "I want someone to laugh with, make fun of the world with, talk about the world with. Charlie has the conversation range of a biscuit."

With a straight face, I said, "Biscuits, I'm told, are not known for their sparkling wit."

"Sparkling wit is a prerequisite. I haven't been on a ton of dates, but I know this much—without sparkling wit, I have zero interest," she said, then offered me some of the popcorn. I took a handful, popped it into my mouth, and chewed.

"Because you give good sparkles. You give good wit. And obviously, you have top-notch taste," I said, then pointed to the popcorn, maybe so I wouldn't be completely transparent.

She smiled, big and wide. "I do have good taste."

I upped the ante. "The best."

Her eyes locked with mine for a beat, maybe more. She nibbled on the corner of her lip, then drew a shuddery breath. "Who won the game?"

That was the end of the moment—a terribly brief one.

At the time, I didn't think much of our conversation. I filed it away in the drawer of Nadia intel.

But in retrospect, it feels like it was the start of something.

At least for me.

Maybe the start of seeing her as something more than my friend's sister.

Seeing her as a woman. With desires, with interests, with dates.

When the ceremony ends and we exit the ballroom, heading into the hotel hallway, waiting for the pics to begin, I want to know what her dating situation is.

Scratch that. I *need* to know. It feels important. In the same way that it felt important to know how prom went.

What if she's seeing someone?

I dive right in. "Now that you're back, are you going to break all the hearts in San Francisco? Like Charlie Duncan's was surely broken the night you declared him duller than a biscuit."

She laughs. "That's a name I haven't heard in ages."

"Your prom date," I supply.

"Yeah, I know. He was sort of . . ." She looks me over, her gaze landing on the lapel of my jacket. "About as interesting as a pocket square."

I tug on mine. "I'd say, 'Poor Charlie,' but I can't muster any sympathy for a dude on the same level as a piece of ornamental clothing."

She laughs. "At least I didn't call him a hanky."

"I might have felt bad for him then."

She shakes her head. "Nah, I don't think you would have."

"You're probably right," I say, then return to getting the info I want. "So you must have left behind a trail of broken hearts, then, in Las Vegas."

She scoffs. "Not even a nicked heart, Crosby."

"How about paper cuts? Did you administer all sorts of paper cuts on the hearts of the men of Vegas?"

With a sliver of a sad smile, she shakes her head. "Not even the tiniest little ache or bruise, I swear."

This I find hard to believe. "Are you really telling me that you've been single the whole time?"

"The entire time."

Whoa.

How is it possible that a babe of the highest order does not leave behind a trail of shattered hearts?

I scratch my jaw, furrow my brow, and part my lips, trying to figure out what to say, because this is insane. "How is that possible?" I ask, taking my time with each word like I'm speaking in a foreign language, but this is foreign to me. And hell, it ought to be foreign to everyone.

I eye her from stem to stern. From knee to breast.

She's gorgeous and brilliant and fascinating.

She clears her throat. "My eyes are up here, Crosby," she says, pointing to those big brown irises that are like pools of the warmest color, with gold flecks at the edges, drawing me in.

Busted.

But I'm cool with that.

It was simply a friendly assessment of the sitch.

"And they are a beautiful brown. I was just doing my due diligence. Assessing everything that you just said. Trying to figure out what kind of fucktangular insanity is happening to the men in Las Vegas?"

"Actually, it's frocktagonal insanity, but to-may-toe, to-mah-toe."

I laugh. "I forgot—you don't swear."

She flutters her lashes. "I'm such a good girl."

Is she though?

My mind wanders once again to images of this good girl being bad. *Shake it off, man.* "Of course you are." I narrow my eyes, goading her. "But someday I'll get you to swear."

"You'll have to work really *forking* hard at that," she says, all saucy as she throws down a challenge.

"You're on," I say, offering her a hand to shake on it.

She shakes back, then gestures to my eyes. "So that whole slide-your-gaze-up-and-down is due diligence? Is that what it's called?" Her lips corkscrew in an *I've caught you* smile.

I square my shoulders, owning it. "Yes. Indeed it is. I'm all about gathering empirical evidence. And I've gathered it with eyes, ears, and brain. You are a goddess, and the fact that men in Vegas do not know this leads me to arrive at only one conclusion. Men in Las Vegas are clearly douche trumpets."

"I was going to go with dingle nuggets, but yours works too," she says.

I snap my fingers. "Dammit."

"Nice try though, getting me to cave," she says in a sexy taunt.

"But is 'douche' actually a swear?"

"Would you say it in a boardroom?" she counters. "That was my father's logic. If you won't say it in a boardroom, don't say it."

"Ah, I don't hang out in boardrooms. Locker rooms for this guy."

"And boardrooms for this gal. So it's 'dingles,' 'forks,' and 'sons of a mailbox' for me," she says, tapping her chest. "Rather than 'sons of you-know-what.'"

"That's perfect—the men of Vegas are sons of mailboxes."

She inches closer, dropping her voice to a conspiratorial whisper. "Or have you considered I scare them off with my anti-man perfume?"

"Like mosquito repellent but for dudes?" I ask, like I'm processing this new development. Dipping my hand into the front pocket of my suit pants, I grab my phone, click on my Amazon app, then speak into it. "Alexa, show me anti-man repellent."

The coolly robotic voice asks if I want mosquito repellent.

Nadia shakes her head, wagging her finger. "You've

got to ask her for anti-man repellent on discount. Don't you want a deal?"

I nod, big and long. "Yes. You know me so well." I clear my throat and speak more slowly. "Alexa, show me your Deal of the Day anti-man repellent."

"I did not understand. Please repeat that request," the voice from my phone chirps.

"Hold on. I've got this." Nadia leans in closer. "Show me douche biscuit repellent."

The phone is quiet for a few seconds, then Alexa speaks. "Here are the results for goose biscuit pellets."

I cringe, shuddering.

Nadia joins me, full-on horror-movie-style. "Who is buying goose biscuit pellets?"

"And are they for the goose or the eater of the goose?" I ask.

"Are they even organic?"

"Organic goose eggbeaters. Here are more results," the phone voice chimes in, picking up on words we both said.

Nadia doubles over, cracking up. "I refuse to believe that's a thing."

"Alexa said it. You cannot argue with Alexa," I say, turning off the app and tucking the phone into my pocket.

"I can, and I will," Nadia says. "Especially since Alexa can't find the anti-man perfume that I clearly bought on Subscribe and Save a few months ago. I mean, how else to explain my absolute terrible luck?"

"Want me to test your perfume? See if it works?"

"You're not worried it might scare you away?" Her

voice dips low, to a tone that suggests I'd be in danger if my nose goes near her.

"I've got this. Hold my beer," I say, handing her an imaginary can.

I draw a deep breath, shake out my arms, and stretch my neck, limbering up like I'm going to battle.

She waggles her fingers by her neck and lifts her chin, giving me room. That is a gorgeous image—her leaning in, offering her neck.

Setting a hand on the bare skin of her arm, I congratulate myself for finding an excuse to move closer to her.

But even so, this is all fun and games.

No matter how sexy she is, we are just friends having a good time.

A damn good time.

I play along with the teasing mood, dipping closer. My nose brushes faintly across her skin. My eyes close. A rumble works its way up my throat, and my senses go haywire.

My fuses trip, nerves fraying like an electrical wire about to snap.

Nadia Harlowe smells better than any fantasy I've ever had.

And I don't want this dream to end.

So I linger, my nose skating along the delicate skin of her throat, getting high off the scent of her.

Like a summer day, but with a hint of something floral under it.

Like a tropical bloom after a summer rainstorm, the

kind of afternoon shower that leaves droplets of water clinging to your skin, roaming over soft, dewy flesh.

That's what she smells like.

Like she's wearing a bikini and a little sarong thing, like we've been wandering through the emerald-green gardens on Kauai, stealing kisses on a hot day as the sun beats down and we hunt for shade.

My mind is officially elsewhere. It's in vacationland with Nadia. It's in Lustville. In Fantasy Arena.

Isn't this the problem? Isn't this my kryptonite? The very thing I vowed to stop at the tux store?

But then, maybe it's not.

Because Nadia and I aren't the problem.

She's not the type of woman I need to resist. She's not an ex, she's not bad news, she's not trouble.

She's the opposite.

A friend.

A damn good one.

And I can be pals with a sexy-as-sin woman. Doesn't mean I'm caving.

In fact, I'm doing just fine on my diet.

Sure, my friend smells mind-bendingly delicious. But I'm not giving her the keys to my car, the code to my bank account, or any piece of my heart.

And boom. Done. Snapped myself out of a Nadia-induced trance just like that. By zeroing in on the friendship. I keep that up, doing my best impression of a cat hacking up a hair ball, Puss-in-Boots-in-*Shrek*-style. Fake retching, I cringe like I'm repulsed by her scent. "Yep, that's it. You're clearly anathema to men."

She swats my shoulder with her bouquet. But I'm a fast motherfucker. Reflexes—I've got them.

I catch her wrist, the one without the corsage, circling my fingers around her. As my hand curls, her breath hitches. She swallows.

Ah, hell.

That's too hard to resist. Even for a friend.

I plant a kiss on her wrist. Soft, gentle, and maybe with a hint of my tropical fantasies.

Then I meet her eyes. "My due diligence is done."

"And what have you decided?" she asks, a little breathy, a lot sexy.

Without letting go of her beautiful brown-eyed gaze, I give her my honest assessment. "Men in Vegas have achieved top marks in the field of dipshittery. And I hereby welcome you to San Francisco on behalf of all the men in the city, such as myself, who were raised to appreciate smart, confident, outgoing, kick-ass, and gorgeous women."

A blush travels slowly across her skin and up her chest, spreading twin spots of pink to her cheeks.

"Thank you, Crosby. I needed that. I truly appreciate that," she says, her voice warm and affectionate. Then she takes a breath, seeming to center herself. She squares her shoulders, and I take that as my cue to let go of her wrist.

She taps my chest with the flowers. "And don't forget, you owe me stories. I want to be fully enter-tained during the reception with all of your tales. I need to know all about your dating break. We're buddies."

Exactly.

We're buddies.

She gets it. I get it. It's all good.

I salute her. "Ready to entertain you," I say, then her sister steps into my line of sight, waves her hand, earth-to-Nadia-style, then shoots us a stare. "Come on, love-birds. It's picture time," Brooke says, her husband and daughter a few feet behind her.

"Lovebirds," I whisper to Nadia, adding a scoff.

"That's as ridiculous as goose biscuit pellets."

We join the wedding party, and as the photographer snaps the first shot, I slide my arm around her waist.

It fits perfectly on the curve of her hips. So perfectly I don't want to let go.

At all.

Not one bit.

And the wrecking ball of obvious slams into my gut.

I am insanely attracted to my best friend's little sister.

But the corollary to that is that absolutely nothing is going to come of it.

I'm okay with that.

I'm okay with that.

I swear I'm okay with it.

7

CROSBY

I'm heading to the reception when a voice booms from around the corner. "Number twenty-two. A word."

That's all I get before a jacket covers my head, arms wrap around my torso, and my world turns dark.

I'm jerked into what's presumably a conference room in the hotel, but the lights stay off and the cover stays on, even after I'm led to a chair to sit in. "What do you have to say for yourself?"

The question comes out like a drill sergeant is speaking, but I know the voice. That's Holden, who plays for the city's other team. Known this guy for a couple years, and though he was only introduced to the rest of our crew since moving up here to San Francisco to join the rival team in the city – the so-called *enemies* – he's fit right in. He's an insane workout partner, since he's so damn regimented. On the field, he takes no prisoners at the plate, and he tells it like it is to the press. To me too. "You're playing with fire, twenty-two," Holden rumbles.

Another voice cuts in, calm, affable. The steady rudder of the Cougars.

"Let's give the man a chance to explain himself," Grant puts in, the easygoing one among the pair. "There could be a perfectly reasonable explanation for all that flirting. Like maybe Crosby's been enlisted to teach a course for friends who are in time-out but want to flirt. Right, Crosby? Isn't that right?"

Grant is the Cougars' catcher. The guy all the pitchers rely on behind the plate, the one who's always looking on the bright side. Every glass is half full for Grant, even when he's dripping with sarcasm. Like now.

"As a matter of fact, you do have some of it right. *Friends* being the operative word," I say.

"You think we believe that? You're a regular Colbert," Holden says.

"It's the truth," I say with a casual shrug, leaning back in my chair like this is no big deal, my head covered with one of their jackets, subject to this Dude-quisition.

But I do need to convince them that they've got this upside down.

Because they do.

They're reading Nadia and me all wrong. They think my harmless flirting with her is something to worry about.

When it's not.

It's going to keep being harmless. No matter how good she smells.

Those flashbacks during the ceremony? To how hot she looked for prom? That was merely the male brain processing a few sexy images it found in the drawers of memory.

I've sorted them out and tucked the pics back into Friendship Town after my brief pit stop in Fantasy Arena. And I want the guys to know. We rely on each other, look out for each other. I have their backs when they need me, and they have mine, so I say, "C'mon. I'm dead serious on this one. I didn't slip. I'm making it to the start of the season with a clean record. I've been reporting in for the last two weeks to you guys, and I'm reporting in today." I take a beat, then punctuate each word. *"I've. Been. Good."*

"You better be," Grant adds. "Because I don't want to have to take myself out of commission just to keep you on the up-and-up."

"There is no need for that kind of solidarity," I say. "But I do appreciate your willingness to lock it up."

"How hard would that be, Grant?" Holden challenges.

"Soooo hard. But I'd do it to support a teammate who's tempted by trouble," Grant adds.

I roll my eyes from under the fabric. There will be no trouble with Nadia. I've merely buddied up with a buddy. "Nadia is a longtime friend and only that."

"So you know her name," Holden says, like a detective in a hard-boiled novel.

I toss my hands up in the air, cracking up. "Yeah, fuck biscuit. You know her name too. We all do. She's Eric's sister. And nothing is going to happen."

Grant hums. Holden growls.

"All right. Let's give him the benny of the doubt," Grant says, the first of the pair to relent, naturally.

"Fine, but I'm watching you," Holden barks.

"We're both watching out for our guy," Grant says as they let go of the jacket, tugging it off my head. "That's our job. But he's passed the test."

My eyes scan the room quickly, adjusting to the dark even in the middle of the day. Holden is the jacketless one. I swipe my hands over my arms as if I'm wiping off dirt or lint from him.

"Had a feeling that was yours," I say, my nose crinkling in-over-the top disgust. "That jacket smelled like Drakkar Noir. You probably doused yourself in it 1980s-style and came here to scam on women."

"Scam?" Holden asks, narrowing his eyes, then shaking a finger in my direction. "Do not even try to turn this around. I *am* allowed to scam. You are not. You made an unbreakable promise to Eric and Gabe, then they enlisted us to have your back," Holden adds, gesturing between him and Grant.

Grant claps me on the shoulder, shooting a smile in my direction. "You can do this, buddy." He drops his voice. "Just don't make me regret supporting you."

"You can clean out my locker and steal all my clothes if I cave."

Grant taps his chin, his eyes going wide with delight, from the look of the twinkle in his baby blues. "That would be hella amusing, but I think we'd rather you admit on national TV that we're both better than you at the best sport ever."

"Yes. That. I want that, twenty-two," Holden says,

too gleeful for my taste. Especially since he's on our rival team.

I wave the white flag. "Fine. You've got it. I'll admit that on TV if I fall, but I won't fall. I've got this. And the tuxes are on me, dickwads. As a thank you for your service."

"Wow. You're so generous. All I've ever wanted is a free tux," Holden says, flinging a hand to his heart.

I flip him the bird as I hop up from the chair. "News flash. I've gone two weeks avoiding the sock thief and amateur photogs of my past. I've got this, just like I've got the hanging curveballs," I say, since those are my favorite pitches to go long on.

Holden arches a doubtful brow. "Nadia is a hanging curveball?"

Grant scratches his jaw. "Not sure that's right. Hanging curveballs are your temptation. You can't resist them. You swing at them every time."

"And I hit them," I say. "I swing at hanging curveballs because I can motherfucking hit them over the fence and into the San Francisco Bay." I pump a fist. "Booyah. Who hit a homer all the way over the bleacher seats and into the Bay last year?" That shit is hard to do, and I pulled it off.

Grant taps his chest. "Did you forget that I hit one out there too?"

I clear my throat. "Listen, this is not an issue. There is nothing to worry about. Nadia and I are friends, and we have been forever. I'm hanging out with her. We're having a nice time. I'm in time-out. She's in time-out," I say, a little worked up because how are they not getting it? How do they not see the obvious? "Therefore, nothing can happen between us." I flap my arm outside the room in the general direction of Nadia, then back at myself. I smooth a hand down my jacket. "And now if you'll excuse me, I have a reception to go to."

I leave, joining Nadia at the table. She smells so damn good, but I am not giving into the temptation.

I've got this.

8

CROSBY

I blame chia seeds.

And kale.

Blueberries are definitely responsible too. They made me the organic monster I am when it comes to food.

My mom, though, is the biggest reason, since she fed me all that before I could walk. She was and is the queen of all things organic, and started her own organic café in San Rafael when I was in grade school.

When the waiter swings by with the chicken entrée, my knee-jerk reaction is to ask the usual question. "Is the chicken organic?"

With a light bow of his head, he answers, "Yes, it is, sir."

As he deposits the plates in front of the other guests, Nadia pats my shoulder. "You're safe here, Crosby. We know you and your mango-loving heart."

"Mangoes and me are like that," I say, crossing my index and middle finger. "Anyway, old habits," I say with a shrug and a smile, because this is what I'm talking about—Nadia and I know each other, down to our families and the nitty-gritty of our food preferences.

Nadia tips her forehead in the direction of my mom, a few tables away, her curly red hair falling down her back.

"How is Sunny?" she asks.

My mom is parked next to Nadia's mom, listening to her intently.

That's my mom. The only way she knows how to listen is intently.

The universe gave us one mouth and two ears, she likes to say.

"She and Kana opened a ninth location of Green Goddess," I say, then gesture to the woman next to my mom, a regal-looking lady hailing from Japan, with sleek black hair. They've been a thing for a few years now, and they're holding hands at the table. "And it's going well."

"And that's going well too, I take it?" Her tone says she's asking about my mom's romantic interest.

Seeing my mom happy again ignites a smile on my face and warmth in my chest. "Oh yeah. Big time. I keep telling Sunny to lock that down, but she insists, '*Everything happens according to its own lunar calendar*,'" I say, imitating my mom and her soothing tone for dispensing adages.

The thing she loves to serve up most, right along with kale and quinoa.

"That sounds exactly like your mom. She has a

mantra for everything," Nadia says after taking a bite of her chicken dish.

"She does. And it absolutely rubbed off on me. I'm a big fan of mantras," I say, because mantras are seeing me through this lady diet right now. On that note, maybe I should start thinking of Nadia as sugar. And cake. And cookies.

All the verboten treats that won't touch my lips.

Resist cookies. Resist Nadia.

There. Perfect.

She lifts her wineglass and takes a drink, her brow knitting as if she's deep in thought. "Is it hard getting used to her with someone else?"

I shake my head. "Nah, she's happy. Honestly, she's just as happy as when she was with my dad," I say, since my mom's always been an affectionate person. She was that way with my dad before he died when I was in college after a quick battle with pancreatic cancer.

"Did it surprise you? That she'd fallen in love with a woman?"

I flash back to the night Mom told my sister and me. In her usual fashion, Sunny was up-front, straightforward. She didn't clear her throat and say, *I have an announcement to make.* She simply took Haley and me out for dinner after an afternoon game and told us that she'd fallen for Kana, and was happy that Aphrodite had smiled on her again.

"Maybe for about two seconds," I say. "But when Sunny said she was pansexual, it just tracked."

Nadia smiles as she spears another piece of the yardbird. "I can see that about her. Knowing how she is with people and how she's always seemed more attracted to hearts than anything else."

"Exactly," I say, digging that Nadia gets it in a way few others have. When Daria met Sunny last year, she couldn't fathom that my mom had been with my dad for a couple decades before falling for a woman. Daria's not the only girlfriend I've had whose expression went all furrowed and confused when they met Sunny. "That was what Haley and I said to each other the night Sunny told us. We kind of looked at each other and said, 'Yep, that makes perfect sense. Pass the blueberries.'" I take a bite of the chicken, chew, then ask, "What about you?"

Nadia brings a hand to her chest, her brow knitting in confusion. "Am I pansexual?"

I laugh, shaking my head. Then I think better of it. "Are you? I guess I sort of assumed from our conversation earlier that you weren't, but maybe you are. I try to operate under the assumption that I don't assume anyone's orientation at all—it's not up to me to try to glean who people love."

She shakes her head. "I like men, despite the few sons of mailboxes."

"The douches," I say, since she won't. "Or as you might say, the duckweeds."

A smile spreads nice and easy across her face. "You've got it."

"So you're really done with men?"

"Confession time," she says in a whisper. "I tried a matchmaker in Vegas, and it was a disaster. We're talking category five hurricane level."

"Does that mean you were caught in the eye of a storm of men?"

Laughing, she shakes her head. "Maybe that was the wrong analogy. More like a black hole. The vacuum of deep space. She couldn't really find anyone for me," she says, with a *what can you do* sigh.

But that shocks the hell out of me. No sighing here. Just a drop of the jaw. "Men ought to be falling all over themselves to get to you."

"I wish I could tell you I was tripping over a long line of men," she says. "It was more like a Tampa Bay baseball game," she says, and I laugh at the comparison to the team with the worst attendance in the Majors. We're talking rows upon rows of empty seats.

"Why on earth would they not want to be set up with you?"

Nadia takes a sip of wine. "Let's just say they were more interested in their own ability to buy tickets for a fancy suite at the football game than going on a date with the owner."

Shock rings through me.

What the hell is wrong with some people? "That doesn't even compute in my world. My dad was an easygoing dude who took a few years off to raise us when Mom was building her business, then he went back to his accounting practice. And my mom's always just been open-minded about everything."

Nadia nudges my arm with her elbow, tossing me an appreciative smile. "And they rubbed off on you." Then she smiles. "But honestly, it doesn't matter. Maybe in the end I was meant to come to San Francisco and be single."

Maybe she was.

Maybe I like that plan.

Because it's easier to hang out with her, I mean.

And hell, it's good that she's as on board with her singletude as I am with mine.

"You think the universe was doing you a favor?" I ask.

"I have so much to focus on with building the team, and I want that to be my priority. Maybe that's why the matchmaker couldn't find anyone for me. Perhaps it was meant to be like this," she says, sweeping her arm out widely to indicate the reception, and maybe this moment too, her and me, hanging out.

Whether it was the universe or bad luck, who knows?

However you slice this night, I'm glad to be here with her, and I want her to know that. She beats me to the punch when she says, "By the way, it's nice to catch up with you."

The grin she flashes me throws me off-kilter for a few seconds. It makes me want to touch her arm, tuck a strand of hair behind her ear, and whisper, *Same.*

I do one of those three.

"Same," I tell her. "Same here."

9

NADIA

I love champagne.

It makes me feel so . . . floaty.

So effervescent.

Like everything is coated in a warm, delicious glow.

Glows are great. Absolutely, officially great.

I would like to commission a glow to surround me wherever I go.

Tonight I'm glowing after the ceremony, after the toasts, after the cake that Crosby didn't touch, of course.

After the moment in the hallway earlier, when he roamed his nose over my neck, like he was drinking in my smell, and then after that fantastic get-to-know-you-even-better chat at the table.

Now we're dancing, along with the rest of the wedding party.

"You promised stories. I need the tales," I say.

He arches a brow. "Are you sure you can handle them?"

"Oh, I'm sure. I love anti-fairy tales."

"That's all I've got when it comes to romance," he says, spinning me in a circle, then bringing me close again, but not plastered-up-against-each-other close. The music is fast enough to shimmy, but slow enough for me to keep my hands on his shoulders.

Translation: we aren't doing that melt-into-each-other slow dance.

His lips curve up in that delicious lopsided grin that he wears so well. That easygoing, lighthearted one. "Let's start with Alabama."

"As in the state?"

"As in the name."

"Her name was Alabama?"

"Yes indeed. Alabama Venus."

I grin. "Where did you meet Alabama Venus? Kinda sounds like a stripper name," I say, then shake my head, thinking better of it. I bring my fingers to my lips, like I'm shushing myself. "Pretend I didn't say that," I whisper.

His blue eyes twinkle with delight. "Oh, you said it, Wild Girl. I heard it. And I sure hope you're not insinuating that only strippers are named after states. Or that there's anything wrong with dating a stripper."

I slap his shoulder playfully. "I have zero issues with stripping. In fact, I'll have you know that I led a campaign to make sure that strip club workers qualified for health insurance in Las Vegas."

"Whoa, look at you, Miss Progressive."

"But the name does sound . . . *deliberately sexy*," I explain as we twirl past other couples on the dance floor, including my brother, who gives us those *I'm watching you* eyes, like Robert De Niro gave Ben Stiller in *Meet the Parents*.

Crosby and I both laugh at the groom.

Friends, I mouth.

Buddies, Crosby adds.

It feels true enough for now.

"Yes, her name does sound overtly sexy," Crosby says. "And I suppose she had stripper tendencies, as you'll learn, but she was actually a fortune-teller."

A laugh bursts from me. "Did you ask her to look into your crystal . . . balls?"

The twinkle in his eye turns into a naughty gleam. "Keep this up. I like this risqué side of you."

Funny thing is, I do too.

I can say things to Crosby that I don't normally say to men. Maybe because I haven't had the chance, since my dating life has been anemic—going to an all-girls college, then heading straight into a master's program where all you do is study, study, study, can do that to a woman who digs men.

But perhaps it's the champagne loosening my lips.

The other option is . . . it's him.

"Maybe you bring it out in me," I suggest, a touch flirty.

"I'll do my best to . . . *keep it up*," he says, wiggling his brows, making me grin. "And to answer your question, I met Alabama Venus at Whole Foods."

I snort-laugh. "Wait, wait! Were you fighting over who got the last basket of organic raspberries?"

"I guess you do have a crystal ball," he says, then dives into the story. "She was an organic food fiend too.

Maybe not the best of commonalities, but there it was. We dated for a while. Seemed to be going well enough. So we went to Cabo, and one night she wanted to go dancing. We went to a club, and we danced our asses off."

Perhaps powered by the "risqué" comment, I jerk back, one hand sliding off his shoulder and landing on his hip, so I can give his rear a quick once-over. Sneaking a peek at his butt, I remark, "It's still here. Did you lose your rear in Cabo then get it back?"

He wiggles a brow. "I had a butt transplant."

I laugh, and as I do, my hand seems to have a mind of its own. Emboldened by champagne, or the wedding, or Crosby's stories.

What if my palm just grazed his rear?

Just a little.

That's all.

We're on the far corner of the dance floor, his backside out of view of the crowd.

And my hand *is* on his hip. I can sort of slide it down a little lower.

The she-devil in me wins, my hand skimming the top of one firm, squeezable cheek.

His eyes widen as my hand travels lower, then lower still.

Oh, thank you, champagne.

I'm feeling floaty indeed.

His eyes darken, a flicker of desire in them, chased with that teasing glint. "Nadia, are you checking out my butt transplant?" he asks, but he doesn't sound like he's busting me.

More like he's . . . inviting me.

Still, heat flushes across my cheeks. I tug my hand away, raising it again to curl over his shoulder. "Sorry. I'm so sorry. It was sort of an accidental squeeze, powered by champagne and dancing," I say, tripping over my apology.

Ugh, that's a lie.

I hate lying.

It was not accidental.

It was deliberate and deliberately sneaky.

His voice dips low, a rough whisper just for me. "Was it? Accidental?"

His sexy tone sends a flare of sparks through my chest. A shiver that makes my whole body tingle.

"Or maybe it was . . . curiosity?" I posit, a little breathy.

"By all means, indulge your curiosity," he murmurs.

My breathing quickens, rushing from my lungs in an unexpected burst that sends prickles of heat along my skin.

"This isn't my normal MO," I whisper, coming close, but not too close, to my virginity confession. Crosby doesn't know I've never had sex. I don't blast that little fact on a billboard. But the least I can do is let him know that I'm not a regular butt squeezer. "Just wanted you to know that. I don't go around accidentally squeezing butts. Or deliberately."

He takes a moment, licking the corner of his lips. "All the more reason to check it out. Deliberately," he says, so warm and sexy on that last word.

Sneaking a glance behind me to confirm the rest of

the guests are caught up in their own world, I snake my hand down to his butt once more.

Cover his firm cheek with my hand.

My insides handspring. My pulse spikes.

His butt feels fantastic.

I squeeze it harder, murmuring my appreciation.

He rumbles his in return, a low growl in his throat that lights me up. "Yeah, it's better when it's not accidental," he says.

"I have to agree," I say, unsure how I'm forming words right now.

Unsure, too, what happens next.

Because the mood has shifted once again.

But when the music switches to Ella Fitzgerald and a love song so swoony you have to sway with your lover, we separate.

Untangling quickly.

"Drink?" I ask, my voice feathery, uncertain. "After all, I need the rest of the dance-your-ass-off tale."

"Let's do it."

We make our way to a bar in the other corner of the room, away from most of the festivities, and order two more champagnes.

After the bartender serves us, we raise our glasses to toast. "To my wedding buddy," I say.

He smiles back. "And to mine."

We clink, and I feel mildly recalibrated.

Only mildly.

"So, Alabama the fortune-teller was a bit of an exhibitionist," he says, returning to the tale. "And when we were dancing, 'Girls Just Want to Have Fun' came on.

She decided to take off all her clothes, right down to her red thong underwear."

My jaw drops. "Are you serious?"

"One hundred percent."

"I guess she did want to have fun."

"When I gave her my shirt to cover her up, that's right when the cops came into the club, and they thought I was involved in her striptease."

I wince, a little nervous. "How did you get out of it?"

"My teammates."

My brow furrows. "They were with you?"

"Nope. But like most ballplayers, I have plenty of teammates who are Latino and speak Spanish. So I made it my mission over the last few years to learn the language. I talk to Juan, one of my starting pitchers in Spanish all the time. So when I was in Mexico, I gave my best effort in talking to the police, and I think they appreciated that. One of them said I should find a nice girl, not a crazy one."

"And what happened to the crazy one?"

He makes a whooshing sound, his arm dipping in the universal sign for an airplane flying. "I flew her home that night. Literally got on the next plane with her, and then I caught a flight to Anchorage. I went whale watching the rest of our vacation. *Solo.*"

My smile spreads to my cheeks. "I can picture that perfectly. I bet you loved it."

"It was so peaceful. Very zen and, I am not afraid to admit, quite emotional," he says. "Watching the whales surfacing out there on the water. Seeing glaciers calve.

Being in the midst of all that wilderness. It was everything I needed."

As we drink our champagne, he dives into his other tales of woe, rattling off a story about a woman who tried to steal his World Series ring, then another who attempted to make off with his Tesla one night, only to forget to charge it, so she ran out of power on the Golden Gate Bridge.

I giggle as he entertains me with his stories.

Then I school my expression. "Level with me, Crosby. Do you think you're attracted to thieves?"

His eyes turn intensely serious. "The evidence would indeed seem to suggest as much. As well as trouble. My cousin Rachel set me up with the last woman I went out with, and she still feels horrible about it. Not her fault, and Rachel's a sweetheart who likes to keep herself busy, since she has a jerk of an ex and I swear she tries to make up for it by setting up others. Sometimes, though, she doesn't make the best matches," he says as I take the last sip of my drink. "Considering the last woman she set me up with tried to sell my dick pic."

The bubbles tickle my nose. They make me cough. But maybe they also go to my head, because rather than laughing, the next words that come out of my mouth surprise me.

"Can I see it?"

That was not what I expected to hear from Nadia.

Not at all.

She's surprising me in all sorts of ways tonight, but then again, maybe I shouldn't be surprised, because she's always been bold.

But about this? About squeezing my ass and seeing my cock?

This is brand-new terrain, and fine, it's *not* friendship territory, but I can't resist trekking across it. Achilles' heel, here I go.

She is it tonight.

She's my weakness, and I take another hit.

"The pic," I say, taking my time, slow and easy, letting my meaning register. "Or my dick?"

With cheeks flushed, she purses her lips, looking right, then looking left. She whispers, her voice edging up in a question, "Both?"

Holy fuck.

She meant it, it seems.

My throat goes dry. My skin sparks. And my mind is all kinds of intrigued with this woman. "Are you serious?" I ask, because I need to know if we're playing jokes, or if we're playing with fire.

She swallows, like she's gulping, then she blinks and breathes out hard. "I shouldn't have asked that. That's crazy. I should *not* have asked that."

"I'm not offended," I say, reaching out and touching her arm just to emphasize my point. "Not one bit."

She lets out a sigh of relief. "I'm not the kind of woman who asks to see that. I swear. Honestly, I don't even think I like those pics."

I can't resist that tidbit either. "But do you like dicks?"

"Didn't I already tell you that? Now stop embarrassing me even more," she says, with a playful stomp of her foot.

"You're truly embarrassed?" I ask softly.

"You're a friend, and I asked for *that*, and I shouldn't have." She waves her hand in the air. "Please just pretend I didn't do that. It was the champagne talking."

But can I actually pretend that she didn't say that?

Didn't seem like just an offhand comment. Or a joke. Seemed like there was a part of her that wanted to see the pic.

And I would have shown her the shot that I paid good money to keep out of the papers.

What the hell is that about?

Am I some kind of dick-swinging pervert?

Why the fuck would I show Nadia a picture of my

cock when I am clearly in time-out? Why would I show her at any time, for that matter?

But an answer flickers before my eyes. I *like* the idea of sharing that kind of naughtiness with her. I like the idea that she wanted to see the pic.

In fact, I'm pretty sure—wait for it—I like her.

And because I do, I want to smooth the landing for her, lest she berate herself more. I lean on our favorite word of the night. "If it makes you feel better, I could just *accidentally* show you the dick pic."

Rolling her eyes, she laughs, some of her embarrassment seeming to slink away. "Thanks. Story of the night —accidental butt squeeze, accidental . . . eggplant pic."

My brain takes a two-second delay to connect the dots, and when I do, I give her a *c'mon* look. "You don't say 'dick'?"

She flutters her lashes ever so innocently. "Maybe I don't. Maybe I do."

"Maybe I'll find out. Accidentally. Now, about that eggplant . . ."

I grab my phone from my pocket.

"Crosby," she says, her tone worried.

But this ought to assuage her embarrassment. I unlock my phone, slide my thumb across the screen, and wiggle a brow, like I'm up to something terribly naughty.

And I kind of am.

I hunt for the perfect shot as she protests, "Crosby, I swear, I was just having—"

I brandish the screen at her.

She flinches.

Steps back.

Then a chuckle burst from her lips. "Sam Spade. That's brilliant."

"He's a private dick," I say, turning the phone back to check out the picture of the private dick that Humphrey Bogart played in *The Maltese Falcon.*

"You are the best," she says, then moves in for a hug.

With my phone in one hand, I wrap my arms around her, enjoying the feel of her in my embrace.

I steal one final inhale of her neck, then let go, and as I do, my boutonniere grazes the strap of her dress, threatening to grab hold of it.

That won't do.

I curl my hand over her shoulder. "Hold still. Let me make sure my boutonniere doesn't cause a nip slip," I say, ·carefully releasing the pin from the slim blue strap.

She breathes a sigh of relief as I detach my accessory from her strap.

"My nipples and I thank you," she says as we pull apart. She waggles her arm, showing off the corsage. "This made the outfit, right?"

"No doubt. The corsage is a winner."

"And your boutonniere is fire," she says. "Even if it tried to mate with my dress."

"Smart boutonniere." I fiddle with it. "It is pretty spiffy, and it's holding up well. I might even be able to use it again at the Sports Network Awards this week."

"You didn't tell me you were going to that. I have to present an award there."

A smile takes over my face. A plan takes over my

mind. "What do you know? So do I," I say, and the gears click. "Are you soloing it?"

"Stag all the way."

I wiggle an eyebrow. "Are you thinking what I'm thinking?"

She glances around the reception, like she's scanning for options, then she taps her chin. "I could take Brooke, or her daughter, or my mom, or your mom. Is that what you had in mind?"

Laughing, I shake my head. "We can put our corsage and boutonniere to good use. Buddy up again?"

Her grin is electric. "We're awesome at it. Let's make it a doubleheader."

I hum appreciatively. "I love when you use baseball analogies. And yes, I'm thinking you and I pair up again before I have to go to spring training," I say, just to make it clear what I have in mind. "We can be, like, each other's event dates."

"Sort of like escorts for various functions?"

I can't resist that. "Do you want the full package of escort services?" I ask, low and dirty.

She nibbles on the corner of her lips, adopting a saucy smile. "Depends on the fee." Then she turns businesslike. "But while you're offering, and since you're off the market, want to be my plus-one at a charity event next weekend? I have a golf thing I'm attending."

I make a purring sound. "Mmm. Golf. Every pro athlete's addiction. Yes, please."

"We'll plus-one each other."

"We have to, especially since Hollywood is making our rom-com—*Plus-Oneing with the Best Man*."

"And I'm glad the best man will be my plus-one," she says.

My chest warms and my mind buzzes at the prospect of another event with her.

Another plus-one.

It's both a terrific opportunity and a bit of a conundrum.

I spend the rest of the wedding trying to figure out what to do with the fact that I like my buddy's sister.

As the night winds down, Eric pulls me aside, clapping my shoulder. "Don't forget I have eyes everywhere. Just because I'll be in the Maldives doesn't mean I won't be watching you. And you asked me to," he says, stern, like he was in the tux shop.

I did ask him. I do know what's good for me. And hey, nothing *has* happened. So I'm still on the wagon.

"And I was already interrogated by your henchmen," I say.

"Good. They'll be keeping their eyes on you while I'm gone," he says, then tips his head to Holden and Grant, who are drinking beers at the bar. Holden is chatting with a woman in a peach dress, Grant with a bearded dude.

"Yeah, they look super focused on their mission to keep me in line," I tease.

"They're focused enough. Nine more days till spring training. You can do it. And then you'll behave during spring training because you'll be busy all the time."

"I've so got this. And you go on your honeymoon. Worship your wife. Fuck your brains out. Drink piña coladas. I will be fine," I tell him, and it feels mostly true.

Until I get in the elevator alone with Nadia at the end of the evening.

I'm not into dick pics.

That's not because I'm a prude. And it's not because I still carry my V card. It's because when I watch porn—and I do watch it, thank you very much, incognito mode—I'm not simply interested in the dick.

I want to know what the man does with it. How it makes the woman feel. But also how she *appears* to feel when he's doing other things for her. Going down on her, kissing her breasts, worshipping her body.

So why does my brain keep planting images of what Crosby's dick might look like?

Not helpful.

As in it's not helpful to staying plus-one-ers.

Especially since he's on a dating diet.

Maybe I need to reassure him that I'm not some kind of perv who's dying for him to whip out his schlong for the camera.

That I'm his friend. That I support his anti-dating quest.

As the elevator shoots us up to my floor, since I booked a room for the night, I set my hand on his arm. "I just want you to know, as we embark on *plus-oneing with the best man*, that I will behave like your friend as we planned. There will be no deliberate or even accidental taking of dick pics, and no deliberate or even accidental asking for them. And I would never attempt to sell them."

He wipes a hand across his forehead in a *whew* gesture.

"Because I live by the belief that friends shouldn't ask friends for dick pics. And they shouldn't take them either," I say, raising my finger to make a point.

He laughs. "I do believe I've seen that on a bumper sticker somewhere. Along with *Friends don't ask friends to bang* and *Friends don't ask friends for boob shots*," he says as the elevator stops at my floor. We step out, and as we walk down the hall, he drapes an arm around me, pals-style. "Also, told you I'd find out if you said 'dick.' I'm pretty confident I can get you to say 'fuck' now."

I fling my hand across my mouth, Bette-Boop-style, playing it up. "Oops! Did I say . . ." I take my time, making him wait for it, before I finish with "*Dick?*"

He licks his lips and growls sexily. "Better than 'eggplant.' Soon you'll be saying 'cock.'"

I have nothing against *cock*.

Hell, I have nothing at all against cocks.

Someday I'd like to enjoy a cock against me.

But since I don't say those words in the boardroom, and since I haven't had the chance to say them in the bedroom, how it feels on my tongue is truly virgin territory.

"You never know," I say with a flirty shrug. "For now, be happy I said 'dick,' since it's way better than 'wiener pic.'"

"How about 'shaft shot'?"

"Oh, that's good. But what about . . . 'member pic'?"

He taps his chin, murmuring his approval. "I like that because it's so euphemistic, the perfect amount of innuendo."

"'Member pic' it is," I declare, banging an imaginary gavel.

"You can accidentally ask me to show you a member pic anytime," he says with a laugh, then the laughter fades as I dip my hand into my clutch purse, fishing out the key card when we reach my door.

He meets my gaze. His irises are rich with possibilities. "You know, if this were *Plus-Oneing with the Best Man*, this would be the scene where he accidentally shows her a member pic, they double over in laughter, she stumbles forward, and he catches her," he says.

The movie reel of that moment unspools before my eyes.

And I like it.

I like it a lot.

Heat flares through me, a match striking. "I wonder what that would look like. The stumbling part."

"And the catching part," he adds.

"And whatever comes next," I say in a softer voice.

Like we're both tempting fate.

Testing possibilities.

"In a plus-one situation, it's important to know those things," he says, his voice husky, a bare scrape of want and wishes.

"I'd definitely like to know," I say, taking my time with each word.

His blue eyes blaze. The vein in his neck pulses. His lips part, and he stares hungrily at mine. "I imagine after she stumbles, there's an accidental kiss."

Those words.

Accidental kiss.

They ignite a riot in my chest. They send flurries of sparks across my skin. They light up my insides.

My heart beats like a wild drum. "I wonder what that looks like."

He lifts a brow, his voice all smoky. "Or feels like."

"A lot like a real kiss?" I ask, my stomach flipping.

There's a charge between us. Ions and atoms are self-replicating, multiplying at an exponential rate, and that electricity tugs me closer to him. "But maybe we should just test it out to be sure. After all, we tested the accidental butt squeeze," I say.

For a few seconds, I wonder who this bold woman is inside me. Who this woman is who's trying to have a kiss with this man. Is it the champagne? Is it him? Is it me? And most of all, will I regret this in the morning? But I don't regret the dancing, I don't regret the talking, and I definitely don't regret the butt squeeze. That was not at all accidental, but totally deliberate.

And because I don't really believe in accidents—I believe in doing things on purpose—I decide to do just that.

If we've made it through this night so far as buddies who flirt, as buddies who squeeze, as buddies who tease and toy, then surely we can weather a kiss.

Taking a step, I pretend to stumble.

Crosby catches me, steadying me. He runs his hands down my arms, brushes my hair off my shoulder, and then presses the sexiest, most tender kiss to the hollow of my throat, murmuring, "You smell so good. All night long. You've been in my senses."

My eyes float closed, and my body screams, *Touch me.*

I whisper, "You're definitely in mine."

His lips travel softly along my neck, closer to my jaw, brushing there and making me shiver. He cups my cheek. "This is what an accidental kiss looks like in the movies," he says.

Then he sweeps his lips across mine.

I melt.

We're talking tingles everywhere.

Along my arms, down my chest, between my legs.

Tingles of desire and longing as he kisses me in a kiss to end all kisses.

It's a kiss that lights up the sky. A kiss that makes you want to write down every detail, record every second, imprint it on your mind for all posterity, so you can recall later on what it felt like to be kissed like this.

It feels like how kissing was meant to be.

A delicious, decadent good-night kiss.

His lips brush mine gently at first, a whisper of a kiss. His breath is soft, a needy exhale, like he's wanted this all night.

And my God, so have I.

I've been craving it while denying it, but I don't want to deny anything now.

Not the tender sweep of his lips, not the delicious exploration, not the way he flicks his tongue across the corner of my mouth.

Mmm, that tantalizing moment sends a wild thrill through my cells.

We linger in the kiss, lips and mouths taking their time, getting to know each other. Savoring every lush second.

His lips are magic.

They make my body perform all sorts of tricks, like the disappearing act of my willpower.

It's vanished, gone like a rabbit in a hat.

And I don't care.

This kiss spreads from the center of my chest to the tips of my fingers. It lights me up from head to toe.

It makes me want him desperately.

Then want him even more when he kisses me deeply.

Hungrily.

Giving me exactly the type of kiss we needed to try out tonight. Like he knows this is the only kind of kiss we ought to have.

A promise.

But it's more than a promise. This cracks open a whole new world of possibility.

And it ends before we let it go too far.

For that, I'm grateful too.

He runs his hand down my arm, giving me a dopey

smile. "Just so you know, I like accidental kisses even better than accidental butt squeezes."

Feeling emboldened, I reach a hand around and I squeeze his butt one more time. "Same here, but I do like both."

His grin is all kinds of crooked.

I can't resist. Leaning in, I drop a quick kiss onto his lips, then spin around. I slide the key card across the reader, open the door, and head inside. But before the door shuts, I pop my head back out, needing the reassurance. "We're still friends, right?"

He rolls his eyes like that's the craziest thing anyone has ever said. He reaches for my cheek, sliding a thumb across my jaw. "We're absolutely friends, even though I would very much like to kiss you deliberately again."

My heart hammers.

My body pulses.

Oh yes, I want all the deliberate kisses.

Everywhere.

And I'm pretty sure that's what's called friends with benefits. Because I'm the kind of woman who says what's on her mind, who likes clarity, I do just that. "That was a friends-with-benefits kind of a kiss, right?"

"And it was a very good benefit of our friendship, wouldn't you say?"

I can't stop smiling. "I would definitely say so."

This time I wave goodbye for real, shut the door, sigh ever so happily, lean my head back against the wall, and close my eyes.

I just kissed the best man.

And it was spectacular.

12

NADIA

Flopping down onto the soft couch, one arm hanging off the side, I can't stop grinning.

It's just not possible. This smile can't be erased.

Running my finger across my lower lip, I let the reel play before my eyes once more.

The way he swept his thumb over my jaw, held my face, explored my lips.

With a contented sigh, I savor the aftereffects of the knee-weakening kiss with the man I've crushed on since I was a teenager.

My skin tingles, and as I close my eyes, the movie screen shows me *A Kiss with Crosby* over and over.

It's a fantastic double feature.

* * *

Morning sun streaks through the window. A heavy breath pulls from my chest. A yawn tugs at my mouth as I rouse.

A slow glance down reveals I fell asleep in my dress. Must have kicked off my shoes, but otherwise I'm still in bridesmaid couture.

Dragging myself up from the couch, I head to the bathroom, brush my teeth, and shimmy out of my dress. I return to the suite, tug a T-shirt from my overnight bag, and find my phone on the table.

I call Scarlett on FaceTime. Her eyes widen the second she sees me. "Someone slept with her makeup on and her hair still done up bridesmaid-style," she says, an *I know what you did last night* grin lighting up her face.

I feign innocence. "And yet I still look fabulous, right?"

"Yes, you look like you were fucked fabulously," she says, mincing no words.

"Is it a good look?" I ask playfully, patting my day-after do. It's a wild mess, hair sticking up everywhere.

"Cover-worthy of a Joy Delivered catalog. *That* fantastic." Scarlett waves a hand airily as she strolls along the Abbey of Saint-Germain-des-Prés in the sixth arrondissement, its gorgeous spires reaching just out of sight of the phone camera. "Now give me the bang report. It's time. You're wearing all the evidence. Look at your hair, woman. It's a wild mess." She peers at the screen, as if hunting for someone else behind me. "Where is he?"

Laughing, I fling myself onto the couch. "We did not bang. Neither dick banging nor finger banging," I say, since I can definitely go full filth with my girlfriends. But girl talk is cone-of-silence-level vault.

"Tongue banging?" she asks, a hopeful pitch in her voice.

A daring tremble runs through me at the prospect of Crosby's tongue exploring me all over.

But now's not the time to daydream about his downtown skills.

Though I want to. Oh hell, do I want to. I may be a virgin, but my imagination is very sexually active.

"We kissed, and it was fantastic," I say in a wild, wondrous confession. "And kissing as in first base."

She blinks several times. "Whoa. I was sort of joking. But sort of not. You really did kiss your wedding date? The one you were just going to go with as friends?"

"Yes," I say, humming as I knit my brow. "Should I feel bad?"

A smidge of guilt wedges into my chest. We were supposed to be buddies. Just friends.

I violated our friendship pact.

"Was it a bad kiss?"

My jaw drops. "Wash your mouth out with soap. It was amazing. Like Paris-lit-up-at-Christmastime amazing. Like kisses-under-the-streetlamp-along-the-Seine amazing," I say, using terms near and dear to my friend.

She brings her hand to her heart. "So it was the perfect kiss?"

"Exactly," I say, then I share more details of the night —the talking, the teasing, the dancing. The dick pic I never saw, the nip slip that didn't happen, our accidental jokes.

Still, was it a terrible mistake to kick things up to the kiss level?

But we didn't let the genie out of the bottle.

The genie is still in the lamp, I'm sure.

"The kiss was quite intentional though?" Scarlett asks, as if needing to confirm it.

"It was."

She sighs. "Interesting."

I sit up, skin prickling, spidey-senses on alert. "What do you mean?"

"Well, you went from going as friends to ending the night with a kiss. That's interesting." She stops at a street corner, the sound of a bus rumbling along the boulevard landing on my ears.

"Interesting good, or interesting bad?" Nerves speckle my voice. My anxiety resurfaces. Did I mess things up? "Should I be worried about something?"

She laughs, shaking her head. "No. At least I don't think so. But how did you end things with him?"

My heart beats faster with worry. Like I did something wrong by tiptoeing across that line. Maybe we both did. "I'm seeing him later this week because he's going to be my plus-one at the Sports Network Awards. Why do you sound like you're worried about me? Should I be worried?"

She shakes her head. "I'm not, my friend. You're a badass woman. An adult. A formidable force of nature and the toughest owner in the NFL." She draws a deep breath as she crosses the street. "But you also entertained a spectacular kiss with a man you want last night."

"Right, but we agreed to be friends with benefits. We were both on the same page. Besides, he has spring training in a little more than a week, so he'll be gone. It's not like there's even a chance for this to continue," I say, telling her and reminding myself. Sure, we crossed the line, but we both agreed to, both wanted to, and both know we can handle it. "We're simply going to two events together, and if something happens, fine. But it's not like we made any plans to kiss again per se."

Though as I give that voice, the words sound odd— like I'm convincing myself.

"Ah, it's the friends-with-benefits plan. That ought to be *quite uncomplicated*," she says, nodding as she marches past a chocolate shop.

The sight of it makes my mouth water, even as her dry words make my stomach churn. "You think I'm being foolish?"

She laughs gently. "I don't think you're being foolish," she says, taking her time, speaking slowly. "But I also think you should be realistic about what this is. Friends with benefits is risky—both to the benefits and the friendship. Even with the expiration date."

I sit up straighter, absorbing her words. "Of course," I say, drawing on my stores of confidence, my internal strength. "I know that. I'll remember it. I swear. And the expiration date just makes sense."

"Good. You always remember your first," she says.

I blink. "I'm not thinking about sleeping with him."

Scarlett laughs, arching a dubious brow. "Did you hear how high-pitched your voice just went?"

"Because I wanted you to know how I feel."

"Yes, how do you feel after kissing him?"

I narrow my eyes. "You're trying to trick me."

She laughs, but it's a reassuring sound. "Fine, maybe *you're* not thinking about it, but I'm thinking about it for you. And I just want you to think things through. Just know the score, Nadia. And go in prepared for . . . *anything.*"

"I will. I promise," I say, both to her and to myself, and try not to think of first times with Crosby.

We talk more, and she catches me up on life in Paris with the dashing and charming Englishman she fell in love with recently.

"Things are fantastic with Daniel," she says. "Since we finished our acquisition of the boutique hotels, we celebrated by going to Amsterdam for the weekend and indulged in dancing, food, and all sorts of decadence."

"Happy sigh," I say, as she entertains me with more tales of her European life and love. They checked out the castles, took a boat tour, and savored every second together.

It all sounds too good to be true, except it's real and she worked hard for her happily ever after. Plus, given how her first husband julienned her heart, she deserves it.

I believe that good people do deserve love.

Scarlett is one of the best people I know, and she's found true love.

Like my parents had.

Like Brooke has with her husband.

Like Eric seems to have with Mariana.

I love that kind of love. I want that kind . . . someday. The forever kind. The true kind.

But not now. I have too much on my plate, and

Crosby isn't keen on dating, so there's no reason why two old friends who've known each other for a long time shouldn't enjoy the benefits of our friendship.

I say goodbye to Scarlett, determined to be prepared for anything that comes my way.

That's all I have to do when I see Crosby again. Just be prepared.

I head to the bathroom to take a shower, checking my phone one last time before I get in. A text from Crosby blinks at me.

Crosby: Just so you know, I slept hard last night. It was an accidental sleep. But it was the best accidental sleep I've ever had. In fact, I think last night was full of all sorts of terrific accidents that should be repeated.

I practically squeeze the phone against my chest, shimmy my shoulders, and fox-trot across the tiles before I reply.

Nadia: Is "repeat" a dirty word?

Crosby: Maybe it is. We'll find out. PS: feel free to send me any pics of what you're going to wear to the event. You know, for my corsage shopping. Think I'm going to get you a new one.

Nadia: When I decide, I'll snap a pic.

Crosby: Can't wait.

I can't either.

I'm giddy and electrified the rest of the day. I return home to finish organizing my new place, including sorting out my *little darlings*—though some are quite large, *big darlings* sounds so gauche. Setting down a satiny piece of fabric in my nightstand drawer, I arrange my favorites, then charge some others in the bathroom.

Another mantra of mine—*there's no excuse for an uncharged vibrator.*

I learned that lesson the hard way one night when I was craving some time with my favorite dolphin.

He sputtered, petered out, and then went dead.

Never again, I said.

That night, the dolphin rises to the occasion.

Oh yes, he does.

And I'm giddy all over again, and in a much naughtier way.

But the next morning, I'm all business.

As I head into the executive offices in the Hawks stadium on the edge of the city, I sweep Crosby from my mind.

It's business time.

I've got my purse, my ovaries of steel, my ultimate poker face, and my *don't be afraid to speak up* mantra.

That serves me well as I meet with my CEO, general counsel, director of college recruiting, and others. They all relocated here from Vegas, but our general manager did not. In the conference room, I set the agenda and expectations for the year ahead, including hiring a new GM—the most important position when it comes to player contracts and hirings and firings.

Then I add as we wrap up, "There's only one thing to do going forward. The Super Bowl was played earlier this month. The fact that we weren't there is all that matters. Next year I want this team to be flying to Miami to win back the Lombardi Trophy," I tell them.

Once the rest of the execs leave the conference room, my right-hand man, Matthew Harris, leans back in his leather chair, looking like a cat who charmed all the pussycats.

With a do-tell grin, I meet his stare, both of us waiting for the other to break first. It's our thing. He's not only the team CEO; he's also a great friend, and the rare Brit who prefers football played on a gridiron. American football.

I drop my chin in my hand and study him, waiting, waiting.

He whistles, then huffs. "Fine, you win."

I make a rolling gesture with my hand. "Spill. What's the tea, as the kids say these days?"

"I might have a solution to the GM situation. I've got some leads on a GM. Some nontraditional candidates."

Color me intrigued. "Keep talking."

With a satisfied glint in his green eyes, he says, "Word on the street is there's a certain woman who rose through the ranks in Dallas and might fancy a post here."

I sit up straight, excitement tripping through me. "Kim Lee?"

"The one and only."

"She's one of the highest-ranking female executives in the NFL. Hiring her as GM would be a huge coup. Plus, she's brilliant."

"Bloody brilliant, some might say."

"Yes. Get her," I say, then press my palms together. "Pretty please."

"I'll make a call. She'd be fantastic."

"I'd tell you you're my favorite person here, but . . ."

He scoffs, like that's old hat. "I know that already. You tell me that all the time."

"It's true, plus you require compliments," I say.

Dragging a hand through his dark-blond hair, he smiles in admission. "I do indeed. The lifeblood of anyone who is a sports exec is a thick skin and an obsessive devotion to praise," he quips, adjusting his tie. The man is the definition of dapper—he wears three-piece suits every day to work, and the vest look is just so spiffy.

"Speaking of compliments, want to order some lunch and work on our plan for Kim?"

"As if I'd want to do anything else."

We order in, devising a strategy, and the focus energizes me. Matthew too, it seems, which makes me happy, since he moved here even though the woman he was dating in Vegas didn't want him to. "How's everything with Phoebe?" I ask.

He heaves a sigh. "Good? Sort of? I think."

I frown. "What's wrong, friend? Is she having a hard time with you being here?"

"Seems she is. Every day we talk, she makes sure to let me know how displeased she is," he says, then shrugs, chasing it with a sigh.

"I'm sorry to hear that," I say, a smidge of guilt wiggling around in me. "I feel responsible."

"Don't be sorry. I chose to move. Plus, you should be with someone who supports your career rather than holds it back." He takes a beat, his lips curving into a grin. "Isn't that what I told you last year when you went through your parade of horrid men?"

"Sons of mailboxes," I say with a smile, thinking of Crosby's saying.

Matthew furrows his brow. "Please tell me that's not a new American saying I need to learn? I've barely come to terms with 'balling,' 'chilling,' and 'slay.'"

"It's something Crosby said to refer to the men in Vegas."

He arches a brow. "Crosby Cash? The baseball player?"

"Yes. We went to my brother's wedding together."

"Oh, did you now?" His eyebrows shoot into his hairline.

"We're friends," I say, but I try to rein in the grin that comes with that.

"Right. Sure."

"I swear," I say, though the kiss didn't feel friendly at all. "And we're going to the awards gala this week."

"Interesting," he says, all catlike once again. "Very interesting."

I wag a finger. "Don't get any ideas about us."

But truth be told, all the ideas about Crosby are mine.

Delicious, tempting ideas.

Ideas I want to act on.

Good thing I have a busy day with Matthew, rolling up our sleeves and making a plan for the next season.

At the end of the day, I'm kicking ass and taking names.

I don't go home till well past ten, after a dinner with the city managers, where I lay the groundwork for expansion plans for the stadium.

Home at eleven, I strip out of my clothes, remove my ring and watch, sink into the tub, and relax.

I've got this.

I can be Nadia Harlowe, my father's daughter by day, and Crosby's plus-one by night.

13

CROSBY

Send the runner home.

That's the goal.

I curl a hand over Jacob's shoulder as he digs a cleat into third base.

The batter at home plate takes a couple practice swings. "If he connects, you just go. Got it? Game is on the line."

Jacob gives me a crisp, eager nod. "Got it, Coach Cash."

I laugh. "Crosby. Just Crosby."

Jacob flashes a smile at me. "Coach Cash."

Across the diamond, Grant mans the first base, while our closing pitcher Chance waits by the dugout, watching the action in the final out in the final inning.

It's pitcher versus batter, mano a mano. The fierce and mighty fourth grader goes into his windup and unleashes a wicked fastball, sending it right across the plate. The ten-year-old batter connects on the first swing, launching a screaming line drive.

My pulse spikes. "Go, go, go, go, go!"

But Jacob barely needs my direction. He's tearing down the third baseline, hell-bent on crossing home plate. The ball screams past the shortstop, skittering across the grass, as Jacob hoofs it. I cup my hands in front of my mouth. "You got it! You got it! Just go, go, go!"

Jacob crosses the plate with the winning run, victorious as the rest of his team pours out of the dugout right as the batter lands on first base.

Grant gives the batter a fist bump. I trot toward home plate, and when the kids break apart from their cheering fiesta, Jacob heads straight for me, a gleaming smile across his young face.

"Thank you, Coach Cash."

"It was nothing," I say, high-fiving the kid.

But it wasn't nothing. I know the coaching mattered to Jacob. To these other kids. That's why we're here. These grade-schoolers have worked hard all season, and they pulled it off, winning their local league championship.

They make my heart swell with pride. I point at Jacob's chest, stabbing a finger into his sternum. "You're the man."

He shakes his head. "You're the man."

I shake mine. "No, you're the man."

Grant jogs over to us, arriving at home plate with a huge grin. "Maybe I'm the man," he says, smacking palms with the kids, then me.

Chance saunters over, joining the celebration. "Yes, it all goes to you, Grant. We couldn't do anything without you," Chance says to the guy who's the steady force behind the plate in our major league games. They are a tough pitcher-catcher combo, one of the best pairings in all of pro baseball, with the kind of tempo that Posada and Rivera had with the Yankees back in the day.

After we congratulate the kids, help them pack up their equipment, and straighten up the diamond, the three of us leave the field where we've served as honorary coaches, playing with a local team of fourth graders in a rougher section of the city.

The kids needed equipment, a field, and some *go get 'em* spirit. So the three of us volunteered to do it, buying their equipment and pitching in as coaches.

Once we leave the field, heading for my cherry-red Tesla, Grant points to the front seat. "Shotgun."

Chance rolls his eyes. "Back seat has plenty of leg room too. You always think you're pulling one over on me, don't you?"

Grant winks at him. "Front seat is better. You can try to justify it. But the truth is I'm just faster."

Chance lifts a brow, his dark eyes taunting. "That's what she said about you."

Grant shoots him a look. He clears his throat. "Maybe that's what she said about *you*. But no man has ever said that about me."

Chance hums doubtfully, his dark eyes narrowing. "I dunno. Weren't you in and out in, like, fifteen minutes with your Grindr hookup the last time we went out?"

Grant shoots deadly laser rays straight at Chance.

"Dude. That was DoorDash. I fucking ordered DoorDash."

"You hooked up with the DoorDash guy? Damn, Grant," he says, whistling.

Grant huffs. "I was on DoorDash ordering some Thai food for when I got home. I'm not even on Grindr, man." He reaches into his back pocket, then tosses his phone across the roof of the car to Chance.

Chance grabs it with one hand. "Cool. You want me to sign you up for it now? Should I put you down as In-and-Out-in-Five Guy?"

Grant rolls his eyes. "I don't have a single dating app on there. Because, wait for it, I don't need 'em."

Chance winks. "Right. Sure. *DoorDash* is your dating app."

Grant cracks up, shaking his head. "It's a miracle you've ever had a date."

I reach the driver's side door, gesturing to the two-man comedy act. "Please tell me we're not going to spend the entire car ride with the two of you debating your prowess in the bedroom with your conquests."

Grant and Chance shoot each other confused looks. "What else would we talk about?" Grant asks.

Chance scratches his jaw. "That's literally our only conversational fodder," he says as he slides into the back seat. "If we can't thump our chests and mock each other, I don't know what we would discuss. So maybe shut your mouth, Crosby."

I hold up a hand in surrender as I slide into the car. "Anyway, that was a helluva good game. A good season too. Glad you clowns didn't fuck it up for me."

Grant squeezes my cheek. "Aw, do we usually fuck it up for you, little Crosby?"

I bat him away. "Sometimes you do. But fair play," I say, shifting to a slightly serious tone as I start the engine. "You fuckers did good today. Did you see how Carson connected on his at-bat in the fourth?"

Grant beams, a grin that makes his blue eyes sparkle. "That was dope. I was so damn proud of him. He's come so far this season."

Chance pats Grant's shoulder. "He's a helluva catcher too. I can see him following in your footsteps, man."

Grant offers him a fist for knocking. "Right back 'atcha. Christian, Vance, Marco—all the pitchers you coached made serious strides this season. Christian is going to be as fearsome at cleaning up the messes on the mound as you are, man."

It's Chance's turn to smile like a fool. "Thanks. Appreciate that."

As the Cougars' closing pitcher, Chance is indeed our cleanup guy on the mound. He's the one we trust to get us out of jams. Bases loaded, no outs? Tough leftie at the plate? Winning run on third? Chance is the man. The team's radio announcers nicknamed him Last Chance Train Is Pulling Out of the Station because of the way he freezes out opponents when he takes the mound at the bottom of the ninth.

His skills with a ninety-eight-mile-an-hour cut fastball are unparalleled, but so is his smile. His laugh. He actually chuckles and grins while on the mound, twin traits that are about as unnerving as his arm speed.

"It's cute to see you two getting along every now and then," I remark as I check the mirrors, then pull out of the parking spot and into traffic.

"It's been known to happen from time to time," Chance says with a shrug.

"Because we're awesome and so are the kids we coach," I say. "And that's why you two will treat me to beers tonight."

"I'm down for that." Grant taps out a drumbeat on the dashboard, then checks out the time. Close to six thirty. "Where do you want to go?"

"Spotted Zebra?" I suggest.

"Good answer. We've got to support my sister," Grant says. "Did you know her bar was named the hippest in Hayes Valley in *SF Weekly*?"

Chance chimes in from the back seat, "Plus, you like to pick up guys at the Spotted Zebra."

Grant shoots us a wicked grin. "I can't help it if the bar draws an eclectic mix of hot men, and even hotter men who are wildly attracted to me."

"You do know the bar attracts women too?" Chance puts in.

Grant waves a hand dismissively. "Yeah. I mean, sure. Have at them."

"Thanks. I really appreciate that," Chance says dryly.

Grant, the wiseass, adopts a disdainful look. "You don't see me going after the same opportunities you're pursuing. I would think you'd be stoked that I'm not trying to horn in on your territory."

I glance in the rearview mirror at Chance. "Yeah,

aren't you so glad we don't have to compete with this ugly fucker for the ladies?"

Grant cuts in. "All I'm saying is, I don't think you cats appreciate what I do for your odds. A thank you would be nice."

Chance leans forward, his hand curling over the back of Grant's seat. "Wow. Thank you so much for digging men so we don't have to compete with you."

Grant nods, long and confident. "That's what I'm talking about. You are most welcome."

"By that same token, you're welcome too," Chance says, all offhand and casual.

"For what?" Grant asks, puzzled.

I slow to a stop at the light, amused by the pitcher and catcher spurring each other on. That's their style. Thick as thieves on the field, prickly as lions in warring prides off it. In the mirror I catch Chance batting his eyelashes as he says. "That I don't ruin your odds."

Grant cracks up. "Well played, bro. Well played."

"And while we're playing," Chance adds, all cool and cucumber-y, "If you ever want to see who can rack up more numbers, you just let me know."

"For real? You think you can pull more babes than I can pull dudes?"

"I think I can."

Grant barks out a laugh. "Love you man, but you do not know dudes. So don't even attempt that or you will be schooled."

I cast a glance back at the pitcher. "Grant has a point. You ever seen the way they flock to him? Time to step down, my friend."

"Fine, fine." Chance huffs, then strokes his chin. "Maybe I'll just chat with Sierra then."

Grant whips his head around all the way to the back seat, staring at the closing pitcher. "Do not. Do not go near Sierra. Do not. Do not. Do not."

Chance grins wickedly. "Maybe I should tonight. What do you think about that, Grant?"

Grant leans back in his seat, closes his eyes, and drags his hand down his face. "You can score as many digits as I can. Just stay away from Sierra," Grant mutters, then turns to me, his tone shifting. "Speaking of sisters, what the hell happened at the wedding with you and Eric's sister?"

"Yeah, how does that dog collar fit around your neck, Crosby?" Chance asks. "Is it nice and tight, keeping you in line?"

I tug at an imaginary collar as I merge into the right lane so I can turn. "It's keeping me away from the women on the other side of the electrical fence."

"Except Nadia. You two looked pretty tight out on the dance floor," Chance says, his tone doubtful. "I couldn't join the guys for the inquisition because I had to talk to my agent then. But it sure looked like you were cozying up with her the rest of the night."

I flip the signal, turning right, and avoiding the question. "As cozy as Grant looked the other night when he met—who was that you met the last time we were at the Spotted Zebra?"

Chance clears his throat. "Crosby, don't deflect. We need to report back to Eric. We're his proxies. What's the story with Nadia?"

As I drive, I flash back to Saturday night at the wedding.

To the elevator, the hallway, the kiss outside her hotel room door.

The way Nadia melted in my arms, her lips all soft and lush against mine, her body like a dream, her scent invading my mind.

Then I replay our texts the next morning.

Do I confess?

Do I tell them we kissed?

But there's nothing to confess.

Not a thing.

We simply made plans to attend an event together that we were both already invited to. Potentially, we're going to enjoy some more perks.

That's not breaking the pact. The pact was not to date. I'm not dating her. I'm only . . . *benefiting* with her.

Ergo, it's all good.

"We're going to the Sports Network Awards later this week. Just like we went to the wedding. We're going as friends," I say, cool and even.

Grant's eyes widen. "As friends?"

"As friends," I repeat.

"Do you actually know how to be friends with a woman?" Chance posits from the back seat.

"Yes, I do, turkey burger. I have been friends with Nadia for years. Since we were teenagers. Since we were even younger. I know how to be friends with her quite well, thank you very much."

"I'm not sure I believe you," Chance says, his tone brimming with skepticism.

"Look, it's all for the best. She's new in town, she doesn't know a ton of people, and she's the owner of the football team, so it's good for her to be seen out and about with somebody when she goes to these events. Likewise, it's good for me to be seen with someone who's not—"

"A train wreck?" Grant supplies.

"A criminal?" Chance puts in.

"Convicted for insider trading?" Chance continues, his voice going all serious. "Do you think maybe you have a problem with picking the wrong type of women?"

I roll my eyes as we near the Spotted Zebra and I hunt for a parking space. "Gee. I wonder if I do."

Grant lets out a sympathetic sigh. "You just let people in too soon. That's all. Got to protect that heart." He smacks my chest. "Trust me."

For a second, Grant's tone is deadly serious, and a little sad.

"Speaking from experience?" I ask, no teasing this time, no mocking.

Chance leans in closer, his tone low and menacing. "Yeah, did some dude hurt you? Because I will cut that fucker."

Grant shrugs like it's no big deal. "I'm all good now. It was a while ago. Right before my rookie season."

"Who was he?" I ask, since I'm not buying the no-big-deal routine.

Grant waves a hand dismissively. "No one."

"He hurt you, and he's *no one*? Was he a spring training hookup?" Chance asks.

"Yeah, he was."

"Were you in love?" Chance presses.

Out of the corner of my eye, I see Grant work his jaw, clench it, then let go. "Doesn't matter. I was young and foolish. It's in the past. No biggie now."

"You sure?" I push.

"Positive," Grant says with a crisp nod, slicing off this line of questioning. "Anyway, back to Crosby." He taps his sternum. "You need to watch out for your ticker."

"So Crosby should keep women at a distance?" Chance asks.

"Hello? I'm still here," I point out.

"Whatever," Chance says. "Let your bros have your back."

"Fine. What sage advice would my bros give me tonight, then?" I ask as I pull into a spot.

"Here's the advice I'll give you. Be careful. Be very careful who you let in. You'll keep your heart safe that way," Grant says, as I parallel park in three perfect moves.

When I cut the engine, I go a little more serious. "Everything is chill with Nadia. We're going as friends, and that's all it is. Honestly, it'd be the same as if, say, Grant went with your brother to some type of event," I say to Chance.

Grant cringes as he swings open the door. "Are you fucking kidding me? TJ? You think I should date his twin?"

"Yeah," I suggest, egging him on. "Like, maybe if you needed a date. A plus-one for an event. Why not take TJ?"

Grant's jaw drops. It comes unhinged. It falls to the sidewalk. He gives me a *duh* look. "He looks exactly like Chance. No way could I kiss someone who looks like my friend."

"Aww. We're friends now," Chance says, bringing his hand to his heart. "I'm touched."

Grant flips him the bird. "Yes, asshole. We're friends. But I'm not dating your brother. That is too weird."

The notion is indeed weird. But it's also distracting.

The debate over dating a friend's twin occupies the two of them for the next hour as we go into Grant's sister's bar, order beers, and shoot the breeze.

Neither one of them even tries to score any numbers. They're too deep in their bar debate.

They decide Grant's chances of dating TJ are less than zero.

Are those the same as my chances with Nadia?

They *should* be zero.

But when I click open my text messages after I finish my brew, a photo loads.

Two pics, actually.

The first is a shot of some silky fabric on her bed, a close-up of her dress. It's the color of wine, and a growl forms in my throat as I imagine how that dress will look on her body.

The next pic, though, knocks the breath clear from my lungs.

She sent me a shot of her feet in a sexy-as-sin pair of heels.

My mind springs several steps ahead, picturing those legs curled over my shoulders.

Wrapped around my waist.

Spread open on the bed for me.

Ah hell.

The chances of me resisting her are not zero.

Not even close.

14

NADIA

I'll see Crosby in less than forty-eight hours.

I am most definitely counting down.

I'm not even going to pretend I'm not.

I'm counting down, and I'm shopping.

Since I've bought shoes when dates have gone awry, I'm damn well going to buy shoes in advance of one that I'm sure will go fantastically.

Okay, fine. It's not a date. It's an event where we're pairing up. Still, events require shoes.

With a pair of red heels in her hand, my mother settles onto a plush pink cushion on a chair at one of our favorite shops on Union Street.

My mother and I bond over many things, shopping among them. Because shopping is great for talking, and that's something we've always done well. We talk, and we share.

"Over a week on the job back in San Francisco. What's your verdict?"

I peer out the window of the store. "It's . . . foggy here."

She laughs as she slides on the shoes.

My lips form an O as I check out the new footwear. "My verdict on those shoes is they are a must buy," I say, pointing decisively at the beauties on her feet.

"I do love them," she says, pursing her lips as she studies the way they fit. "Where would I wear them though?"

"Anywhere," I say, as the sales associate returns with a gorgeous pair of amethyst velvet shoes for me. I thank her, then continue my ode to Mom's cherry-red pumps. "Everywhere. Gardening. Jigsaw puzzling. Shopping. Going out for tea. Heck, I'd wear those babies walking around the house. And I'd stop and admire my feet in the mirror every time I walked past one."

She taps her chin. "All good ideas. I wonder if I should . . ."

The light bulb goes off. "Wait. Are they for a date?"

She dips her head, her shy smile giving me the answer I need. She confirms it with a nod and a soft, barely audible squeal.

I sit down next to her, grabbing the jewel-like shoes from the box and sliding my left foot into one. "Tell me everything, you secret keeper."

She lifts her face, sporting a smile she can't contain. "I have a dinner date this weekend in Napa."

"With who?" I ask, desperately needing the answer.

"Crosby's mom is setting me up with a man she knows," she says, borderline giggling. It's the most adorable thing I've ever seen.

"Who is he? Is he an upstanding citizen? Does he recycle? Does he have a decent job? Did he go to college?" I ask, peppering her with the same sort of questions she'd pepper me with. "And, most important, does he like dogs?"

I fasten the strap of the shoes as I wait for her answers.

"He's originally from Sydney. He owns a couple of vineyards."

I smile. "Great. So he likes wine. Point in his favor."

"He donates to a local animal shelter. In fact, he's one of the biggest donors."

Nice, I mouth approvingly.

"He came here for college. Went to UCSF. He recycles *and* composts."

I sigh dreamily. "And I bet he has a dog."

She holds up two fingers. "Both rescue mutts. And he likes live music."

I glance at the ceiling, hands up, like angels have sent this man from on high. "Let me guess. James Taylor, Melissa Etheridge, and Jackson Browne. Am I right?"

She smacks my leg. "I'm not *that* old."

"You're right. Melissa Etheridge is not quite as old as those guys."

"Did you think someone my age would prefer Katy Perry?"

"No. You're so not a Katy Perry person. But you are *so* a Jackson Browne person." I raise a finger to make a point. "And therefore you are exactly *that* old."

She rolls her eyes. "Fine, fine. I love Jackson Browne. My '70s heart is pitter-pattering. I can't help myself."

"Is he taking you to that Jackson Browne concert this weekend? I heard there's one in downtown Napa."

She shoots me an *I'm so impressed* look. "Yes, that's where our date is. You know everything."

"Hey, it's my job to be knowledgeable about all things Bay Area. Also, I'm talking to a number of people for the GM job and one of the people I interviewed this week lives there, and he mentioned that he's going to it too."

"How is the quest for a GM going?"

As I try on the shoes, I tell her about the candidates I've met so far this week and the others to come in the weeks ahead. "I want to find someone who can negotiate the trades and the personnel changes I need to make a big splash. Someone who knows exactly how to bring the Lombardi Trophy back to the Hawks. I want to live up to Dad's reputation."

She pats my leg, flashing me a warm smile. "He would be proud of you, holding your own in the job. You've done a great job the last few years, and you'll keep doing it."

A lump forms in my throat. "Thanks, Mom. I needed to hear that. Some days are hard and busy." I gesture to the shoes. "But shoes make hard days easier. You need to buy those shoes. Actually, I'm going to get them for you as a gift for your date."

She smiles. "Thank you. That's very sweet of you." Then her expression falters, her smile fading away. "Nadia, do you think it's terrible that I'm dating again? Would he be upset?"

I squeeze her shoulder, shaking my head adamantly.

"He loved you so. He'd want you to be happy. Don't forget that note he wrote."

She brings her hand to her mouth. A tear slides down her cheek.

Tears well in my eyes too as a memory flickers before me. My father's decline was fast and furious. In some ways that was for the best. He didn't have to suffer for long. When I was at the hospital with him, he asked me to help him write a note for his wife.

He wanted her to be happy again. He wanted her to go out and find love. The kind that they'd had.

"Don't let your mother mourn me for too long. She's young and vibrant. She'll want to love again. And you need to keep reminding her that that's what I would want for her," he told me.

We wrote a brief instructional manual for me to give any man dating her after he passed. Though, not on a first date.

Instructions for dating my wife: You must keep up with her, like puzzles, enjoy gardening, recycle as much of everything as possible, be able to banter about the news, cook a meal now and then, but also take her out to the best restaurants in the city, as well as a dive bar occasionally because she loves those. It helps, too, if you can bake, because she has quite a sweet tooth. Most importantly, she has the biggest heart in the world, and if you break it, I will haunt you forever.

I memorized every beautiful word. Replaying them in my head brings a surge of emotion to my heart. A lump to my throat.

"He doesn't want to have to haunt this guy," I whisper, fishing in my purse for my handy tissues to dab the threat of tears. "So yes, Mom, he'd be very happy."

She nods a few times, a small smile playing across her lips, rearranging her frown. "I think he would too." She takes a beat to compose herself. "What about you and Crosby? You seemed to enjoy each other at the wedding."

Enjoy is putting it mildly.

I savored it.

I fantasized about it.

I've gotten off to it.

But I'm not telling *that* to my mom.

I zoom in on the practical matters of Crosby and me. "We're going to the Sports Network Awards later this week. I'm looking forward to it," I say, trying desperately to maintain a straight face even though I'm giddy with excitement about seeing him in less than forty-eight hours.

She arches a wry brow. "Are you dating him?"

I kind of wish I were.

But there's no space in my life for it. It's for the best that he's already erected walls. "He's taking a break from dating. I'm focused on work. Truly, I'm just going as his friend." *Friends with benefits perhaps*, I add silently, reminding my lips not to curve into a naughty grin as I imagine some of the benefits.

More kisses?

More than kisses?

Kisses all over?

A shiver runs through me . . .

Pressing her palms together, my mom gazes ceiling-ward. "Someday you might date him."

I swat her playfully. "Don't be silly. I just said neither one of us is in the market for a relationship. I'm busy with the team. He has spring training and then, you know, the regular season. Which lasts for six long months."

"To that I say—*blah, blah, blah.*"

I laugh. "Glad you have your own opinion."

"I do indeed. And I've been rooting for you two ever since he looked at you the night you went to prom."

I jerk my head back. "What? How did he look at me?"

"Like he wished *he* were Charlie Duncan." She shrugs, a little devilishly. "I saw something in his eyes then."

I'm still for a moment, flashing back not to eight years ago, but to a few nights ago. At Eric's wedding, Crosby mentioned Charlie and his *broken heart.* Is my mother right? Did Crosby look at me like he wished he'd taken me to prom eight years ago?

Just as quickly as it arrived, I wave off the galloping-away thought.

That was the past.

But in the present, is he wanting more than our *plus-one*?

We *did* leave the door open.

Does he want to kick it all the way open?

Do I want to?

My stomach flips as I imagine his hand on my face again, his lips sweeping over mine, our breath mingling.

And more. So much more.

I return to the moment. "And I saw something in *your* eyes when you gazed at these shoes." I point at the red pumps. "Let's go buy them."

A few hours later, I take a sip of chardonnay, enjoying how it warms me.

How it fuels thoughts of *benefits*.

What type of benefits are on the table?

Sinking onto my plush duvet, my mind indulges in a meander down friends-with-benefits lane, checking out the scenery. Right there are the words Crosby said to me the other night. *We're absolutely friends, even though I would very much like to kiss you deliberately again.*

I wander around the bend to check out his text from the next morning. *In fact, I think last night was full of all sorts of terrific accidents that should be repeated.*

What comes around the next curve in the lane?

What do I want to come next?

I'm not entirely sure, but I know this much—I want more.

As I scroll through our recent texts, I land on one where he invited me to send him a pic of what I'm wearing to this weekend's event.

Why not?

I set down the wine, slide on the shoes, and arrange myself on the bed.

This will be fun. Just more of *plus-oneing with the best man.*

I send him a picture.

Me in bed, wearing these shoes, my feet crossed at the ankles.

Along with a few words.

Nadia: I bought these for our event, my plus-one.

His reply arrives lightning fast.

Crosby: I didn't have a foot fetish, but now I do. I really fucking do.

Nadia: I like this fetish of yours.

Crosby: And I would like to kiss your ankles very much.

I tremble, picturing his lips on my ankles, him brushing his mouth along my skin. It's not a *plus-one* type of response from him. It's so much better.

Nadia: I think I'd like that.

Crosby: You know what I'd like?

Nadia: What would you like?

As I wait for his reply, I savor the sensations floating through me, the shivers running up and down my body, the tingle in my chest. It feels so good to flirt. So good to kick us up beyond *plus-one*.

Crosby: I would like to slowly, deliciously unbuckle them, take them off you, and kiss my way up to your knees.

Fire flickers through me, scorching my veins. My God, did it get red-hot in here all of a sudden? Yes, it did.

Nadia: I bet that would feel so damn good.

I'm no expert at flirting, and I hope I'm doing this right. But the speed of his reply tells me that I'm doing it exactly as we both want.

Crosby: Kiss you behind your knee, lick you along your thighs, press my lips to your legs.

Nadia: I'm . . .

Crosby: You're what?

I draw a deep breath.

Am I doing this?

Smashing past this friendship wall? Knocking it down? Sending this banter into officially naughty terrain?

I squirm, my body hot, my center pulsing.

Yes. Yes, I am doing this.

I type out my greatest wish right now. I feel daring and bold as I write it, no matter how risky this might be. We've sped up to sixty miles per hour in the span of one hot picture of my feet in heels.

But maybe that was all we needed, a match to our kindling.

Nadia: I'm wanting you to kiss me all over.

Crosby: Fuck, Nadia. I'd love to. You're going to look so damn good in those shoes. And I bet you taste so good everywhere. Every inch of you.

I wave a hand in front of my face, as if that will lower my temperature. But my skin is flushed, hot with lust and need. I'm dangerously wet and wickedly turned on.

There's only one solution.

. . .

Nadia: On that note, I need a moment. Be right back.

Letting go of the phone, I slide down my panties, kicking them to the floor. Opening the nightstand drawer, I grab my most favorite rabbit. Turning it on, I lift up my knees, then let them fall apart as I close my eyes.

The rabbit's ears buzz, tantalizing my wet clit.

A gasp falls from my lips, hungry and wild.

I glide the rabbit's head through my hot center. It moves easily. I'm that slick, that aroused.

That ready for Crosby.

My skin tingles all over, cells bursting with electricity, sparking with pleasure as I rub.

My legs part farther, and I hike up the speed, seeking friction, sweet friction, as I chase relief. I breathe harder, rocking my hips, abandoning myself to the feelings igniting in me.

To the tendrils of desire curling in my toes, coiling in my stomach, pulsing in my aching center.

As I imagine Crosby.

His face. His mouth. His lips. I breathe his name on a harsh pant.

"Crosby."

Then I say it again, loving how it feels on my tongue in the heat of the moment, what it does to my body, the way it makes me ravenous with lust everywhere. How

I'm hot with the prospect of bliss. I punch up my hips, pushing the rabbit into me.

I moan, letting my legs fall open wider as the silicone shaft sinks deeper and I imagine it's Crosby.

Pushing, sinking, thrusting, until he fills me all the way and I gasp.

Crosby.

Oh God.

Please.

Yes. More.

Like that, fucking myself with the rabbit, its ears wildly caressing my clit at rocket speed, I moan and groan. I writhe and melt.

I picture. I imagine.

My mind plays dirty image after dirtier image, switching ruthlessly between him licking me, eating me, then fucking me.

The thing I've never had. The thing I want desperately now.

Sex, gorgeous, beautiful, hot, hard sex.

I want him inside me.

Taking me, having me, fucking me.

I detonate, coming hard and fierce as I call out his name.

It sounds so incredibly right. I picture him leaning over me, braced on strong arms, dipping his head, brushing a soft, gentle kiss to my lips.

Telling me how incredible that was for him too.

All of that. I want all of that. I want more than plus-oneing with the best man.

* * *

After the rabbit's gone back into its burrow, I pick up my phone. Read a new message.

Crosby: What kind of moment did you need? Everything okay? Did I cross a line?

I reply, as more than a friend.

Nadia: I needed a moment . . . to cross all sorts of lines myself.

Crosby: Are you saying what I think you're saying?

Nadia: I'm saying I'm feeling very satisfied right now.

Crosby: And I bet that was not an accident at all.

Nadia: It was very deliberate satisfaction.

15

CROSBY

After a gallons-of-sweat-inducing StairMaster workout, some pretzel-like stretching worthy of a YouTube yogini, and a punishing session with my personal trainer at the gym—because sessions with personal trainers should always be punishing—a quick glance at the clock tells me I'm seven hours away from seeing Nadia.

I grab my water bottle and zip up my hoodie, tipping my chin to one of my workout partners. Juan, a pitcher on my team. He's tearing up the treadmill. He yanks an AirPod from his ear.

"You almost done?"

"Do I look like I'm almost done?" he fires back, breathing hard, attacking the machine with ferocity.

"Looks like you're taking a walk in the park."

He laughs, then flips me the bird. "Fuck off."

"Fuck off to you too."

"Hey! You want to babysit again?"

"Anytime. You let me know."

"Thanks, man."

I turn to Holden. "Over and out for you?" I ask as he tugs on his LA Bandits sweatshirt, his former team.

"I am. Logged my four miles already this morning. So this was just extra."

"Show-off."

"You could work harder too. Might make your stats better," he says, an evil glint in his eyes.

"My stats destroy your stats."

He scoffs, then laughs. "You wish. Ready for some grub?"

"You sure you can fit it in your schedule? You probably have a one o'clock session with a sandwich, then a two o'clock to do your laundry."

"You're right. I'll dine alone."

I clap his shoulder. "Let's go. Lunch with you will kill an hour."

He rolls his eyes. "Thanks. Glad I'm a way for you to pass the time."

"That is indeed one of your benefits. Along with the occasional display of friendship and support," I say with an *I'm a smart-ass* wink. I gesture to his sweatshirt. "Any word from your agent or from the team about whether the Dragons have a new manager yet?"

He shakes his head, sighing heavily. Holden joined the Dragons after a recent trade. Once the city's vaunted baseball franchise, the longtime team is now the scourge of Major League Baseball after a sign-stealing scandal that would put a certain Texas team to shame. Our fans call The Dragons our mortal enemies, saying the city isn't big enough for two teams, when one's best known for cheating. The cheating ran up and down the lineup, with the manager enlisting players, pitchers, pinch hitters, bat boys, camera operators, field crew, and more in an elaborate ruse to steal opposing teams' catcher signs to rack up ill-gotten wins. So many wins and so many sign thefts that the team won two World Series in a row.

Two *tainted* championships one right after the other.

When an enterprising sports reporter broke news of the scandal, the Dragons owner was an apoplectic-level of livid. He cleaned house like a biohazard crew on steroids, gutting the organization with a stem to stern roster shake-up.

Every player on the cheating lineup got the hook. Every coach too, from manager down to first base, third base, pitching, and so on. The owner brought in new talent, like Holden.

But one of the last pieces to fall into place is a new skipper.

"No idea when that's going to come. It'd be nice to know who's going to be determining the batting lineup," Holden says as we head up Fillmore.

"What's the vibe like so far with the new players? Any idea yet from talking to the guys?" I ask.

He shakes his head. "I've only met a handful. They seem decent and as disgusted with the sign-stealing as they should be."

"Hell yeah. If I were the baseball commissioner, I'd ban the entire former team for life."

"Ban them right now. Right the hell now." He shakes his head in obvious disgust. "Consider yourself lucky that you're on the team in the city with a squeaky-clean image."

We stop at the light. "I definitely consider myself lucky for that. In fact, I might have to get a new pair of lucky socks just to celebrate being on a fine-ass team."

On that note we pop into Gabriel's Tuxedos on the next block. "I need a new pair for tonight. Every event needs its own inaugural socks," I say, heading for a display of the sartorial item in question. Flicking through pairs, I find one that suits my fancy. Fox socks. "I deem these my new lucky socks."

I hold the pair above my head, Simba-style.

"Those are ugly as sin, so they're perfect for you," Holden says.

"Or maybe I'm just a fox and they match me."

"Keep telling yourself that."

At the register, Gabe says hello then shoots me a *give me news* stare. "How's it going with the plan?"

"Yes, inquiring minds want to know," Holden adds with avid eyes of his own. The man knows my temptation. My *particular* one.

But I haven't fallen too far off the wagon. I'm holding on to the wheels. I give them two thumbs up. "I am all good."

"You're being a good boy?" Gabe asks, wanting to be sure.

"So good."

That feels true enough for now.

We take off with my socks in hand, heading to my favorite salad-and-grain-bowl spot for lunch. As we eat, Holden and I chat more about his season ahead, and what he wants to do differently to distance himself from the old guard.

"I feel for you, man. It can't be easy. But I have faith that you're going to do a great job. You just have to work on your media persona," I say, since he's not known for being a smiley-faced favorite among reporters.

He sneers, then narrows his eyes. "That's going to be one tough task. Last time I sat down with a local sports reporter in Seattle it didn't go so well."

"Did he burn you?"

"More like stabbed me in the back, made shit up and totally invaded my family's privacy."

"Ah, so that did it. That's why you don't like talking to the media?"

"I don't have many warm fuzzies for the press."

"I hear ya. It's a balance, man. It's part of the job though. Helps with sponsorships."

"True. And my agent says the same. So I'm sure I need to work on it. Someday." As he takes a bite of his lunch, his brow furrows. "Hey, if you said at the wedding that nothing was happening with Nadia, then why the hell are you counting down the time until the awards ceremony tonight?" He strokes his chin, like a detective cracking the case. "I sense a plot twist, Watson."

"No twist. The answer is as simple as the evidence in front of you."

"What evidence?"

I lean in closer, adopting a satisfied smile. "She's prettier to look at than you."

He lifts a forkful of his chicken salad. "No argument there. She's gorgeous."

I bristle, but don't disagree.

Facts are facts.

* * *

Six hours later, I'm in my black tux. I pull on my new lucky socks, adjust my bow tie, and grab the corsage and boutonniere from the fridge.

I frown at the plastic container in my hand. This is cheesy, right?

Like extra-slices-melting-down-the-burger-patty levels of cheese.

Does she really want this for each event?

It's kind of . . . teenager-y. It was kind of funny when it was required at the wedding.

But tonight? For a gala?

We don't need to walk down Prom Memory Lane.

Fuck these flowers. Nadia is a sexy, sophisticated woman. I'm going to get her something to match her mystique.

I check the time on my phone then open the picture she sent me of her dress fabric, and then hightail it out of my house, googling the nearest stores as I go.

Bounding down the front steps, I reach the limo door just as the driver steps out.

"Good evening, Mr. Cash."

"Hey, Jasper," I say. "Can you take me to that store on Fillmore that sells those things women wear around their shoulders?"

"Wraps, sir?"

I snap my fingers. "Yep. Those."

He doesn't even blink—probably not even close to the strangest request he's gotten. "Right away."

My phone buzzes in my pocket as I slide into the back of the limo. When I click on the text from my cousin, attached is a photo of a cute blonde with a heart-shaped face.

Rachel: How about Caitlin? She teaches preschool! And fosters kittens! She's soooooo good.

Crosby: Rach, I love you, but I'm not interested. Plus, I'm taking my old friend Nadia to the Sports Network Awards tonight.

Rachel: OMG!

Crosby: It's nothing. I swear it's nothing.

Rachel: Squee! I want a report!

Crosby: I will give you no such thing. But hey, maybe I should find a guy for you. Payback, cousin!

Rachel: You say that like it's a bad thing, you setting me up with someone. I'm pretty sure you know some fabulous men. Ideally, I'd like a man who loves his job, likes to unwind with something quirky and creative, and would be passionately, madly devoted to me, talking and trying to make the best of a life together.

Crosby: I'm on it.

I tuck the phone into my pocket when we reach the store I passed the other week, the one with scarves and shit in the window.

"Be right back," I tell Jasper, and race in. I show the dress fabric to a sales associate, and three minutes later, I walk out with a gift for my . . . old friend Nadia.

Hardly seems like the way to describe her though.

I'm back in the limo when Rachel replies with another message.

Rachel: But back to you and Nadia. All I will say is I'm so excited for you, but please be careful. You let people in too soon.

Crosby: Funny. Grant said that too the other day. I promise I'll be careful.

But at Nadia's door a few minutes later, I don't know that I feel *careful*.

Hungry—that's what I feel when she opens the door.

A dress the color of a rich merlot hugs her curves

and shows off her fantastic breasts, which are dusted with some sort of shimmery powder. All that glimmering skin makes me want to haul her against me, bury my face in the valley of her breasts, and kiss her every-fucking-where, starting with those lips, all sensual, pink, and glossy.

Her chestnut hair falls loose over her shoulders in thick waves I want to run my hands through. And her face. Those cheekbones. That mouth. Those big brown eyes.

My brain kicks into an overdrive of desire. My breath catches, and lust hums in my bones.

"Nadia Harlowe," I say, "there is nothing accidental about how sexy you look, or how much I want to kiss you right now."

Her lips part, her tongue flicking across her bottom lip, and she shudders. "Kiss me," she whispers.

I set the gift bag on the entryway table.

This time, I'm careful about one thing only. *Don't mess up her hair.*

I step inside, kick the door closed, and cup her cheeks. I haul her close. With a groan already rumbling up my throat, I cover her lips with mine and kiss her so goddamn deliberately.

The opposite of our first kiss.

A kiss stoked from fire.

One forged from the flames of lust licking between us, fanned by nights of flirty, dirty texts.

Or maybe, just maybe, from years of latent feelings.

Whatever it is, I need to touch her, consume her, taste those lips crushed against mine. Her tropical island scent dances in my head, making me dizzy, buzzed on her.

I kiss her like I can't get enough of her. Like we're both pouring years of longing into this moment. Like our kiss is fueled by bone-deep need to surrender to this desire.

To this kiss.

To this connection.

I run my thumb along her jaw as I kiss her rougher, more passionately, my tongue exploring her mouth, my lips brushing over hers, our breaths mingling.

She sighs and murmurs, kissing me back just as fiercely, her hands traveling up my chest, spreading over my pecs like she wants to own my body.

Hell yes.

Have at it.

I drop one hand from her face, sliding it down over the curve of her breast. She trembles as my fingers roam around her and down her spine till my palm curls over her ass, and I jerk her against me so she can feel the outline of my cock.

"Oh!" she gasps.

It's so goddamn sexy, that one syllable and the way she says it, tinged with desperation.

I break the kiss, panting hard.

"I think I need a moment," I say, echoing her line from the other night.

"I think I need a moment too," she says.

We both grin like we share a secret, and we do—the truth of how we feel for each other.

But there's no time to explore these feelings now.

She glances at her watch and shoots me a rueful smile. "I think we better go. I do have to present an award," she says, her breath still uneven, laced with desire.

"Me too." Gently, I run my fingers along a soft curl of her hair. "But know this—I'd love nothing more than to play hooky, unzip your dress, strip you down to nothing, and kiss every inch of your naked body." I meet her gaze again, locking eyes with her so she can see in mine how much I want her. Reaching for her wrist, I run my thumb over it and feel her shudder under my touch. "I'd love nothing more than to kiss you, touch you, fuck you."

She shivers, her eyes fluttering closed for a second. "I want that too," she whispers, and I don't know how I'm going to make it through the next few hours.

"We better go," I growl. "Or I'm going to take you right now."

"Can't have that," she says, sexy and teasing.

Somehow we separate for real this time.

No touching.

She grabs her purse, lifting a brow as she checks its contents. "I don't need my Leatherman, but I do need these two necessities." She takes out a tissue to wipe away her smeared gloss, then leans into me and dabs my lips too, a delighted grin on her gorgeous face. "There. Now you don't quite look like you were kissed six ways to Sunday."

"But I was. I definitely was."

She tosses the tissue into the trash can, snags her lipstick, and reapplies it.

I raise a hand. "Um, back up a sec though. Leatherman?"

"Every woman should carry one. How else would I remove a porcupine quill if I'm out hiking?"

"There you go."

She snags her keys and drops them into her purse. "Let me grab a wrap."

I grin. "Let me."

She shoots me a curious look as I reach behind her for the small shopping bag.

"I ditched the corsage. Tonight isn't the prom. It's a gala, and this seemed more fitting." I hand her the bag, anticipation skating over my skin, along with the hope that she'll like it.

Pulling out the tissue paper, she dips her hand inside and tugs a length of wine-colored fabric from the bag. "It's one of those wrap thingamajigs," I say. It comes out gravelly and a little awkward.

A smile lights up her face. "You can just call it a wrap," she says, then runs her hand over the soft fabric. "It's silky and gorgeous."

My heart thumps at the compliment. "Glad you like it."

She tosses it around her shoulders and hugs it across her breasts. I breathe out hard, groaning my appreciation for how goddamn good she looks in everything—especially in something I got her.

"Gorgeous. Like you."

"Thank you," she says, all whispery and sexy, and I am dying with desire for her.

We step out into the hall, and she shuts the door

behind us. In the elevator, she turns to me, her expression pensive but determined.

She steps closer, fiddles with my tie, then meets my eyes. "Before we do any of those things you said, there's something I want you to know."

16

NADIA

Funny, I don't normally tell a guy the status of my V card on a second date.

Not on a third or fourth date either.

For the longest time, I thought my virginity was a whispery secret, a closely guarded little nugget of privacy. Right now, right here, I'm seeing it for what it is—not a secret, but a fact.

Having sex or not having sex says nothing about who I am, what I want as a woman, or what I want in bed.

I flash back to my choices with other men.

By the time I was ready to have sex, the men I dated were uninspiring. In college, I never dated anyone long enough to want to give him the keys. Then, in my master's program, I liked a guy well enough, but when my pants were off for the first time, he groped me like I was a Thanksgiving turkey.

Kind of a turnoff.

I didn't want any more with him or the others.

So I never told them I was a virgin.

No one has earned need-to-know status yet, because I've never met anyone I wanted to sleep with.

Until now.

I want the man standing across from me in a tux.

My friend.

My friend with benefits.

My brother's best friend.

I want him, unequivocally, passionately, and so damned soon.

This awareness dawns on me all at once, like the lights turned on in a house that's been dark.

Switch.

Every room illuminated.

And I know beyond a shadow of a doubt that I want to have sex with him.

And so, I'm not confessing my virginity. I'm sharing it.

As the elevator doors whisk shut, I meet Crosby's gaze. "So, everything you just said to me—take me, have me, have sex with me?"

His eyes widen, sparkling with the desire I've seen in him since he showed up at my door tonight. "Yes?" His voice is full of anticipation.

I draw a breath but find it's remarkably easy to tell him. Maybe because we've known each other for years, or because we're friends.

Or maybe because we've been up-front about what we are.

Friends with benefits.

I finish the thought. "I want that. I'd really like to have sex for the first time ever. And to have it with you."

That was easy.

As easy as buying shoes, as easy as talking to a friend, as easy as being with family.

"Tonight," I add. It's a relief to say because I want this so badly. I want it with every part of me, and I want it with him.

But Crosby is frozen.

He breathes out. Breathes in.

Fine, he blinks a bit.

But that is all.

I laugh, a nervous sound. "Maybe I do need a Leatherman to get you to talk." The nerves missing before now clobber me over the head like a criminal sneaking up on me in an alley, and I twist my fingers together. "Crosby? Say something, won't you?"

That's what I ask.

And then I wait, terribly, awfully worried that I've broken him.

17

CROSBY

Why am I not freaking out about deflowering my best friend's sister?

Maybe because resisting Nadia has never been about her being Eric's sister. It's because I asked Eric to be my no-sex sponsor.

But Eric's not here.

And I'm so damn grateful because I don't want to stop.

I want to say to her, *Absolutely, let's go right this fucking second.*

All right, her truth bomb does knock the breath out of me, and I have to get it back before I can answer her. She's vibrating with nerves, and I can't leave her like this.

"Yes." I knock the side of my head, kick-starting my shock-stalled brain. "Yes. Yes. Yes."

Her shoulders relax, and she lets out a laugh, chased with a long sigh of relief. Then she smiles like a sexy and innocent vixen.

That's what surprises me the most. Nadia is a conundrum. "I wasn't expecting you to say that. You're so . . ." I have to hunt for the right word. "Bold and confident. You're a woman who knows her own mind. You're so . . . sexual. I didn't expect you to be a virgin. You don't seem innocent."

The elevator doors open, and she steps out first. "I'm not innocent, Crosby. I'm simply inexperienced. But nothing is virginal up here." She taps her temple.

I would love to know all her filthy thoughts, and I'm dying to know if they match mine. "What's in there, Wild Girl? Tell me. I want to know every dirty thing."

Her smile is devilish. "The other night? When I took a moment?"

I nod, my neck hot, the collar of my shirt suddenly too tight. "Yeah, I remember perfectly."

"I imagined you on me, over me, in me. I want to feel all of that with you."

I drag a hand over the back of my neck, letting out a low groan, my temperature shooting up to dangerous levels. With my other hand on the small of her back, I guide her out of the lobby and into the waiting limo. I tell the driver where we're heading then raise the partition so we're alone in the vast back seat.

I take her hand, linking my fingers through hers. "I want you so fucking much. But this is big. This is huge. I don't want you to have any regrets."

She furrows her brow, glancing down at our clasped hands, then back up. "Regret is not what I'm feeling now."

I laugh lightly. "Me neither. But I don't want you to feel it later."

Funny, how telling Nadia how I feel is so much easier than anything I've ever done with any other woman, light-years easier than talking to anyone else has ever been.

"I want to do everything with you, for you, to you. I want it to be spectacular for you. You deserve that. You deserve to feel incredible," I say.

Her eyes shine with lust and a warm kind of happiness. The sort of happiness that comes from within, from someone knowing you, understanding you.

"I'd like to feel that way," she says in a tempting whisper.

My God, she is my undoing—so sweet and still so bold.

I run a hand down her arm, savoring the way she shivers. My other hand squeezes her fingers more tightly, and I don't want to stop touching her. I don't want to break this connection. "You deserve to feel like a queen being adored. A goddess being worshipped. A woman being consumed."

Her eyes float closed, and her breath catches. When she opens those big chocolate eyes again, they're glittering with desire. She parts her lips, her voice a little softer, innocent and hopeful, as she asks, "Will you consume me, Crosby?"

"Will I? That's not even a question," I rasp out.

Every inch of me is burning up with a lust so strong, so powerful, it feels like madness.

I gaze at the sensual curve of her mouth, at the

inviting skin of her sensual shoulders, at the tops of her soft and wondrous breasts. I want to touch her, taste her, please her. But we should talk about expectations.

I trail a finger down the top of her hand. "Let's just set the rules first."

She waggles a brow. "We're both in sports. Rules are good."

My grin goes crooked. "We'll call this the Virgin Rule Book."

"Can rule number one be we have sex?"

I laugh hard. "Yes, woman. But let's set the less obvious ones. Look, we're friends, right?"

"Obviously."

"You want to stay friends?"

She rolls her eyes. "Of course. And you aren't interested in dating, so we're just friends with benefits. I'm down with that. Is that the second rule? We stay friends?"

"Yes. Let's make that rule number two."

She makes a check mark. "Friends with benefits now. Friends always."

"Good. I like that rule a lot." It means I won't lose her.

I won't fuck this up. Because I *can't* fuck this up. I won't let someone in too fast, because she's already in. Ergo, this thing brewing between us doesn't count as a relapse. This isn't me cheating on my cleanse.

This is the opposite. This is safe. This is fine. This is so much more than fine. This is a call to service.

To service her. And I can't deny my duty.

"This is part of the whole plus-one thing," I say.

"Is that a rule, though, or more of an addendum?"

"It's an addendum."

"The Friends with Benefits clause." Her expression is confident, professional. Probably the same way she looks when she's negotiating deals.

Reluctantly, I tell her, "But rule number three is no sex tonight."

She pushes out her bottom lip, giving me a big ol' frown. "Why not?"

Damn, this is hard.

Pun intended. I glance down at my crotch. My dick is as hard as granite. Yeah, this is rock-fucking-hard. But there can be no wavering on this.

She matters to me. In ten years, I'll still be her first. And in ten years, I still want to be her friend.

"I care too much about you. You're so damn important to me. I want nothing more than to fuck you right this very second and to make love to you later tonight, but I want to make sure that you'll have no regrets. And I want it to be special for you," I say, my hand roaming over her shoulder and down her back.

She trembles in its wake, then nods. "I get that. But I kind of hate you for being right, because I'm so ridiculously turned on right now." Her fingers thread through mine even tighter, her grip getting needier. Desperate, even. The look in her eyes is completely wild.

A groan works its way up my throat. "Maybe I could do something about that so you won't hate me."

"What do you have in mind?"

I dip my face, kissing her bare shoulder. "Rule number four. I get to make you come. A lot."

Shuddering, she gasps. Her voice is smoky, full of longing. "Like, right now?"

I growl a *yes*.

Then I heed the call to action, tugging on the skirt of her dress, yanking it up higher, then higher still. There. Perfect. "Why don't you climb onto my lap and rock that beautiful body against my cock while I play with your pussy?"

She bites her lip, grinning like she won two tickets for a trip to the moon.

That's exactly what I intend to give her.

18

CROSBY

With her dress bunched up by her waist and her legs straddling mine, I savor my first glimpse of the woman's panties.

Let the record reflect that Nadia could wear granny underwear, boring gray ones that go all the way above her belly button, and I'd still want her.

But instead, the lace matches her dress. *Burgundy.* They're lace, tiny, and the color of desire, as enticing as the rest of her.

Every inch of her.

With one hand gripping her hip, I slide my other hand between her legs, the pad of my thumb touching that delicious wet spot on the cotton panel.

A throaty gasp rewards me.

"Ohhhh."

Her hands fly to my shoulders. She steadies herself, curling her fingers around them, gripping more tightly.

A grin breaks across my face. I love that she's holding on for dear life. That she's taking charge already, rocking against me, rubbing her sweet, hot center against the ridge of my cock.

The only issue is . . . my pants.

"Gimme one second," I say, unzipping my tux pants, since, well, I don't want to walk into the event with a wet spot on them. I push them down but leave my boxer briefs on, thinking it's a little presumptuous to just whip out my cock for her riding pleasure.

Besides, it's hotter like this anyway.

I tug her hips back down on the outline of my dick, rubbing her against my erection.

She groans when we make contact again, then swivels her hips.

"You feel so fucking good," I growl as we work in tandem, rocking, rubbing, thrusting.

My hand coils more tightly around her hip. She tilts her pelvis, seeking the friction that she needs, using the outline of my erection as her pleasure device.

Fine by me.

"Use me, Wild Girl. Use my cock to get off. It's all for you."

She nods wildly, panting, letting her face fall into the crook of my neck as she whispers, "Please touch me now."

"Touch you where?" I ask, teasing. "I'm waiting."

But Nadia doesn't hesitate. "My pussy," she whispers.

My skin sizzles. My dick hardens impossibly more. "God, it's so fucking sexy when you say dirty words." I dip my fingers below the lace, pushing it to the side and touching her flesh for the very first time.

My fingers travel over tufts of soft hair, finding her hard clit.

I shudder with lust.

She trembles with desire.

This is bliss, perfect fucking bliss, this evidence of her arousal in the delicious rise of her clit.

She's so wet, so slick. Her moans are like jolts of electricity as I stroke her, traveling along her soft, wet folds.

She pants and moans. "Yes, do that. I've never . . ." But she doesn't finish the thought.

My ears perk up, hearing what's unsaid.

Never.

Does that mean what I think it does?

Her pace riding my cock quickens, as her breath comes faster, her groans and moans more frenzied.

With one hand still gripping her hip, my other hand delights in the paradise of her sweet, wet pussy. I follow her noises, touching her clit exactly the way she seems to want.

A way that makes her murmur and sigh, moan and writhe.

She's a sight to behold as she chases her pleasure.

An absolute sensual beauty rocking on me.

My dick is a steel rod in my boxer briefs. Hell, it's her fucking dildo right now, and as horny as I am, as turned on as I am, I'm so fucking happy she's using me like this, like a horse she wants to ride. May she gallop away on me into the sunset of a massive orgasm.

"Use me for whatever you need, baby," I say, urging her on as she grinds and dips and fucks. I kiss my way up to her ear. "Love the noises you make. Love the way you ride me."

She gasps, words seeming out of reach as she treats me like her bucking bronco.

I'm a furnace, but I don't care if I overheat—all I want is for her to shatter. She lifts her face from my shoulder. Her jaw is tight, her eyes squeezed shut. When she opens them, they're glazed over with lust.

Pushing harder against my dick, she drops her lips onto mine, kissing me savagely, then so damn sloppily. "Yes, oh God, I'm coming."

With another stroke of my fingers, another rub over her diamond clit, she trembles and shakes, crying out her release.

Her whole body seems to flush with pleasure. And God knows mine is too. She raises her face and meets my eyes, looking so damn happy.

She smiles the most wonderful smile I've ever seen, and God, I'm horny as a lion in heat. I grit my teeth because we'll be at the gala soon and I need to rein this in.

Time to picture baby animals.

Ducklings floating across the pond, kittens nursing on their mamas, anything to forget that all my blood has rushed south of the border.

But then Nadia slides off me, drops between my legs, and gets to her knees.

I barely have time to think.

Hell, I don't *want* to think.

She looks up at me as she sets a hand on the steel outline of my cock in my boxer briefs. "Can I?"

Well, I'm not saying no.

I'm saying, "Fuck yes."

I shove my briefs down, freeing my cock.

Her eyes widen, and her grin turns fully wicked. "I like your cock."

I pump a fist. "I knew you'd say 'cock.'"

"I can say 'cock,' and I can suck your cock," she says. My dick twitches its thanks.

She draws the head between her lips, then I groan as she takes me in farther. My hips jerk up. My muscles tense with pleasure. She wraps a hand around the base and licks a long teasing stripe up my shaft.

"Yes," I rasp.

And then everything becomes a blur of lips and heat.

Of pleasure and lust.

I thread my fingers through her curls, careful with her hair. I wrap my other hand around the back of her neck, letting her set the pace. I won't need much. I'm already on the edge. I'm already primed, ready to shoot.

She doesn't need to deep throat me. Her mouth covering most of me is all I need, and she gives me that as she sucks and kisses and licks. Sensations sizzle down my spine like an electrical wire snapping with a burst of sparks.

I hit the edge in seconds, my orgasm blasting through me at breakneck speed, and I grunt, "*Coming.*"

My friend, my plus-one, the virgin on her knees, sucks me down, drinks my come, then lets me fall from her lips with a loud, wet pop as she runs a tongue over her bottom lip.

I bring my hand to the bridge of my nose, pinching

it in delicious disbelief.

She's a woman who knows her mind and her body. She's the sexiest innocent vixen ever, and I want to experience all of her.

I reach for her hand, pull her up next to me, wrap my arms around her, then press a kiss to her lips. "You're stunning, and now I want you even more."

"Funny how that works. I want you too."

I swipe her hair away from her face, helping to straighten it. "Question for you though. You said 'never' when I was touching you. Have you never come like that before?"

She grins, then gives an impish little shrug. "Others have tried. Others have failed. This was another first."

Pride suffuses me. But it's more than pride.

It's something else entirely.

Delight?

No.

Happiness?

That seems too obvious.

Maybe I'm simply happy to give this woman so many firsts.

She deserves them, yes. But I love, too, that she's experiencing them with me.

She finds some mouthwash in the limo—props to the driver for being well stocked—and we straighten up thoroughly then step out of the limo, put together once more.

On the street, she eyes me up and down. "Looking good, twenty-two. No one would suspect we've been up to anything."

"Exactly. Just that we've been following all the rules."

She chuckles like we have a private joke, and we do. "We have definitely been following *our* rules," she whispers.

"Our rules are important," I add.

She turns to head into the hotel then spins around again, her gaze roaming over my face.

"Wait," she says, stopping to neaten an errant strand of hair on my forehead. Her fingers brush lightly over my skin. Her soft touch feels unexpectedly familiar, like we do this when we go out, like she fixes my tie or smooths my hair, and like I'd do the same for her.

So I do, tucking a chestnut curl behind her ear.

She raises her chin, her eyes meeting mine. A charge rushes through the air, but it's not buzzing with lust this time.

It's humming with . . . something else entirely.

She flashes me a soft smile. "You look good, Crosby," she says, and her words send an unexpected tingle down my spine.

That tingle—it doesn't feel sexual. It feels . . . warm, and I don't know what to make of that either.

So, I offer her my arm, and she takes it. As we enter the gala together, my heart beats a little faster. A little harder.

A rhythm that's less like we're friends with benefits and more like that other thing.

The thing I don't know how to name.

But it feels hopeful.

And it feels dangerous.

19

NADIA

An attendant scurries up, asking to take my wrap.

A private thrill rushes through me—my wrap.

My gift from Crosby.

"Thank you." I hand it to her as she gives me a ticket, which I drop into my purse.

Next, a woman in a silver dress and cute red glasses strides over to us, an iPad in her hand.

She can only be a publicist.

"Hello, Ms. Harlowe and Mr. Cash. We'd love to take your photo on the red carpet."

Crosby shoots her a smile, then me. "Of course."

"That would be great," I echo, though my shoulders tense briefly.

How will we look together with lights flashing?

In many ways, this picture is no different than the wedding photos from last weekend.

And at the same time, it's a universe apart.

We just *came together* in the car.

Mouthwash and neatened hair aside, do I have an

orgasm aura about me?

I want to lean in close to Crosby, to whisper, "Do I look . . . *obvious?*"

But then, I'm not sure I want to let on to him, either, that I'm still floating on a cloud of climax dust.

Just smile for the camera.

The silver-sequined, no-nonsense publicist guides us along the red carpet to a backdrop splashed with the Sports Network Awards logo.

A young photographer with a Russell Wilson charm greets us with a quick hello then lifts his Nikon. "Let's get one of the woman who's going to bring us a Super Bowl victory."

I grin. "That's the goal."

He snaps a few shots of me. "Fantastic. And now one of the Cougars best known for . . ." He stops, flashes an evil grin at Crosby, and continues, "His long ball."

Crosby rolls his eyes. "Thanks, Leo."

The photographer shrugs. "I call it like I see it. But then, no one saw it. Such a shame."

"Ah, you're so sweet, Leo. Missed you so much," Crosby says, smiling for the guy he clearly knows.

"And now how about a few of beauty and the beast together?"

Crosby points to Leo. "He's a regular Seinfeld."

"*Hey, what's the deal with dick pics?*" the photographer asks, imitating the famous comic.

"I don't know. Why don't I send you one later?" Crosby fires back, and the barbs delight me, the way they juggle them like lit torches.

"Let the countdown begin," Leo says, then gestures

for us to move closer together. "There. Pretend you like him, Ms. Harlowe. Act like you can stand him."

Laughing, I inch even closer.

He has no idea that I'm not playing make-believe at all.

Snap, snap, snap.

"Perfect. Just one more. Put your arm around her waist, Crosby. Sorry, Ms. Harlowe. I promise this will only hurt for a second."

"No pain, no gain," I say as we smile for the camera.

When he's done, Leo waves us on. "Next season, I need you to go long more often. It'd help my fantasy stats," he says to Crosby.

"Fantasy and you, Leo. The two go hand in hand," Crosby says, then returns the guy's wave.

As we enter the reception area, I say, "You two were friendly. How do you know him?"

"He's a freelance photog. He snapped our team head-shots last year. Leo's a good guy. Takes the time to actually get to know everyone, which is why I can rib him like that," he says.

I hum then nudge his elbow, dropping my voice to a whisper. "Hate to break it to you, but I think he did the ribbing, Crosby. And well too."

He smiles in acknowledgment. "He did. But guess what? I got the last word. Or the last laugh, rather, since those pictures gave me another chance to get my hands on you."

Sparks shimmy over my skin as we head to the bar.

Orgasm aura indeed.

* * *

The thing I like best about the Sports Network Awards is that it includes fans. Most awards galas are industry only—players, agents, owners, publicists, and so on.

But every year the sports network makes tickets available to a handful of regular folks, usually via charity auctions.

It gives the fete a different energy, makes it more real. Keeps you on your toes.

On one hand, a bunch of thirtysomething investment bankers dropped to their knees and gave me a *Wayne's World* "We're not worthy" welcome, thanking me for bringing the Hawks back to California. On the other hand, I was serenaded with John Denver's "Fly Away," the words changed to "Fly away, Hawks." Message received.

The team is both loved and reviled.

That's sports for you. Little else can engender such passion, and that passion is why I love my job.

Heck, it's why I have a job.

"Safe to say it's a love-hate thing here," Matthew says, leaning casually against the bar as we snag a few minutes to chat post-serenade.

"Don't I know it," I say.

"But it's all in a day's work," he says, squeezing my shoulder.

"Exactly. It's just part of the job. And that's what we're doing."

"Speaking of *doing*," he says, dipping his voice, "are you on the pull tonight?"

"What?" I whisper, shocked.

He rolls his eyes. "Oh, come now, Nadia. We know each other well. You can't fool me. There's something happening with Mr. Interesting from the wedding. I saw the way you looked at him too when he presented an award earlier. So, is there?" he asks, with a nod toward my . . . date.

Yes, Crosby feels like my date.

My eyes roam to the man I want. He's chatting with Holden, as well as Juan Rodriquez, one of the Cougars' starting pitchers. I love how close he is with his teammates, how they're good friends and look out for each other. He told me recently that he and Chance babysat Juan's toddler son when Juan wanted to take his wife out to dinner.

As I check out the man I shared a limo ride with, I fight off a grin, then change the subject. Matthew's my friend, but what's happening between Crosby and me is private right now.

"You never know," I say evasively. "What's going on with Phoebe? Has she changed her tune at all?"

"The opposite. She's turned up the volume on her complaints."

"Let's hope it's just a rough patch," I say.

"I have a feeling it's more like a rough road to the breakup," he says, and I frown, but he waves it off. "It was probably destined to happen anyway. And look, when she throws me in the rubbish bin officially, I fully intend to take up wine and painting."

I laugh. "Why's that?"

"Well, can you think of a better way for me to meet a

lovely woman in San Francisco than to go to one of those wine-and-painting classes?"

I burst into laughter. "Gee. I hadn't thought about your backup plan. But clearly *you* have."

"I'm truly joking. I don't actually have a plan. And I certainly don't have a plan involving wine and painting."

"For now," I say.

He gestures to the stage, then taps his watch. "Better get on, love. It's nearly your turn to present."

I head backstage, waiting for my chance to present an award.

A voice booms from the podium—the pretty, confident soprano voice of Lily Whiting, the main anchor at The Sports Network. I've met Lily in Vegas a few times. She's a fantastic reporter who was recently married, but went back to using her professional name rather than her married name. I admire that about her. It's not easy being a strong woman in a high position and she wants to stand on her own merits. She's proof you can be ridiculously in love and be your own woman in business.

"And now presenting the award for the best sportsman or sportswoman is a woman I admire greatly," Lily says. "A woman who fights hard for equal pay for other women in this male-dominated field, who's making strides at bringing more women into sports and who has already brought a top team back to the Bay Area. She embraces community with her team's involvement in local charities. I am so proud to welcome back one of our own with the return of the Hawks to San Francisco, helmed by Nadia Harlowe."

I stride onto the stage, thank Lily, then head to the mic to present the award.

As I gaze out at the audience of team owners, reporters, athletes from all over the country, and plenty of fans, I smile, imagining my father watching over me. I send a silent wish to him that I'm honoring his vision, what he built from the ground up with the fortune that he'd amassed in other fields before pursuing his dream of owning a football team.

I am so lucky to have inherited it from him, and I want to always make him proud.

That's what I hold on to so I can flash a smile at the crowd. My eyes lock ever so briefly on the friendliest of faces, and Crosby grins back at me, mouthing, *You've got it.*

I wasn't looking for encouragement, but it sure is nice to know that man has my back. I haven't felt that before in this setting, but I relish the sense of partnership.

It fuels me. It's another first.

"It's an honor to return to the city I love," I say.

A boo rings through the audience. "Go back to Vegas with the showgirls!"

"Quiet down!" another voice shouts.

"Women can't run teams."

"Women *do* run teams."

I simply grin. It is what it is. Even at an awards ceremony, there is heckling, and it's a reminder of the work I need to do.

"I know to some of you the Hawks are still interlopers, but I fully intend to do this city proud. San Francisco is big enough for many sports teams. After all, I bet we have Cougars fans here. And Dragons ones as well."

Next to Crosby, Holden claps.

"But this isn't about me," I continue. "This moment is about an award that means a lot to so many of us. That perhaps is the highest honor. This is an award for the man or woman who exemplifies giving back. And tonight I am thrilled to share that the recipient of the Best Sportsman award goes to . . ." I stop to slide a finger under the envelope flap, then take out the embossed card.

I grin when I see the name. One of Crosby's good friends and teammates. "Grant Blackwood, catcher for the San Francisco Cougars, who exemplifies giving back with his volunteer efforts for several local charities, including supporting underprivileged young athletes and LGBTQ athletes. Congratulations, Grant."

I clap as the catcher jogs to the stage, a grin lighting up his eyes. The man is damned handsome, all-American, from the dark-blond hair, to the sky-blue eyes, to his friendly, outgoing personality. I shake his hand once he's onstage, but he pulls me in for a big hug and swipes a kiss onto my cheek. "Thank you. But keep your damned hands off my third baseman," he says in a deliberately teasing tone.

I laugh, pat him on the shoulder, and say, "I promise to do my absolute best."

I move aside as Grant gives a quick and heartfelt thanks from the podium. When he's through, I clap for him once more, then head backstage with him before I exit into the crowd again, looking for Crosby.

Before I find him, though, a tall, dark, and handsome creature leans back from a clutch of athletes and agents, catches my eye, and winks.

"Declan!" I beam, closing the final feet to the tuxedoed shortstop for the New York Comets. He steps away from his crew to meet me.

"Future Baseball Team Owner," he says in that sexy guy-next-door voice of his, then yanks me in for a hug.

I laugh, throwing my arms around him. "Why are all the men in my life trying to get me to buy a baseball team?"

"What?" he asks as we separate. "I'm not the only man in your life? Who is he? Who's this other guy?"

I swat him as I roll my eyes. "Please. You're the only one," I say, teasing my friend, a guy who's most decidedly only ever been a friend. We met a few years ago when I was in New York for business and hit it off, bonding at a party over a shared love for breakfast food and the same loud rock music.

"How long are you in town?" I ask.

He looks at his watch as if it includes his calendar. "I take off tomorrow afternoon."

I shoot him a wide-eyed glare. "Hello. Why are you not on my schedule for breakfast tomorrow?"

"I could say the same to you."

"You, me, tomorrow. Let's do it."

"All I heard was you're taking me out for the best omelets in the city," he says.

"You have such selective hearing. And I'll text you a breakfast spot."

I give him a kiss on the cheek and resume my hunt for Crosby. I spot him at the edge of the ballroom, and head over. He's hanging out with Holden, who's slung his tux jacket over his arm and rolled up his shirt-sleeves. A tattoo adorns his forearm, an illustration of a tree extending over his muscles down to his wrist.

Holden offers a fist for knocking. "Well said, Nadia. I dug the bit about room for both teams."

"Thank you," I say, knocking back.

"It's hard when you feel like you're ten steps behind from the start."

"It is. But I find it's best to try not to let the negative comments affect how you do your job." I tilt my head, studying his face. "I take it you're dealing with some of the fallout from the Dragons' cheating scandal?"

"So much of it." He sighs heavily, dragging a hand over the back of his neck. "The media constantly wants to talk about it, even in the off-season."

Crosby gestures to his friend. "I keep telling him that he needs someone to help him handle the media. Someone beyond the team."

I meet Holden's green-eyed gaze. "What do you think, Holden?"

With a scratch of his jaw, he shrugs. "I guess I'll see about that when the season starts."

I give him a sympathetic smile. "Let me know if I can help. I know some sharpshooters who can give you lots of tips."

His eyes glimmer with the hint of a smile. "Thanks. I appreciate it."

Holden turns to Crosby, tipping his forehead toward me. "She's cool. Maybe I'll let this one slide," he says.

Crosby's brow furrows. "Let what slide?"

Holden rolls his eyes, claps Crosby on the shoulder, and says, "I'll catch up with you tomorrow. For now, don't do anything in front of me that'll require a call to the Maldives."

He saunters away. Once he's out of earshot, Crosby leans closer, his voice warm and tantalizing near my ear, making me shiver. "But privately, I'd like to do all sorts of things to you."

Pleasure zings through my body, and I can't wait for this event to end.

Soon, it does, and we make our way out of the ballroom. Lily Whiting catches us, stopping Crosby to ask if he'll do an interview before he leaves for spring training.

"Absolutely," he tells her.

"Great. I'll be in touch to set it up."

As she leaves, Crosby turns back to me. "See? I'm good with the media."

"If I were your team's owner, I'd be very proud of you."

"If you were my team's owner, I'd still want to bang you," he whispers.

I laugh, shaking my head.

"I mean it. Your job is hot. Smart women are hot. Powerful women are hot. Also, *you're* hot."

I am indeed, thanks to his compliments—ones that

are the polar opposite of what I heard my last year dating in Vegas.

Crosby is the opposite of so many men, and I love that he's not threatened by me. That he admires me rather, and supports me.

Still, once we're outside, I put on my big-girl pants and say the hard thing.

20

NADIA

Outside the event hotel, I take a step closer to my plus-one and slow the train even though I don't entirely want to. "I want to invite you over, but I think I'd break rule number three," I say, my voice low and just for him as I tug my wrap a little tighter around my shoulders, the mercury dipping as the stars twinkle in the night sky.

Crosby heaves a sigh then nods in agreement. "You read my mind. If I'm alone with you tonight, I'm going to have the hardest time keeping my hands off you."

"It's not your hands I'm worried about," I say in a flirty tone as the limo pulls up.

He lets his gaze drift downward, straight to his crotch. "Aw, that's so sweet of you to worry about my cock."

"Oh, I'm not *worried* about your cock at all," I toss back.

Crosby grabs the door before the driver gets out, shaking his head in admiration as I slide into the long black car. "You're a woman unleashed. As soon as you say one swear, you're saying them all."

"That's poppy . . . *cock*," I say with a wicked grin.

"Speaking of . . . let's go get a *cock*tail."

* * *

Fifteen minutes later, we walk into the Spotted Zebra.

The fun decor fits the name perfectly. One wall is pink. Another is black. Yet another is brick. Alt rock plays on the sound system, and hip bartenders and servers in monochrome uniforms circle the joint with drinks.

Low couches with black-and-white stripes beckon patrons, inviting them to lounge.

We swing by the bar, saying hello to Sierra, Grant's sister, who flashes a grin at us as she tucks a pink-streaked strand of her blonde hair back into its messy bun.

"Hey there." Ink dances up and down her right arm, and both her earlobes are pierced many times over.

"Hi, Sierra," I say. "Good to see you."

"Welcome back, prodigal daughter," she says dryly, then leans in to give me a quick hug across the bar.

"Ha. That'll be my new nickname."

She waves her hand dismissively. "Don't let the boos get you down. We'll play the Hawks games here." She nods to the TV blasting a hockey game in the corner. "Well, when it's not hockey season."

"Hello? How about baseball?" Crosby chimes in.

Sierra yawns, big and over-the-top. "Baseball is sooo boring."

Crosby clutches his heart. "You're killing me."

Sierra slaps some napkins down on the bar. "What can I get you two?"

Crosby orders me a wine, then a beer for himself, and when Sierra hands us the drinks, we grab a spot in the corner, settling onto a striped couch.

He already shed his jacket and bow tie in the car, so now he rolls up his shirtsleeves, showing off his strong forearms. I admire the sight of them for a second, imagining how they'd look with him braced over me, his arms pinning me.

Wild sensations kick through me, a hot rush of adrenaline. I cross my legs, trying to keep my desires in check.

He lifts his glass. "Let's drink to . . ."

"To not calling the Maldives?"

His lips curve up in a naughty grin. "So tempting though."

"I couldn't agree more."

I take a sip of the wine, then set it down. He does the same with his beer. "I was impressed by you onstage," he says. "You are poise personified."

I beam, grateful for the compliment. "Thank you. That means a lot to me. Especially considering what other men have thought about my job."

"Fuck them," he scoffs. And that's all. That's literally all he has to say. "You have your plate full, and you still handle yourself like the badass you've always been."

I smile. "Stop, or you'll make me blush."

He shakes his head. "You're not a blusher. I know you."

"True. I'm not a blusher at all."

He leans a little closer, his voice dipping to that low and husky range that I love. "But are you a blusher in the bedroom?"

Tingles spread across my shoulders. "I don't know. Maybe we'll both find out."

He laughs, then moves a little closer. But rather than whisper, he clears his throat. "So, have you never met a man you wanted to have sex with? Were you waiting for a relationship? Or was the timing never right? Or was it something else entirely? Which, of course, I guess raises the question of . . . *why now?*"

I love the lack of judgment, the genuine interest in the elephant in the room—the *why*.

But I slide in with a joke first. "You mean other than your prowess and pure masculine raw sex appeal?"

He gives a casual shrug. "Well, yeah, obviously that."

I tell him the basics, about college and the lack of men there, then about my focus on classes during my master's program, and finally about the matchmaker woes last year, though he mostly knows those details.

"But more than that," I finish, "I've never wanted to go there with anyone before. I never felt the desire intensely enough. Don't get me wrong though—I have *a lot* of sexual desire."

His eyes glint. "I can tell."

"And there are plenty of things I want to do. There are plenty of things I fantasize about. And, hey, my toys get quite a workout."

He drags a hand across his brow as if wiping off sweat. "You're not helping with keeping rule number three tonight."

I lean my head back and laugh. "Trust me, it's hard for me too. Whatever the case before, I'm very interested in sex now. And I'm very interested in sex with you."

He waves a napkin like a white flag. "I surrender."

I swat his arm playfully. "What I'm trying to say is this—I wasn't holding on to my virginity because it's some precious thing, or because I have some notion that I'll walk down the aisle in five years, or whenever, still a virgin."

"Five years? Is that the wedding plan?"

A surge of embarrassment rushes blood to my cheeks. "I don't have a wedding plan. I was just throwing that out there."

"So no pressure, then, for you or your future hubs." His grin is playful, but he catches my gaze on those last couple of words, almost like he's testing them out.

I wince a bit, not entirely sure why that gnaws at me —*future hubs*. "Sure," I say. "He can just deflower me on our wedding night," I say, making a big old joke about whoever the future hubs might be because that's easier than dealing with this nagging sensation. Instead, I turn more serious. "But yes, I do want, someday, what my parents had. Not now, but down the road. I want what your parents had. What Brooke and Eric have." I draw a breath, letting it fill me. "Right now though? I have my work cut out for me with the team, so I like this thing you and I have. And I don't want to keep having sex with myself anymore," I say, our eyes locking with want flaring between us, like a shimmering heat mirage.

"Like I said, rule number three is very hard to resist tonight. But I can wait for you. I *want* to wait," he says, his dark-blue eyes locked with mine, and I can't look away. I don't want to, because the way he says *want to wait* makes my heart catch in my throat. Another odd feeling I should truly ignore. Too bad it feels so good.

I take another drink, turning the tables on him, since these boomeranging emotions in me are a ping-pong game I don't want to play. "And you? What's your story? You seem drawn to dating. Not like you're a player, but more like you enjoy having girlfriends. Fair to say?"

Nodding thoughtfully, he lifts his beer, drinks more of it, then sets down the glass. "I suppose I'm the same as you, Nadia. I'd like what my parents had. Hell, what my mom has now with Kana."

My chest warms, my heart feeling *glow-y* from that lovely sentiment, one you don't hear as often as you'd like, from women or from men. "Most people are afraid to admit they want that—love, connection, intimacy. I like that you just put it out there. In general. I like that you're saying it in general," I add quickly, since I don't want him to worry that I have ulterior motives. "Don't worry. I'm not going to get all clingy. I understand the rules. *We stay friends.* Rule number two," I add, like I'm proud of myself for recalling the laws we laid down.

He gives me a reassuring smile. "I wasn't worried. At all," he says, lifting a hand to squeeze my shoulder. A sort of friendly squeeze.

Hmm.

Is it weird that I want a non-friendly squeeze right now?

But I keep going, glad he's on the same page. Truly, it's good that he's not worried. I do want to stay friends after we work our way through the Virgin Rule Book. I absolutely want to remain buddies. I shake away any wayward notions that extend beyond friendship.

This *plus-one plan* is fantastic. Besides, I'm lucky to be friends with someone who's so easygoing and so open at the same time. And someone who's so . . . bangable.

"It's kind of heartwarming when anyone admits they want what we all truly want," I say.

Smiling in acknowledgment, he knocks back some of his beer. "I hear ya. I blame it on my mom. She was all about being in touch with your emotions. *'Don't be afraid of your feelings. A real man can admit when he's fallen,'*" he says, imitating his mother.

"Funny, you sound just like her."

"I suppose I'm glad she's like that. Trouble is, I'm not so good at following her advice."

My brow creases. "What do you mean?"

He exhales heavily, scrubbing a hand over the back of his neck. "My dating woes? All those ex-girlfriend stories? They're all my fault."

"Why do you say that? You just . . ." I trail off though, unsure how to finish the thought fairly. *Pick the wrong women?* I don't need to say that—he knows it.

"Choose the wrong women?" he supplies.

"You said it," I say, laughing.

"It's my Achilles' heel. Grant and my cousin are right

when they say I don't take my time getting to know a woman before I let her in. They say I trust too soon. That's true, and it's all on me." He holds up his right hand like he's taking an oath in court. "Swear on it. Like I told your brother. I happen to have horrible taste. I'm kind of drawn to bad girls."

My stomach dips with worry.

He reaches out a hand, clasping mine. "I *was* drawn to bad girls. Present company excluded."

"I have nothing against bad girls, but I don't think I'm one," I say, perhaps a little apologetically.

He squeezes my hand harder. "You're not a bad girl, and I'm wildly attracted to you. Maybe my taste is changing."

I hope it is. "Perhaps," I say noncommittally, not sure what else to say.

"Or maybe I've always had a thing for you," he says with a shrug. "Maybe you're the only good girl I've ever wanted."

"Is that good or bad?" I ask, genuinely curious.

He runs a finger over the top of my hand, making my skin heat up.

"Feels good right now," he says. "And this thing between us *is* good. We already know each other."

"We do," I echo, and as if to prove it, the conversation sails away on its own while we catch the end of the hockey game, complaining about some calls, cheering about others, debating who's going to win as we finish our drinks and then make our way out of the bar after saying goodbye to Sierra.

Crosby takes me home, gets out of the limo, and

walks me to the front door of my building. He stops before I unlock it, dipping his hands in his pockets and rocking back and forth on his heels.

It's the *what's next* moment. Nerves thrum through me.

"So," he begins. "We have the golf thing this weekend. Before I jet off to Arizona."

"Cactus league time," I say, using the insider lingo, the term for baseball teams who do their spring training in Arizona.

"I'm leaving on Monday," he says.

I try not to dwell on him leaving. Who cares that he's leaving after all? He's coming back. Spring training doesn't last forever. Nor does friends-with-benefits, so there's no need to be all moony.

"But there's plenty of days on the calendar before then," he adds, and it comes out like an invitation, a little flirty.

"So very true," I say, waiting, hoping he wants the same thing.

He inches closer, dips his face to my neck, and breathes me in. I tremble as his nose runs along my neck, traveling up to my ear, where he nibbles ever so gently on my earlobe then pulls back. "I don't want to wait till the golf thing to see you again."

My heart tap-dances across a Broadway stage. "I don't either."

He murmurs as he brushes decadent kisses along my skin. "Invite me over tomorrow night, Nadia."

My body is throwing an *I'm ready* parade. "Come over tomorrow," I say.

He separates from me, his gaze roaming over my figure one last time. "I'll bring dinner."

"I'll bring an appetite," I say.

"I'll see you at eight, then, Wild Woman."

He returns to his limo and drives away, having bestowed a new nickname on me.

Am I a wild woman?

Maybe we'll find out.

I can't wait for tomorrow. Though, as I head inside, I'm also missing having him here tonight.

A lot.

21

NADIA

Brooke bats first, with a text message flashing like a neon sign as I apply makeup the next morning.

Brooke: Called it. Lovebirds. Like I said at the wedding.

What is she talking about?

As the new album from my favorite singer ever—Stone Zenith—blasts through my bathroom, I set down my mascara wand and click open the photo Brooke sent.

My chest flutters. My lips form a stupid grin.

"The Guy in the Picture" fills the bathroom, the love song echoing across the tiled walls as I stare at a shot of Crosby and me from the red carpet posted on the Sports Network Instagram feed.

I zoom in on the image, and a barrage of questions slams into me.

Was his hand really wrapped possessively around my waist like that?

Were his eyes staring at me like I'm the only woman for him?

Was his grin telegraphing how much he wanted to follow rule number one? To sleep with me?

My stomach sashays, then does a rumba. Maybe a samba too. Hell, it could be taking a Zumba class for all I know.

This photo is a damning piece of evidence that shows two people who are *into* each other. Really into each other.

Because I'm looking at him like he's the only one I want with me.

Last night, tonight, any night.

My heart beats faster and music floods my ears as Stone reaches the chorus.

The song takes over my senses, lodges itself into my heart and mind.

Something is happening between Crosby and me.

Something that's more than friendship.

And I don't know what to do about it.

I've tried to deny it.

I've played the logic card.

But logic has slipped away, and emotions are dealing the deck now.

That man just does something to me.

Something that's not only physical.

That's why I want to see him tonight, why I want to have sex with him. Not because I'm horny, not because I'm friends with him, not because I'm attracted to him.

I'm attracted to him because I like him.

The phone slips from my hand, clattering to the floor with a bang.

With a loud sigh, I stumble back, grab hold of the wall, and proceed to freak the hell out.

For about ten seconds. Then I get my act together, pick up my phone, turn down the music, and dial Scarlett.

"Emergency," I say the second she answers.

"What is it?"

"This," I say, then send her the image. "Check your texts."

A few seconds later, she says, "Ohhhh. That looks complicated."

"I know," I say, pacing to the tub, sitting on the edge, and dropping my head in my hand. "I think something is brewing . . . No, that's wrong," I say, quickly correcting myself.

I lift my face, inhale deeply, and lean on the boardroom side of me. The woman who speaks up.

"I don't think—I *know*. I like him so very much."

The admission is both a relief and a brand-new burden.

Scarlett's words and tone are kind. "So, what are you going to do about this friends-with-benefits thing, then?"

It's a great question. As I picture tonight, him coming over, us connecting, I can't see a path to resistance. Not one I want to take. Once more, I go with the full truth. "I suppose I'm going to sleep with him, and deal with whether it'll hurt my heart later."

I can hear a sympathetic smile on her face when she says, "At least you have your eyes wide open."

I suppose I do.

I say goodbye as a new text lands on my phone.

Mom: Looks like you had a great time last night.

Nadia: I did. I absolutely did.

Mom: Is that someday coming soon?

I close my texts, because how can I answer whether the someday of us dating—the someday she envisions—is coming?

I have no idea.

I finish getting dressed, then head to a nearby café for breakfast with Declan, where we catch up about life and love in New York.

"So, what's the latest? Any new, hot, brainy men in your life who rock your world?" I ask as I lift my cinnamon latte and waggle a brow.

He shakes his head. "I've kind of been taking a break."

That surprises me. He's always seemed like such a serial monogamist. "A break? Like, from dating in general?"

"Yep. Last time I even saw someone was more than a year ago."

I can't *not* ask. "Is there a reason for the break?"

"Just trying to make some changes in my life."

Well, now I really have to know. "Good changes?"

"Let's just say if I was a superstitious guy I'd be wearing lucky socks," he says with a hopeful glint in his expression.

I laugh. "Funny, I know someone just like that." I take a beat, study my friend, try to read his eyes, and see what's going on behind them. "So these *hypothetical* lucky socks. Would you be wearing them, if you *were* wearing them, in the hopes of finding that someone special?"

He smiles. "You're getting warmer."

And I think I know why. "Wasn't there *once* someone special?" I ask. I had the sense once upon a time that he'd fallen hard for someone. He'd never shared the details though, and I hadn't pried. Maybe that's the reason he's taking a break?

"Yes." His answer is emphatic. For a moment he seems lost in time, then he returns to the here and now. "Someone very special. Maybe he will be again."

A smile takes over my face. "There's nothing quite like finding your someone special, is there?"

"I couldn't agree more." He lifts his coffee, takes a drink, then asks thoughtfully. "And you?"

"I haven't had anyone special before."

"And do you now?"

A grin dances across my lips. "Maybe," I say into the latte.

"Elaborate," he instructs.

I don't give him the sordid details. I don't divulge

name, batting average, or uniform number. Declan's a ballplayer too, but even if he weren't, I wouldn't serve up the personal intel.

But I give him enough.

"I hope he's your someone special," he says as he knocks back the rest of his coffee.

"We'll see," I say, trying to hide the smile that won't go away.

* * *

After breakfast, I head to the stadium and bury myself in work. Matthew and I interview the fantastic woman named Kim who's been an assistant GM for two other teams. She's sharp, smart, and confident, and she knows her way around arbitration, analytics, and scouting.

The three of us talk for two hours, and during that span of one hundred twenty minutes, I don't think about tonight at all.

It's a wonderful slice of time.

It reminds me that I can do my job. I can do what I came here to do.

Sure, even if I get my emotions bruised, even if my heart is knocked around, I'll be fine.

I'll come out on the other side of friends-with-benefits unscathed.

Surely I will.

When I say goodbye to Kim and let her know we'll be in touch soon, Matthew and I conduct a postmortem.

"She's great. We should offer her more than you make," I say, teasing.

But he flashes a warm smile and nods. "If that's what it takes, do it."

I scoff. "Matthew, I'm joking."

"I'm not," he says, intense, serious. "I'm not sitting around counting who makes more money. Or who has the bigger post. I just want what's best for the team."

I sigh happily. "I would like to clone you for literally every job I ever need to fill."

"I'd like to clone myself sometime. Can I send one of my clones out to eat cake and pie all day long, while I stay fit and trim?"

"I want one of those clones too," I say with a laugh.

"In any case, we've got a few more candidates for the job, but we should make sure we know exactly what Kim wants. And then offer it to her."

"It's like we share a brain."

He narrows his eyes. "Sometimes. But, call me crazy, I think it's for the best that we can't read each other's mind."

With a laugh, I agree. "Truer words."

I'm glad no one else has access to my thoughts when I check my phone a little later.

Anticipation zips through me when I see Crosby's name on the screen.

Just flies through my body, lighting me up.

Crosby: Don't know about you, but I've spent the morning getting harassed about that pic Leo took of us.

I mean, in the harassers' defense, I do look like I want to devour you. So fair's fair. I want to, and I plan to, and I will be doing just that tonight. Before then, I need to know—do you want pasta, Thai, or a grain bowl from Mom's café tonight?

Leaning back in my chair, I grin like a fool as lust roars through me.

This man turns me on and makes me laugh.

That's the problem.

I write back, asking for the grain bowl. At least that much is easy.

22

CROSBY

I toss the question to my priest. "Am I supposed to confess?"

Raj taps his chin, his brow furrowing as I work through the insane number of crunches he ordered me to do.

"In situations like this, I ask myself, 'What would Kenneth do?'"

"Who?" I ask as I twist my obliques.

"Kenneth from *Thirty Rock*. He's my point of reference for decision-making," Raj says, crouching next to me at the gym.

"Kenneth? The ultimate good guy? The sweet, innocent Kenneth who's basically a proxy for Mister Rogers and Kermit the Frog?"

Raj grins, his white teeth gleaming, as he nods. The former Bollywood stuntman is now a kick-ass personal trainer, and I was lucky enough to snag a spot on his client list. "Yep. And hey, those guys all knew how to make good choices."

"So you're saying I should tell my buds I fell off the wagon?"

Raj rolls his eyes, grabs his phone, and brandishes the shot from last night at me. "Do pictures lie, man? Switch to bicycle crunches stat."

"Everyone has shown that to me," I say, taking my phone from the floor, opening it, and shoving it at him before I shift to the new exercise. "Open my messages."

He clicks on them, then cracks up, his hand flying to his belly. "Dude."

"I know," I say, rolling my eyes as I twist my elbow to my opposite knee, then the other, and so on.

Raj clears his throat, reading out loud. "From Grant at nine thirty: *Dude. I know she didn't steal your socks, your ring, or your car, but have you no self-control?* From Chance at nine forty-five: *Dude. Busted.* From Holden at ten fifteen: *Dude. Guess who's admitting on TV that we're better at the world's greatest sport?*"

Raj flops down on the mat. "Looks like you don't need to confess, Cros. They figured you out."

"From a picture. What the hell is so obvious about that pic?"

"Switch to side planks," he says, studying the shot. "Oh, I see."

"What is it?" I ask as I hold myself up on my right side, left arm straight up in the air.

"It's the eyes," he says, tapping on the phone, then showing me a close-up of my peepers. "Do you see it?"

"What am I looking for?"

"You look at her like you're falling for her."

I fall on my hip, slipping out of the plank, landing splat on my side with an *oof*.

Recovering quickly, I ask, "What are you talking about?"

As I pull myself up, he sits crisscross next to me then proceeds to explain in detail how my eyes give everything away.

"Huh," I say, studying the picture, the way I'm gazing at Nadia, how my lips are crooked into a grin, how my hand is curled tightly around her waist.

Maybe I do look at her that way.

Maybe I am falling for her.

Holy fuck.

It's like I just learned that a pitcher I've batted against for years is now throwing a knuckleball.

And I don't know how to hit it.

The rest of the day, I try to figure out what the hell to do with this knuckleball of Nadia's.

The situation gets worse when I stop by my mom's café in the city to pick up dinner.

She hands me a paper bag full of food. "So how are you going to deal with the fact that everyone seems to think you have it bad for Eric's sister?"

"Because of the photo?"

She laughs softly, shakes her head, and sits me down at a table. "It's not because of a photo, sweetie." She shoots me a knowing grin. "It's because of years."

23

NADIA

I pace my home.

Set my hand on my chest.

Breathe in, breathe out.

It's T-minus one hour till . . . hymen send-off?

But no, that ship went bye-bye a long time ago. I mean, I don't know for sure, but my family of little darlings and big darlings surely broke my maidenhead long ago.

Ugh.

Maidenhead.

Who says "maidenhead"?

Who says "hymen" for that matter?

But hey, maybe those ridiculous words will calm me down.

"Maidenhead, maidenhead, maidenhead," I mutter, but still, the word repetition does nothing to settle the overdrive my body's in.

My heart skitters.

It's like a rabbit in my chest, racing in circles, frantically beating.

Settle down.

I flop down on my couch, drop my head into my hands, and try to breathe.

My lungs won't fill.

My breath is short, sharp.

Nothing is working.

I'm going to jump out of my skin. And why?

Why am I so wound up?

I want this. I want him. I'm ready.

But tell that to my nerves that are jackhammering in my cells.

I head to the bathroom and turn on the tap for the tub. I planned to shower anyway, but maybe a bath is what I need.

A little relaxation session.

I strip out of my clothes, turn the temperature to hot, and toss in a tropical island bath bomb.

I close my eyes, letting the steam swirl around me as the marble tub fills. I step into the bath when it's nearly full, dancing the oh-my-God-it's-so-hot hula for a few seconds before I gingerly lower myself into the water.

And I burn.

I'm broiling.

Whose idea was it to make this so forking hot?

I stand, step out, grab a towel, and wrap the fluffy material around me.

I sneer at the cauldron.

Draining the tub, I head to the shower stall, turn the water to lukewarm, then take a shower.

Baths are officially not relaxing.

Five minutes later, I'm out of the shower, but my heart is still trying to run away from me.

Music? Do I need music?

Should I take up yoga real quick?

Maybe champagne would do the trick?

On my way home from work tonight, I picked up a bottle. Organic, naturally. But I can't pop it open without him.

So, as I slather on lotion, then get dressed in jeans and a casual pink blouse, I try—truly try—to figure out what'll ease my nerves.

Not a hot soak.

Not a drink.

And not some more girl time.

I look in the mirror, studying my face, asking the hard questions.

What do you want? What do you need?

I want the man.

And I want to know we're good. I want to know we've got this. I want to talk to him, or text with him.

So I pick up my phone, open our text thread, and write him a note.

Something that'll set the mood.

The mood of who we are.

Nadia: Remember that time I asked to see your dick pic?

. . .

I put the phone down on the bathroom counter as I swipe on some powder and blush and then mascara, feeling a little more settled already. He writes back quickly, for which I'm grateful.

Crosby: You're changing your mind about tonight and you want a pic instead of the real thing? I SUPPOSE I can live with that. But the bigger question is—do you still want the grain bowl?

Nadia: I wanted to say I'm secretly glad you didn't show the picture to me, because I liked experiencing it live last night.

Crosby: Whew. So you want the grain bowl *and* the sausage? Good thing, because I'm on my way over with both.

Nadia: Excellent. I'll be ready with this . . .

I step away from the mirror, unbutton my shirt to a scandalous degree, then send him a picture.

Of the tops of my breasts.

His reply is instantaneous.

Crosby: Did you hear that? It was the sound of me tripping and falling flat on my face from the ABSOLUTE

HOTNESS of you. I hope you have a Band-Aid for my nose.

Nadia: I have Band-Aids with foxes on them. I know you love your cute animal socks, so these will match.

Crosby: You do know me well. Also, thank you for the world's sexiest image.

Nadia: You can see them live in a few minutes.

Crosby: I intend to, Wild Woman. I fully intend to see, touch, feel, lick, kiss, and devour them.

Nadia: Mmmm . . .

Already, my pulse is slowing, warmth returns to my cheeks, and my mind is calm, but eager.

And because talking to him seems to settle my nerves, I'm guessing that making him laugh might do the trick even more, so I do a quick Google search.

Then I send him a shot of a cat lounging seductively across a bed.

Nadia: Here's a naughty shot for you.

Seconds later, my phone pings.

Crosby: Meow! Also, here's your shaft shot.

Crosby: I meant, here's your wiener pic.

I crack up as the shot of a dachshund fills the screen.

I am officially relaxed. All I needed was *this*. This banter, this connection, this fun.

When the clock strikes eight, he texts that he's in the lobby. I buzz him up, and a minute later, I open the door.

"Hey, you," he says in a tender voice that sends a charge down my spine.

"Hey to you too."

I'm still nervous.

But I'm also ready.

* * *

Champagne and food help.

My chest flutters as I take another bite of the food, another sip of the champagne.

"Did you know this is organic?" I ask, holding up my flute.

He takes a bite of his dinner then smiles, speaking when he finishes chewing. "You might have mentioned it a few times."

"Oh, right," I say, waving a hand. But I'm still rattling

off randomness about champagne. "See, when I went to the store this afternoon, I wanted to make sure it would work for you. The champagne. It's made without sulfites. And no chemicals either. Also, it's made from sustainable grapes. Hey, what are sustainable grapes? Are there unsustainable grapes? What makes a grape unsustainable?"

He sets down his fork and reaches for my hand. "It's a grape that's wildly nervous."

I let out a long, heavy breath. "I'm not nervous," I say, lying, patently lying.

"We don't have to do this, Nadia."

Tension slices through me as I stare daggers at him. "Don't say something so awful."

He smiles, stands, and offers me his hand. "Come with me."

"But the table is a mess," I say, grasping at straws.

"We'll clean it up later."

He takes my hand, guides me to the couch, and gently sweeps out his hand for me to sit. I do.

He goes back for the champagne flutes then sits next to me, reaching for my hand, running his thumb across the top of it. "If you're not ready, no hard feelings."

I swallow roughly. "I am ready, I'm just . . ."

"Nervous?" he supplies.

I nod, admitting it at last. "I am."

"Do you want to talk about why?"

I take a sip of my drink then set down the glass, waiting for the floaty feeling to kick in.

But champagne isn't the answer.

Crosby sets his glass on the table next to mine,

waiting for me to tell him the truth I'm holding in.

I part my lips, draw a shaky breath, then blurt out, "I don't want to be bad in bed."

A laugh bursts from his chest. "Nadia," he says softly, then weaves his fingers through mine. "Would you think it's crazy if I said the same thing?"

I scoff. "There's no way you could think that."

He gives a *but I do* shrug.

My jaw drops. "Do you really worry about that?"

He inches closer, clasping my hand tighter. "I want this to be good for you. Fuck, that's wrong," he says, dragging a hand through his hair. He stops like he's collecting his thoughts, then his blue eyes lock with mine. His blaze with heat, but something else too— something sweet, something vulnerable. "I want it to be spectacular."

My heart lodges in my throat, and I swallow past a lump that appears out of nowhere.

What the freak?

Now is not the time for my crying-on-cue gland to activate. I draw a steadying breath. "I don't want to be unspectacular," I admit, feeling terribly vulnerable too. "I want you to feel good as well."

He cups my face in his hands and presses his forehead to mine. "It'll feel good because it's you, and it's me, and it's us." His heady whisper sends me spinning into a whirlwind of lust and longing and something else too—something that feels dangerously close to another *L* word.

He brushes his lips against mine, a hint of a kiss, then he pulls back. "But we can put the brakes on this for now. Or forever, if you want. There's no pressure. Hell, if you want to play poker or watch SportsCenter or scroll through Netflix in the hopes of finding a new comedy you haven't seen, we can do that."

I shake my head. "I do like poker, but I don't want to do that. I think . . ." I do a status check, and my heart is finally beating normally. "I think I just needed to talk to you first. I feel better now."

"We can talk all night if you want. I meant what I said last night. No regrets. No pressure." He sweeps some hair off my shoulder, making me shudder. "Do you want to talk more now?"

The truth is . . . I do. Because talking to him settles me. This connection with Crosby is what I like. This is why I want to be with him tonight. My eyes drift down his body, taking him in again—his navy-blue Henley stretched snug across his firm pecs and showing off his strong biceps, his faded blue jeans fitting him just so, then finally his . . . corgis?

I peer at his purple socks, then up at him, arching one *are you serious* brow. "Are there corgi butts on your socks?"

He waggles a foot. "Why, yes, there are. These are my new lucky socks. Bought them today."

I laugh, truly laugh, from deep within. "So a dog's rear end? Those are your getting-lucky socks?"

He slides his foot up my leg. "What's hotter than corgi butts?" he asks, his covered toe reaching my knee.

I laugh harder, pushing his foot away. "You really love your good-luck charms."

"I'm a superstitious mofo."

"So without the new socks, nothing would happen tonight?"

He slides his arms around my waist and shakes his head, the mood shifting, intensifying. "Honestly, Nadia, I just like socks a lot. They're kind of my thing. And maybe the ritual makes me feel calm, makes me feel centered."

"Do you feel calm right now?"

He licks his lips. "I feel certain."

My body hums at his words, at his gaze, all possessive and open at the same time. "Certain about what?"

"About you," he says, a husky sound that ignites a shiver of sparks down my spine.

"What about me?" I ask breathily.

"This." He leans in close again, takes my face in his hands once more, and reconnects with my lips.

He's torturously slow and deliberately gentle, like he's kissing me in slow motion.

He flicks his tongue across my bottom lip, and I shudder. We're talking full-body tremble here, pleasure spinning through my veins.

He's achingly tender, kissing me like he's luxuriating in every second, like he's exploring my mouth in the most unhurried way. He slides his tongue across it, then nips on the corner, sucking my bottom lip between his teeth.

"Ohhh," I moan, and the melting begins.

It starts as a warm, hazy sensation gliding over my skin. Then it becomes more intense with each brush of his lips, with each sensual graze of his mouth on mine.

I go boneless, my knees weakening even though I'm

sitting, as he cups my face and kisses me like I'm the answer to every question.

His hands slide into my hair, his fingers tangling through the strands as he deepens the kiss.

And I deepen it right back, kissing him the way he kisses me.

Because he's the answer too. He's the answer to all my questions about sex, about intimacy.

Especially, maybe, about why I waited.

I waited for *this*.

This connection.

This sense that we're the only ones in the world, that our kisses are all that exist.

That no one has ever touched the way we touch.

These are endless, floating, hungry kisses that become full-body experiences. Soon, he's shifting, stretching me out on the couch, sliding next to me, taking me in his arms.

We don't stop making out.

We go at each other's mouths more intensely, breaths coming faster, legs wrapping around each other, bodies tangling.

His hard-on presses against my pelvis, and the feel of him sends a wild, erotic thrill whirling through me, settling between my legs.

Yes, I have officially melted in his arms.

And at long last, we break the kiss, coming up for air. His lips are red, and his eyes are shimmering with something more than desire.

Something wildly powerful.

Maybe the same thing I feel.

I grab his shirt collar and own this moment. "I'm not nervous. Not anymore."

"So, the corgi butts worked," he murmurs.

I laugh softly then run my hand over the back of his head, my fingers curling into his hair. "Crosby?"

"Yes?"

I gaze up at him, speaking from the heart. I don't want games, or plus-ones. "You're the one I want. I want this with you. You know that, right?"

A grin tugs at his lips, playful and happy.

Wildly happy.

"I do," he whispers. "I do know that."

"Good." All those nerves are long gone, and I'm so here, so ready.

So sure.

"And I want it to be so good for you," he says. "Do you know why?"

"Why?" I ask, feeling like we're hovering on the edge of something new.

He's quiet at first, then he licks his lips. "Because this doesn't feel like just friends with benefits, Nadia," he says, unexpectedly intense. "Not at all, not anymore."

My breath hitches, and tingles light up my body from head to toe. But they aren't just tingles from desire. They're from my heart. From the possibility that he feels the exact same way.

My chest is glowing, my heart is squeezing. And the rest of me? The rest of me is wanting.

Craving.

I tug on his hair, dragging him closer. "I'm aching for you."

His lips crook up. "Let me take care of that."

He sits up and unbuttons my blouse, keeping his gaze pinned on me the whole time. "I want to taste you first, sweetheart," he says, and I arch my back, arching into that new word.

Sweetheart.

I'm no longer Wild Girl, or Wild Woman.

I'm *sweetheart*, and the significance isn't lost on me.

The affectionate name, the possessive tone.

"I want that." I help him along, unbuttoning my jeans, unzipping them. "But I have to warn you about something."

He shoots me a curious look as I shimmy down my jeans. "What's that?"

I take a beat, smiling wickedly, because I might be virginal, but I'm not innocent. "I'm outrageously wet right now."

The groan that falls from his lips is carnal, and somehow it makes me even wetter.

We're a blur of clothes and nudity as he tugs off my jeans and I push down my lace panties.

He slides down the couch, moving to the end, kneeling between my thighs as he parts my legs and gazes at me like I'm his next meal.

And I am.

"Fuck, you're soaked, sweetheart."

I have nothing else to say.

Nor does he.

Talking is overrated when there's *this*.

This man sliding his hands up my thighs then pressing the most decadent kiss to my center.

CROSBY

The instant I brush my lips over her heat, she trembles.

And she moans.

It's the most fantastic sound ever, the kind of *ohhh* that says her toes are curling.

Hell, maybe mine are too.

Because . . . my God.

She tastes spectacular.

So slick and soft and aroused.

I want to bury my face in her sweet pussy, but I want to take my time too, to savor every second of the unraveling of Nadia Harlowe.

She's a delicious conundrum, and unwrapping her sexuality is the best gift I've ever received.

As I kiss her wetness, I groan, an electric charge zapping through me. My God, she's incredible, and so damn responsive.

Writhing.

Moaning.

Sighing.

I want to imprint each sound she makes, every lift of her hips. My hands run along her thighs as I kiss her, letting her scent go to my head, flood all my senses. She tastes like longing, like lust, like that dreamy escape into a tropical garden.

It's wild and heady, and I want so much more. But I need to pace myself with Nadia, so I press gentle, tender kisses to her pussy, my hands traveling up and down the soft skin of her thighs. When I flick my tongue across that delicious rise of her clit, she arches her back and unleashes a strangled *oh God*. Her hands fly to my head, her palms curling around my skull.

Oh yes, sweetheart. Grab my fucking face. Grab me hard.

I will happily spend hours devouring her pussy.

With a wicked grin, I listen to her cues, giving her more kisses, more flicks of my tongue, and long, lingering licks as I lap up all the flavors of her desire.

Sweet, salty, desperate.

She tastes like the woman I've been craving.

She ropes her fingers tighter into my hair as I press a little harder, kiss her more deeply.

My hands travel behind her legs, over her ass, curving over her flesh.

That sends her reeling. Her hips jerk, and her voice hits the ceiling in a long, loud "Yessssss."

So my Nadia likes a little ass attention. I'm down with that. I'm definitely down with that.

As I worship at the altar of her clit, I grip her flesh, squeezing her cheeks harder.

"Please," she murmurs.

Consider it done, sweetheart.

I knead her ass as I devour her wetness, kissing her harder, licking her faster, and squeezing this most fine ass as I go.

Hard as steel, my cock throbs in my boxer briefs. Hell, my dick is leaking, and I don't fucking care, because she's losing it. Arching and moaning. Crying out and rocking her hips.

It's beautiful and wanton, the way she seeks her pleasure.

She's so shameless.

So bold.

And I love that I'm the lucky recipient of all her desire.

All her want.

She spreads her legs wider, opening herself up, a debauched invitation to consume her flesh.

Why, yes, I will gladly accept.

I break contact for a second, raising my face. My mouth is covered in her slickness. "Fuck my face, sweetheart. Go wild on me," I rasp.

She gazes down at me, her brown eyes glimmering with darkening desire. She parts her lips, licks them, then locks eyes with me. "I'll fuck your face," she whispers, saying that filthy word for the first time.

Letting go of her ass for a second, I run my hand up her body and brush a finger over her lips. "Your naughty mouth."

She nips my finger. "Fuck me with your naughty mouth," she murmurs, and I nearly die of being ridiculously turned on.

This woman. Her words. Her need.

She delivers.

I return my hands to her ass, my face to her pussy.

And we go wild.

She lets go, rocking and thrusting, having a field day. I'm her toy now, my tongue is her vibrator, and she's using me fiercely, expertly, her hips arching up, up, up.

As my tongue goes flick, flick, flick.

As my hands grip her ass, digging in deeper, squeezing her.

"Yes, oh God, yes," she moans, her fingers gripping my skull.

We work together to find her bliss. Hands, hips, mouth, tongue, and sweet, frenzied friction.

That's what she needs.

That's what I give her as she begs for release.

She cries out, a delirious, keening sound that's half my name and half "*Coming.*"

And wholly hot as fuck.

She tenses, then shudders, her thighs squeezing my face as she comes on my tongue, my lips, my mouth.

I devour her climax, losing my mind at the taste of her release.

At her moans.

Her pants.

Her *oh Gods* as she comes down from the high.

When she lets out a soft laugh, I take it that she's hit a wall, that she's too sensitive. Letting go of her ass, I look up, meet her gaze, and smile like a happy fool.

Because, fuck, that's what I am.

I'm so damn happy with her.

She's blissed out, her hair wild, her smile gloriously filthy, and her cheeks flushed orgasm-pink.

"Hi," she whispers.

My heart slams against my chest.

My cock thumps inside my jeans.

For the first time in a long time, the two organs are utterly in sync, working in tandem, and that's terribly dangerous.

But it's a risk I'm taking.

I need more of her.

Wiping a hand across my face, I crawl up her, brace myself on my palms above her, and meet her gaze. "Hi."

A smile comes my way. "Which rule number was that? I can't think."

I wiggle a brow. "Rule number four, sweetheart. And it's still in effect."

"Right." Her sex-drunk frown is adorable. "And rule number four says . . ."

"Rule number four," I say, "says that I get to make you come." I pause. "A lot."

I push back onto my knees, then offer her a hand. She takes it, and I tug her up. "And now I'm going to take you to your bed, where I'm going to fuck you and make love to you," I tell her.

She lets out a satisfied sigh, her lips twitching in a grin. "Thank God for the lucky corgi butts."

* * *

In her bedroom, Nadia tugs on the hem of my shirt, her heated gaze drifting downward, checking out my clothes.

I'm still dressed. She's half naked, which mostly works for me. That blouse needs to go. The bra too.

Stat.

"Do I get to undress you now?" she asks, playing with the fabric of my Henley, lifting it a few inches so her fingertips trail over my abs.

Her touch ignites goose bumps across my flesh. I want to feel those hands all over me, turning me on, making me crazy.

"Take it off. Take it all off." I want everything off. Her clothes. Mine. I want to get naked and roll around with her all night long, arms and legs wrapped around each other. I want to feel her bare skin. Explore every inch, discover every reflex.

Laughing, she pulls the fabric over my head. "Don't you want to admire my candlelit seduction, roses, and soft music?" She gestures to her bedroom as she tosses my shirt on the floor.

With a quick glance, I appraise her decor—no candles, no flowers, no tunes. Her bedroom is simple—a cranberry-red cover on her king-size bed and gobs and gobs of pillows.

"Woman, where is the seduction? How do you expect me to get turned on without rose petals all over the place?"

She spreads her palms over my chest, and I draw in a sharp, hot breath as sparks shoot through me.

Her touch is electric, and it short-circuits my brain.

"I don't know. Are you turned on, Crosby?"

My eyes narrow as I rope a hand around her bare waist, jerking her against the ridge of my cock. "You tell me."

She murmurs, "Seems so." Then her busy hands continue their journey, traveling over the planes of my stomach on a path for the button of my jeans.

Working the snap open, she heads for the zipper next.

I waste no time either, fiddling with the rest of the buttons on her pink shirt, spreading it open, revealing the tops of those luscious tits I've only sneaked a peek at.

Tonight I get to gawk. I get to indulge in them.

She lets go of my jeans to shrug out of her shirt. I help the nudity cause by unhooking her bra, letting the white lace fall to where-the-fuck-ever.

"Fuck me," I groan as I free her tits—gorgeous, perky breasts with dusky rose nipples that stand at attention. I cup one in each hand, and she lets out a throaty gasp, arching her back, pushing into my touch as I knead these beauties.

"I like that," she purrs.

My dick tries to wrestle its way out of my jeans, jerking against my clothes, doing a skyscraper impression to get some attention.

But fuck my dick.

Because . . . these breasts.

I drop my face between them, nuzzling, licking, sucking.

Groaning too. I could spend all day here. I could get

lost in the valley of her breasts. Don't bother with a search and rescue crew; I'm not leaving.

Doesn't seem she wants me to either. Nadia grips my hair, tugs me closer, urges me to lavish attention on her gorgeous globes.

"Yes, Crosby. God, yes," she says, but then a few seconds later, her hands still, and she whispers, "Hey."

At the sound of her alarm, I instantly look up, searching her face.

"I love second base," she whispers, not actually alarmed at all, but encouraging, it turns out, as she says, "but I kinda wanna get to home plate."

I grin, then laugh, shaking my head. "What's wrong with me? Getting all stalled out on second, when it's clearly time to score." I clear my throat and lecture sternly, "For the record, though, the rule book dictates that I get to return to second base and spend all night here. There's so much I want to do to these beautiful tits."

"And so much I want you to do with your . . . baseball bat?" she asks as she cups my hard-on.

"Dick, shaft, cock." I cover her hand with mine, pressing hers more firmly against my erection.

Ah, yes. Fucking yes. That feels so good.

With a mischievous grin, she mutters, "Fuck, fuck, fuck."

I sigh happily, at her words, her deeds, her palm stroking my dick through my jeans. She's where I want her to be.

Well, I do want to move us horizontal.

Gently removing her hand, I bend to take off my

socks, because no woman should see a man in only his lucky socks—that's how they become *unlucky*.

Next go the jeans, and soon she's shoving off my boxer briefs and my dick is greeting her with a hello and a *Let's get intimately acquainted right this second.*

Her breath rushes out sharply, and she goes still, standing in front of me with her hands at her sides.

"You okay, sweetheart?" I ask, worried at how awkward she suddenly seems.

She presses her lips together then takes an audible breath. "It just hit me. I don't know what to do next."

Her voice is small, but not shy, not nervous. It's an admission and a request for guidance.

"I've got you, sweetheart," I whisper. All I want is to be her guide.

But then, as I lead her to the bed, gently laying her on it, I know that's a lie. I want to be more.

More than her friend.

More than a fuck buddy.

I want to be her man.

Why the hell did I have to be in self-prescribed time-out when I reconnected with the woman of my dreams?

Because I'm pretty sure that's what Nadia Harlowe is.

Bold and beautiful, open and vulnerable, spread out on her red bedcover and waiting for me to make love to her for the first time.

As I crawl over her, reaching for a condom, I stop, cup her cheek, and ask, "You still sure?"

Her brown eyes are so deep, so beautiful as she locks

them with mine. In those irises I see trust, certainty, maybe even . . . *years*.

"I think I've been ready for this for a while," she whispers, reaching for me, curling her hands lightly over my shoulders. "With you," she adds, and my dumb heart trips over itself, racing to get closer to her.

That's what I want.

To be close to her.

Maybe it's what I've always wanted. Maybe this wish has been knocking around in the back of my mind for a long time.

Only now, she's front and center.

I'm not sure she can stay there, but that's where I want her. For tonight and beyond.

I drop a soft kiss onto her lips, whispering, "That's why I want it to be good for you. Because this is so much more than sex."

She trembles all over, and it's a beautiful sight.

Even more beautiful is the way the happiness spreads to her eyes.

A happiness that says we're in this together.

The question isn't are we ready to screw, but are we ready to stay together?

Goodbye, virginity. Hello, better-than-my-rabbit action.

At least, I'm pretty sure the real thing will be better than silicone. Though, in defense of that plastic material, sex toy manufacturers can mold some seriously life-like schlongs.

Girth-wise, my rabbit isn't that far off from this man, or his length either. Which means, yes, Crosby could be a cock model.

The thought brings a smile to my face.

But the smile disappears when he moves closer, settling between my legs, making it all much more real. I swallow roughly. "What do you want me to do?" My voice pitches up, threaded with nerves once again.

"Just relax, sweetheart. I'll go slow. It'll probably hurt for a bit. But I'll stop anytime you want, okay?"

I nod a few times, my hands curving over his shoulders. "Okay." I gulp, taking a breath. "Leave my hands here?"

"That's perfect. You can put your hands anywhere, but shoulders work," he says, then he settles between my legs, rubs the head of his cock against me, and I jump.

But it's a good jump.

A pleasure jump.

My pulse spikes, and my heart skips a beat at the intoxicating feel of his dick on me—of hardness against wetness.

Breathing in purposefully, deeply, I let the air fill my lungs, my whole body. And I imagine relaxation flooding me.

My legs fall open wide as he continues rubbing the head against me. I stare down at us, mesmerized, utterly mesmerized, by the erotic sight—his big hand curled around the base of his cock, the slow and sensual way he rubs the crown through my wet folds, then how he presses it against my clit.

A blast of pleasure smashes into me, and I curl my hands tighter around his strong shoulders, digging into his muscles, his flesh.

"Feels so good," I murmur.

A smile curves his lips. "You fucking bet it does."

His eyes darken, arousal coming over them, but passion too—passion for me.

I feel it.

I sense it.

This is not just sex.

We're not just fucking.

We're connecting.

Anticipation ignites a fresh rush of tingles down my spine. Pleasure rolls through me as he pushes in.

My thighs clamp, tightening for a second, gripping his hips. Then I laugh, letting go. "Hi."

"Hey," he says, bracing himself on his palms. "You good?"

"So good," I whisper as I hook one leg over the back of his thigh, tugging him a little closer, a little deeper.

He sinks in another inch, and I arch up, savoring at once the utter intoxication of him starting to fill me at the same time as I bite back a burn.

He goes deeper, and I'm being stretched.

It's good, but uncomfortable too.

So much pressure, so much pushing, like an invasion.

My fingers dig in. I need to grip him, and as I grasp him tighter, he groans, a long, slow sensual sound that sends a wave of hot sparks across my skin.

From his reaction.

From his unrestrained response to sinking into me.

His noises help me to relax, and relaxing helps me to take him in.

He's halfway there, maybe more, and I coax him deeper, my thigh hooking more tightly around him as I grit my teeth momentarily.

His eyes lock with mine. "Nadia, it's hurting you. I can tell."

Shaking my head, I breathe in, out. "It's a good hurt. Let me feel it."

"Are you sure?" His question is desperate, like his eyes, like his expression.

He wants this as much as I do. He wants me like I want him.

And I do want him.

In every way.

Deep in my bones, far into my heart.

Thank God I am a toy aficionado.

I've done this, I've been here.

Yes, the real thing is different, but I can handle this, and I want to.

I want to so much. I wrap both legs around him, hooking them over his firm ass, then I jerk him closer so he sinks deeper into me.

"Oh God," I gasp.

"Fuck, sweetheart," he groans, then grits his teeth, clenches his jaw.

The realization that he's as affected, as lost, as I am unravels me.

It wrecks me and takes me apart.

I inhale deeply, slide my hands down his body, cover his ass, and hold on tight, closing my eyes as he sinks all the way in.

All. The. Way.

I tense, tremble, bite my lip at a rush of pain.

It radiates in my center, a burn, and a sting.

But I breathe through it, again, again.

And soon, the pain ebbs, like a tide flowing out to sea and leaving a gentle lull in its wake.

A tender push, a delicious pull.

And the sensation of being filled, of being one.

That's how I feel with Crosby.

Connected.

And also insanely turned on.

I lift my hips, seek him out, ask for more.

He grits his teeth, a bead of sweat forming on his forehead. He pulls out, inch by inch, until he's almost all the way out, then he swivels his hips and sinks back into me.

"Oh!" I gasp, arching into him.

"Yes," he grunts, then eases out, pauses, and slides back in, his shaft grazing my clit as he goes.

And that right there is better than a bunny.

Hotter than a dolphin.

And way more intense than any battery-operated little darling.

I wrap my arms around his neck, my fingers playing with his hair as my legs slide up his body, my thighs gripping his ass.

He lowers himself onto his rippling forearms, his muscles taut. His expression is torture and bliss all at once, but then soon it's sensual determination as we find a rhythm, hit a pace, and move together.

I moan, writhing under him, gripping him, loving *this*.

Savoring this connection.

What I love most of all is when he dips his face, brushes his lips against mine, and then sighs a needy, dreamy sigh, like he can't get enough of me either.

My whole body is coated in bliss.

Dusted in desire.

I don't want this to end, but I desperately crave the explosion of an epic orgasm.

And I think I'm going to need a little help to get there.

I lean my head back, part my lips, and ask for what I want. "Will you touch me? Play with me till I come?"

"Fuck yes," he rasps out, then pushes up on one strong arm and slides the other down my body, between my legs.

Strokes me.

Oh God.

Yes.

That.

His fingers slide across my clit, and he rubs me where I want him most, faster, then faster still, pushing me, pressing, and taking me closer to the edge.

As he rolls his hips, as he fucks deeper, he strokes me, and I grip him. In a flash, the pleasure crackles in my veins, bursts like bright neon lights, and then flares all at once.

A bright, hot, powerful surge inside me.

I cry out as my whole body succumbs to beautiful, newfound bliss.

Coming with the man I'm falling in love with.

Part of me feels like an utter cliché—the virgin falling for the first guy she sleeps with.

Another part feels like the luckiest woman in the world.

And still another part is completely frustrated. Not over the sex, but over the absolute inconvenience of these feelings.

The terrible timing of my emotions.

Why now?

He's leaving for spring training in a few more days.

He's off the market.

I'm up to my earlobes in responsibility.

But those worries fade away as these luxurious sensations steal my senses, and I gladly let them go.

26

NADIA

I have a million questions.

But only one answer.

There is only ever one answer when life gets too complicated.

Okay, fine. Two answers—shoes and ice cream.

But since it's late and shops are closed, Crosby and I are on my couch, cuddled in a blanket, sharing sea salt with caramel ribbons ice cream from Salt & Straw after he dashed down the street to fetch a pint.

Which certainly doesn't make me want him any less.

Should I stop wanting him? Every logical part of me says yes, and every other part says I don't want to stop anything.

The trouble is—I'm not sure where we go from here.

From cozy on a couch, noshing on post-sex dessert, to whatever's next.

We're a whirlwind. My brother's wedding was only a week ago. I went into that feeling knocked flat and stomped on by Cupid, rejected even by the top matchmaker in Las Vegas. Now I'm having the time of my life with my good friend and new lover.

This is what I've wanted—the real deal.

I wanted *this* with a friend.

And I'm having it.

But can we trust something that ignited in a week? A week when we were supposed to be off the market?

Crosby dips his spoon in one more time. "Best ice cream ever?"

I consider the pint container, then I'm floored. "Wait. Is this even organic?"

He wiggles his brow and lifts a finger to his lips. "*Shhh.* I'm breaking all the rules tonight."

Maybe that's what we're doing. A little rule bending, then we'll return to the way we were.

But when we put the ice cream away, he tugs me close and loops an arm around my waist. "Ask me to spend the night. Hint: I'll say yes."

I grin from the depths of my soul. "Spend the night."

"Yes."

He takes me to bed, tugs my back to his chest, and asks if I want to go again.

"Hell yes."

This time he slides behind me, hooks my leg over his thigh, and enters me like that, taking the lush and scenic route to pleasure. He makes love to me as we spoon, until I'm coming, and he's coming, and it feels like we're new lovers, old lovers, true lovers.

Especially when he draws me close afterward. When he threads his hands in my hair. And when he whispers, "You do make me break all the rules. I'm pretty sure rule number five was don't fall for each other." He shrugs, his lips curving into a *what can you do* grin. "But I broke that."

My heart leapfrogs over itself. My smile won't be denied. "Guess I broke that one too."

Problem is, the rules don't say what happens now.

* * *

In the morning, I know I want this much to happen: food and orgasms.

We shower together, and when Crosby asks me to turn around so he can wash my hair, I shoot him a dubious look.

"Is that code for something?"

"You think I'm going to do something naughty to you while I wash your hair?"

I shrug. "Maybe."

"Do you want me to?"

"No, but maybe once you rinse out the shampoo, I'll want you to," I say, dragging a hand down his pecs and over his abs before he turns me around. "Or maybe now."

He presses a kiss to the back of my neck, making me shiver. I murmur as his lips sweep over my skin, down my back, along my spine. The sound of his knees touching the tile echoes in the steamy shower stall.

He brushes his mouth over the curve of my ass, then nibbles on my flesh.

And oh my.

That feels . . . incredible.

I had no idea butt-biting was *the best*.

But it is. Oh, holy hell, it is.

He works his mouth over my ass cheeks, biting and nipping.

A storm gathers inside me, building in intensity as he nibbles.

I moan and groan, louder and even louder, as his tongue maps my flesh, as his teeth mark my skin.

A pulse beats between my legs, insistently, exquisitely.

I'm pretty sure he's discovering that my ass is an erogenous zone. I'm discovering it too, because I had no idea. Now I do, and I like it.

I like the attention he's giving to my rear. I love his hands on my flesh, his mouth on my skin, his teeth sucking and biting.

Is he going to take my ass someday?

Dear God.

What's come over me? I tossed my V card into the bonfire of pleasure, and now I'm going to give up my ass virginity too?

Also, hey, isn't he supposed to be washing my hair?

But who cares about clean hair when his tongue is caressing the outline of my cheek right where it meets my thigh, right where it feels spectacular?

He travels along the seam of my ass, and I'm pretty sure my bones turn molten and my blood is lava.

"Is it supposed to feel so good?" I moan.

Crosby growls then nibbles on my butt again. "Had a hunch you'd like that," he whispers, then rises up and slaps my ass.

I yelp and I smile at the same damn time as a delicious cocktail of pleasure and pain wings through my cells. "You did? How did you know?"

Lips land on my shoulder. Hands slide up my stomach, traveling to my breasts. Firm arms cage me in. "Because you loved when I played with your ass last night while I went down on you," he whispers. "When I squeezed you hard as I ate your pussy."

A shudder rips through me, igniting an intense, powerful wave of sparks. Like fire shooting through my veins.

I gasp, aching for him. "Can you do that again? Knead my ass as you finger me? I think I'll love that too."

His teeth land on my neck, possessive and hungry, chased with a groan that sounds like it was ripped from his chest. "I love how you ask for what you want, Nadia. You're so damn bold. It turns me on so much. Everything about you turns me on," he rasps, pushing his cock against my ass, the hard length of him pressing against my cheeks.

"I like asking you for what I want. I love that I can," I say, opening up to him in yet another way.

I shudder against him, then he lets go of me, spins me around, and meets my gaze. His eyes darken to midnight blue, shimmering with wild arousal. "You can ask me for anything. I want you to. I want to give it to you."

"Thank you." I loop my arms around his neck. "I mean it. I've had all these desires, all these wants. And to act on them with you . . ." My voice catches, and I'm not entirely sure how to finish. We're talking about sex, but we're also talking about intimacy.

True and real intimacy.

That's what I feel with Crosby.

Dipping his face, he drops his lips to my jaw, bites me, then pulls back. "I want you to share them with me. Your desires. Your wants," he says, his tone edging toward desperate. He sounds as lost as I feel. "Share them anytime. I'll give them to you."

I shake with the emotions and lust surging through me all at once, twining together like strands of a rope. "I will."

"Good," he says, low and smoky. "Now, let me give you what you asked for."

He backs me into the shower wall, dragging one hand down my body to glide between my legs while the other snakes around to my ass.

Panting, I rock my hips, seeking out his touch in an act of sheer desperation. His fingers connect with me in a burst of heat. The fire in me licks higher, burns brighter.

He works me over, stroking my clit, squeezing my ass, then slamming those lips to mine.

I'm hemmed in by desire, by the sweet torment of touch everywhere. Of the way he drives mad pleasure through me, and the way I need it, crave it.

Lust claws at me.

I feel out of control, wild and animalistic.

I feel like I'm losing my mind. Losing my reason, my logic, my inhibitions.

I feel like I never want any of them back.

As he crushes his lips to mine, thrusts his fingers inside me, sweeps his thumb across my clit, and grabs my ass, I nearly die of bliss.

My climax seizes me, taking hold of my body, my mind.

It shakes me to my bones. He breaks the kiss, and I cry out, gasping his name, God's name, every name.

I don't even know what I'm saying.

I'm only feeling.

Feeling ecstasy vibrating from my core out through every cell.

At some point, who knows when, we separate, and I am a noodle.

A spent noodle.

I blink up at him, and he stares at me with a new intensity in his dark-blue eyes.

Yes, that was intense.

But it was intense because I trust him. Because he's discovering me. We're discovering how we are together.

He swallows roughly, his eyes flickering with passion. "What have you done to me?"

My throat tightens with emotion, with the need to touch him, to be touched. "What have *you* done to *me*?"

He shakes his head, maybe in disbelief, then he dips his face near my ear, brushing his cheek against mine. "Need to get close to you right now, sweetheart. Want to be inside you."

Desire squeezes my chest. "Yes. Please. God, yes."

He steps out of the shower, grabs a condom, and returns to me.

The water still beats down on us as he slides the

condom on his cock, wraps my leg around his hip, and tells me to hold on.

Then he slides into me.

We gasp at the same time.

We stare at each other in the same way.

And when he sinks into me, we're both feeling it—something else. Something new.

I might not know much about sex.

I might never have been in love.

But I know this much. Somehow I've fallen for him. Hard, fast, relentlessly.

I'm pretty sure it's the same way for him.

That's how he fucks me in the shower.

Like he wants me, like he needs me, and like he's as utterly floored by what's happened in a week as I am.

When he reaches the edge and I follow him there, coming again, coming together, I don't want to stop.

I don't want *us* to stop.

And I don't want to pretend at all, not one bit.

Maybe he doesn't either, since he cups my cheeks, presses his forehead to mine, and whispers, "I'm so crazy about you, Nadia."

My heart flutters wildly. "I'm pretty mad about you, Crosby. And there's nothing accidental about it."

He laughs softly, then his laughter fades. "What the hell are we going to do about this?"

I shrug. "Wash my hair, then let's get some breakfast and figure out what kind of frocktangular mess we've made of our friends-with-benefits plan."

"It's a fuckerrific mess, that's for sure."

27

CROSBY

I know three things right now.

These eggs at Helen's Organic Café around the corner from Nadia's place are moan-inducing.

The tea is life-giving.

And the woman across from me is quite possibly the reason I've picked the wrong women for ages.

Was I waiting for Nadia all along? Had I already met the right woman when we were younger, so I torpedoed everything else with terrible choices?

I'd bet I did. Everything about Nadia feels right.

We laugh. We talk. We connect. We share.

And we smolder.

She's a friend and a lover.

This thing we're doing right now? Eating breakfast after making love? After that kind of sex, that kind of soul-deep intimacy?

Hell, I want it. I want it with her—badly.

But something nags at me from the back of my mind.

Several *somethings*.

The deal I made with her brother. The same one I made with Gabe and the guys too.

It's the same promise I made to myself. A few weeks ago, I was so fed up with my own poor judgment that I asked my friends to be the rubber band I snap on my wrist to break my bad habit. Because I'm tired of wading through my own relationship wreckage.

I know I don't make the best choices.

That's the crux of the issue.

What if *this choice*—wanting to be with Nadia—is another disastrous decision, only I don't know it yet? Like I didn't realize Camille was bad news? Like I didn't know Daria would be terrible for me?

Here I am untangling from the remnants of girlfriends past, and while Nadia isn't one bit like my exgirlfriends, I'm still me. I'm the one who needs fixing, needs a hard reset.

I don't want whatever this thing is with Nadia to backfire simply because I have a bad track record.

I set down my fork, then drag a hand through my hair. "I don't know what to do."

She blinks, as if shifting mental gears, but she asks, "About what?" like she already suspects the answer. Maybe she's been thinking in the same circles.

"About how the hell we became a *we* in a week."

She shrugs a little helplessly. "I know. I came to town to focus on the team. You needed a break from relationships." She scoffs lightly. "And now look at us."

I slide my hand across the table, gripping hers. "I don't know if I should trust myself. A few weeks ago, I was telling your brother how I was radioactive. That I needed to detox. And that's what scares the shit out of me."

"Detoxing?" she asks, a little confused.

I shake my head. "No. That I needed to do one thing, but I did the opposite. I *intoxxed*. I intoxxed you." My heart fills and empties at the same time. "I'm falling so hard for you, Nadia," I say, and it feels wonderful to give her the truth of my heart, but terrible too.

"I'm completely falling for you," she says. In her voice I hear the same kind of hope I feel, and a thread of the same worry too.

That's the trouble. Is this a false hope?

"But the last thing I want in the whole entire universe is to screw this up, Nadia," I say.

She nods slowly in understanding, maybe even agreement. "Because it's happening so fast?"

"It's like a wild roller-coaster ride we're on, and I don't know how to pull the brake, or if we even should. I want to be with you, but I also don't want to ruin this by rushing things when the timing is wrong, or the timing is against us?"

She winces, but nods too, taking it on the chin. "I feel the same. I wanted nothing to do with a relationship when I moved back, and now . . ."

I finish the thought. "We're practically having one?" It comes out heavily.

So does her reply. "We are. Instant relationship, just add water."

I scrub a hand over my jaw. I'm pretty sure falling in love should make you stupidly happy, not constantly worried you'll torch the best thing that ever happened to you with one false move.

But maybe there's a way to pull this off. Maybe we can pull *us* off the way we originally planned.

There has to be a way to get back on track. To salvage our initial intent. If it's friends-only or lose her completely, I'll do it.

I brace myself for what I'm about to propose. "I know what we should do."

Her eyes flick to mine, hopeful. "You do? Please tell me."

"The plan was to stay friends, right? We need to adult the fuck out of this. We need to adult it for real this time. We never truly tried to buddy up. We said we would, but we didn't."

She jumps in, picking up the thread like we're solving a business problem. "You're right. We planned to buddy up, and instead we fell into bed."

"We're supposed to try being friends. Try for real. Not get all wrapped up in each other."

"Exactly," she says, agreeing, her brown eyes intense, how I suspect she is at work. "We can't just get together that quickly. That's not how relationships work."

"We need to do this the smart way. The measured way. We need to be patient."

She lifts her mug, taking a long drink of her coffee, like she's giving herself time to analyze the problem. When she sets down her cup, her brows are knit, her words slow and serious, almost cautious. "Did we just agree to be friends?"

I look down at her hand, still joined with mine, and

then let go. Friends don't hold hands like they're crazy for each other. Friends eat breakfast and go their separate ways. They don't text each other later in the day, and they don't ask when they'll see each other again.

My heart pinches like a rope is tied around it, tightening it.

I don't want to be *just* friends.

I don't want to level down with Nadia Harlowe.

And I sure as shit don't want to be less than lovers with her.

But being friends without benefits feels like the first responsible decision I've made about this woman in weeks.

It's what I *need* to do.

"I leave on Monday for spring training. I'm going early this year to get in some extra workouts when pitchers and catchers report. Then I'm gone for a little over a month anyway." I can't quite fathom how I'm willingly ending something that has barely begun. But I have to do this. I have to know I'm not nuclear any longer.

I force myself to think with my head rather than the pathetic organ in my chest that wants to smother her with kisses, hide out with her in bed the rest of the day, and never let her go.

Brain, you're at bat.

Just take a fucking swing.

"And while I'm in training, since we can't be together," I continue, doing my damnedest to be rational, "maybe we use the time to be apart. To take it slow and measured. To be patient." I swallow roughly. "We can go to the golf event tomorrow as friends," I offer, like I'm dying to go platonic with her.

Being just friends only sounds like a forking awful consolation prize, but it's the opposite of my past mistakes, and that's what I need to do.

"Sure," Nadia says, a little uncertain. But she takes a shuddery breath and seems more resolved. "It's what we were supposed to do anyway. Besides, I need to focus on finding a new GM, and all my plans for the team. There's no lack of work for me to do," she says, crisp and professional.

In a similar tone, I say, "Then we'll see how things are after spring training. After we've done the friend-ship thing for real." I sound much more decisive than I feel. "We'll wait for our pitch. That'll be our new rule. Rule number six."

She gives me a faint smile, drains her coffee, then nods like it's all settled. "Friends."

"For now," I agree. We're not calling it relationship-quits forever. We're just sensibly slowing down.

So why do I feel like we just broke up?

28

NADIA

My niece, Audrey, brandishes a paperback in each hand, waggling one then the other.

"Girl spy or girl warrior?" she asks, debating her purchase as we peruse the shelves at An Open Book.

I screw up my lips, tapping my finger on my chin, studying each cover. "That's a good question. But with books, you truly can have it all. I vote for both," I declare.

She nods resolutely, her black ponytail bouncing. "You're right. I'll ask my dad to buy me both."

This is one of my favorite bookstores in the city, perched at the edge of the Marina, a soaring view of the Golden Gate Bridge beyond. I scan the titles and tip a copy of a sports biography into my hand. "While you're at it, maybe add this one. Girl athletes are cool."

She takes it with eager hands, reads the back jacket, then glances up at me with inquisitive eyes. "Will you ever have a girl athlete on your team?"

"There have been some female kickers. You never

know. We might have one in the NFL someday. But you want to hear something cool?"

"I do."

I lower my voice to a whisper. "I think I might hire a female general manager."

"You're so cool, Aunt Nadia." She spins on her heel and rushes off to find her father in the travel section, thrusting the books at him.

An elbow nudges my side. "Did I just hear you say you're hiring a female GM?"

I turn to my sister, Brooke, who's joined me in the kids' section, some new thrillers tucked under her arm. "It's looking that way. She's the leading candidate."

"Dad worked hard to create equal opportunities and build a diverse workforce. He'd be proud of you for carrying that on."

"Thanks," I say, a lump sticking in my throat. Emotions are riding me like I'm a surfboard today.

Breaking up with a guy you weren't technically dating is the worst.

Especially when you're falling hard for him.

Brooke studies my face. "You don't seem as happy about that as I'd expect. What's going on?"

That's my sister, seeing right through me.

"Nothing is going on," I say with fake cheer.

Cheer she bludgeons with one sharp snort. "Right. I don't buy that. What's the story with *the man*?"

I sigh heavily, slumping against the Jenny Hans. "I wish there were a story." My voice is tight, my chest heavy. But I'm not one to dwell, to go all "woe is me" over a man. Then again, I've never experienced a man like Crosby.

Brooke sets her hand on my arm, squeezing gently. "What happened?"

I'm not sure I want to open the wound again. This morning's adulting session at the café felt necessary, but in the way a dental exam is. You need it, even if it hurts like hell when the hygienist gets that tooth scalpel thingie out and scrapes off any plaque, all while chatting cheerily about her day. "Nothing happened," I say, though, really, a tooth scalpel thingie isn't nothing.

She grabs my arm. "Oh no, you don't."

"It's fine. I'm fine." I pinch the bridge of my nose, trying to dismiss all these feelings I didn't want to face when I returned to town. I simply wanted to be Take Charge Nadia. Boss Nadia. Nadia with her Leatherman that can open any door. My father's daughter. I didn't want to be Nadia with a soft, squishy heart that could be stepped on, smooshed, and stomped into a pulpy mess.

"Is this about Crosby?" Brooke asks, a little too insightful. I shake my head, and she rolls her eyes. "You can't fool me, buttercup. You two are in love. What's going on?"

Those words are a burst of sunlight in my chest. *In love.* She's not wrong. But the timing is. It's utterly and completely wrong.

"Timing is a tooth scalpel," I say.

She arches a *what the hell* brow.

"It can hurt like a son of a banshee, but sometimes the timing doesn't work out."

"That's just an excuse, Nadia."

My shoulders sag, and a kernel of sadness expands in my chest, the roots extending throughout my body.

Am I upset with Crosby?

Maybe I am.

But maybe I shouldn't be.

He might have dealt the fatal blow to our *benefits*, but I agreed with him from the beginning to the middle to the end.

His choice was smart.

Logical.

Right.

I would have made the same one.

I think.

"Look, I tried the whole dating thing in Vegas." I square my shoulders, digging into my metaphorical purse for my ovaries of steel. "It didn't pan out. But that's okay. The universe clearly wants me to be single and to focus on the team right now."

Brooke clears her throat, her eyes drifting pointedly to the front of the store. David is laughing with Audrey as they reach the counter and she plops down the three titles. He ruffles her black hair. She tosses her head back and laughs.

"I'm in love, and I can focus on work," Brooke points out.

My heart lurches at her words then squeezes as David tosses Brooke an *I love you* grin.

From all the way across the store.

She throws one right back at him.

It's everything.

Everything I've ever wanted.

That kind of love. That kind of trust. A relationship that's born from talking, falling, caring.

Like my parents had.

But I bet they didn't start as friends with benefits.

Relationships should start the right way, in a proper sequence and specific order. They shouldn't begin with a request for a dick pic, then turn into an accidental kiss in a doorway, then morph into a virgin rule book for defining friends-with-benefits behavior.

Ugh. I did everything upside down and backward.

I should have known better.

"But you and David met through a friend when you were working in China. You went on dates all over Beijing. You romanced each other. He proposed to you before you moved back to California. That's how it should be," I point out.

Brooke shakes her head. "There is no rule for how good relationships start."

"There should be," I say in a dead voice.

"Do you truly believe that?"

"I do." But I don't really know what I believe. All I know is that I miss Crosby, and I have a mountain of work to climb tonight.

I join Brooke and her family for lunch, try to be decent company, then head for the office, where I blast my friend Stone's latest single and get to work.

This is why I'm here after all.

Nothing more.

29

CROSBY

Holden tosses up the ball at home plate, swings, and connects with it, sending it down the third baseline.

Jacob fields it perfectly for the hundredth time in a row.

I clap his shoulder. "Dude, keep that up. You've got this."

The kid grins at me. "Can we go a few more times?"

I cup my hands over my mouth and shout to Holden at home plate, "Give us a few more screamers!"

My bud nods crisply and hits another ball down the third baseline.

Jacob fields it again neatly.

"You barely need me to tell you what to do," I say, proud of this dude.

He shoots me a dubious stare. "Maybe you forget how many line drives I missed at the start of the season?"

"Are you saying my memory stinks?" I ask.

"Maybe a little," he ribs me back.

We wrap up, and as we head off the field, the kid thanks us. "I'm glad you remembered enough that I could convince you to give me some extra practice."

"We've got you addicted now, is that right?" I ask.

"I think so," he says. "I can go again tomorrow."

"That's the way to do it, man," I say, clapping his shoulder. "Practice like it's all you ever want to do. Right, Holden?"

"That's what it takes," Holden adds sagely. "That's what I did when I was your age. Practice, practice, practice. That's what I still do."

"That's the key to success," I say. "Gotta put in the hours before the season if you want to have a shot at the pennant at the end."

That's where I went wrong with Nadia—not putting in the hours. Not dating properly, not taking my time. And when I realized things were moving too fast, I should have slowed down.

But nope. It's like I've learned nothing whatso-fucking-ever from my mistakes. I'm still diving headfirst off the relationship cliff. And what has that ever gotten me? Legal fees, stolen socks, the prospect of jail time in a foreign country.

And I can't fix it, can't go back and date her properly, because I'm leaving for Arizona in two days, and that's that.

Holden and I walk Jacob home, then I call a Lyft from outside his house, zipping up my hoodie as we wait, and cursing the cold-as-balls weather. "I won't miss San Francisco in February, that's for sure. Give me the Arizona desert, I say."

"Bet you'll miss something about here," Holden says dryly.

I lift a brow. "Yeah?"

He gives me a look as we pile into the car, heading back across the city. *"Yeah,"* he says, imitating me dead-on.

"Dude."

"Why are you *duding* me? I've been waiting for a report. You and Eric's sister. What's the deal? Obviously you have it bad for her."

"And obviously I made a pact to do nothing about it," I say defensively.

Holden laughs, shaking his head. "I don't give a shit about your deal."

"C'mon. You kidnapped me a week ago. You Drakkar Noir jacket-boarded me."

He lifts an imaginary violin, pretending to play it. "Poor Crosby."

I flip him the bird. "Goose biscuit," I mutter.

"Goose biscuit? What the fuck? You can't even swear properly?"

"Evidently I can't. And I paid for your tuxes. I'll honor the deal. I know I blew it."

"Whoa. I'm not saying this to get you to cash in."

"Then why are you saying it?" I fire off, pissed at him, at myself, at the whole damn universe.

"Someone is testy."

I drag a hand down my face, breathing out hard, trying to let go of all my frustrations bubbling up inside me. "Sorry, man. That's on me."

"No worries," he says as the driver heads into Grant's hood, swinging past a coffee shop I know.

"Can we stop here? I need a pick-me-up. They have organic black tea," I say, a little embarrassed.

"No problem," the driver says, pulling in front of Doctor Insomnia's Coffee and Tea Emporium.

Once we're out of the car, I level with Holden. "Look, there was something going on with Nadia. But now it's nothing."

He scoffs. "It didn't look like nothing the other night."

"What did it look like?"

He takes a beat, then locks eyes with me, like I'm the target. "Everything. It looked like everything."

My chest seizes up. Were we that obvious? Maybe we were. Because it felt like everything with Nadia. "But that's the problem. I need to slow the fuck down. I need to practice being single," I say as I head into the shop, order a tea, thank the barista, then head back out with the steaming cup.

"But do you truly need to practice being single?" Holden asks as we walk up the street.

"Hello? Have you met me? You guys all lit into me the other night about my horrible taste," I say, then take a scalding sip.

The tea burns my tongue.

"We've all made mistakes though. Maybe you just need to recognize when something isn't a mistake." Holden scratches his jaw as he turns philosophical.

I go pensive too, considering his words of wisdom. Trying to understand what is and isn't a mistake.

"How do you know though?" I ask, wanting his advice now, no longer testy.

"Maybe when you can't get her out of your system," he says, stuffing his hands into his jeans pockets. "Because there's always a woman like that, right? The one you can't get out of your head? Maybe you had one night with her, one kiss, one conversation. Your what-if woman."

"You're talking from experience, aren't you?"

"It was a while ago," he says as we cross the street.

"Who is she?" I ask, more intrigued now by his sitch than mine.

"Doesn't matter. I don't even know what she's up to anymore."

"You going to look her up?"

"Maybe," he says with a shrug, then a shake of his head. "But maybe I should just focus on the team."

I nod, getting it, understanding confusion completely. "That's what I'm talking about. That's what I need to do too. But in the meantime, tell me more about your what-if girl."

He cracks a smile. "She's definitely the what-if woman. It was one night. A couple years ago."

"The one-night stand you can't get out of your mind?"

He doesn't laugh. He doesn't scoff. He only sighs wistfully. "Almost. But not exactly. It wasn't even a one-night stand. More like a great conversation and an out-of-this-world kiss, a great time. Kind of crazy, right?"

We turn the corner, and then I stop in my tracks when I spot a familiar face. It's Declan, ducking out of another coffee shop—this neighborhood has them springing up like baby bunnies. He's got a Hawks ball cap on his head, and a cup in his hand. He lifts his chin in greeting. "Hey, guys."

I give him a curious look. "You're still in town? Figured you had left."

"I've got friends and family here," he says. "I stayed an extra night, but I'm catching a flight back to New York in two hours."

"Was it good to see peeps?" Holden asks.

Declan's lips twitch, maybe with the hint of a grin. "Yeah. Mostly." Distracted, he looks at his watch. "I should go. I'll catch you on the first home stand. You'll be on my turf, and we plan to destroy you," he says to me.

Ah, that's the Declan I know. He's the most competitive bastard in the league.

"As if the Comets can do anything but choke on our dust," I say.

"You'll be choking at the plate," he says with a wicked grin, then tugs on the bill of his cap before he tips his forehead in the direction of the airport. "Gotta take off."

"See you," Holden says.

Declan takes off, and we head up the block and around the corner, ready to rap on Grant's door. But he's already bounding down the steps in his workout clothes, his hair a wild mess, like he stuck his finger in an electrical socket.

I shoot him a look. "You've been DoorDashing on a Saturday afternoon?"

He rolls his eyes, flipping me the bird. "Yeah, I had a burger and a blow job. Let's go hit the gym."

We do, and the three of us all seem a little lost in our own worlds as we're working out.

As for me, I can't stop thinking about Holden's comments.

Not the ones about what-if women.

The ones about recognizing mistakes.

30

NADIA

Back when I was in my matchmaker phase, I read dating columns religiously—articles on the latest trends in dating, on where to go, ideal topics for discussion on the first date, and how to read between the lines.

And I want to issue a complaint right now.

Someone needs to pen a column on how utterly awkward it is to be friends with the guy you gave your virginity to the night before last.

Here we are at a golf course on the edge of the city, making small talk.

Small talk is painful. Hell, it's worse than having your plaque scraped. *Loudly.*

"So, you're looking forward to spring training?"

"Absolutely. I love it," Crosby says, all chipper and upbeat.

"It must feel like everything is possible," I offer, equally peppy so I don't think of him doing bad things to me or whispering sweet everythings in my ear.

"Yes, that's exactly it. The world is your oyster," he

says as we chat by a golf cart as the event is winding down. "We have a lot to work on with our oyster, but I'm stoked to do the work. It's always good to get back in the saddle."

Ugh, I want to gag.

He's talking to me like he's chatting with a reporter at the end of the game.

I chuckle, but it's mirthless, maybe even frustrated.

Crosby arches a brow. "What's that for?"

Should I just let it go? Screw it. "You just sounded like you were giving me a PR answer," I say.

He laughs. "I guess I did. The truth is, I'm kind of ridiculously excited. I always feel a little bit like a lion pacing in a cage, or maybe a bit of a lost soul, without baseball."

"See? That's a better answer. Because you love it," I say, glad to be talking honestly now.

His smile is magnetic, genuine. Like a kid riding a bike for the first time. "I do. It's definitely my first love," he says.

In some ways maybe I should feel jealous. But I don't. I'm glad he has something that he loves that much. That baseball is *it* for him. "That's how it is for me too. I'm not out on the field playing, obviously, but I grew up with a football-is-life worldview because of my dad. I can't imagine doing anything else. Is it crazy that even when I was a little girl, I wanted to run my dad's football team?"

"No *frogging* way," he says, smiling widely.

"I see I've rubbed off on you."

"In more ways than one," he says, wistful, his eyes a little lost.

I feel the same. My God, I feel the same.

"It was good to talk to you," I say, gesturing from him to me. "Like this."

"It was, Nadia. It was great," he says, and we both shuffle closer.

It's that awkward moment when you don't know if you should hug or not.

We go for the full awkward embrace, and the scent of him, the mind-bending, knee-weakening soapy scent of him, makes me feel lost all over again.

My heart is empty, but I know exactly how it would feel full again.

* * *

When I return home, I'm ready to write to the dating sites and tell them what to say. How to deal with this *frogging* mess.

Deal with it by saying it.

I want the friendship.

I want the love. I want to be the girl warrior and the woman who falls hard for the man. I want to have it all. Is that so crazy?

I send a note to Scarlett.

Nadia: Is it insane to think we can actually have it all?

. . .

The hour is late in Paris, and she doesn't answer, but that's okay. I think I know the answer.

* * *

I grab a late dinner with my mom that evening.

After we order yellowtail and edamame at my favorite sushi restaurant, I give her a wide-eyed look. "So, did Jackson Browne grease the wheels for you this weekend, Mama?"

A flush crawls up her cheeks, and my jaw goes slack. "Are you kidding me, Mom? For real?"

"That's not what I'm saying," she says, hushing me, but it's a half-hearted denial.

"So what *are* you saying, Mommykins?" I bat my lashes.

She lifts her green tea and takes a sip, her brown eyes sparkling with the kind of delight I haven't seen in them in a while.

"What I'm saying is I had a lovely time and I'm going to see him again. I want to see what happens. It seems kind of foolish not to."

I repeat her words in my head—*kind of foolish not to.*

They feel true.

They feel important.

They feel like one of those statements someone makes that stays with you.

That becomes a brand-new mantra.

More powerful than the one about speaking up.

Or maybe it's the perfect corollary. "Are those words to live by?"

"I think they are," she says, then tilts her head, studying me. "Is there something you'd be foolish not to do?"

The answer is as obvious as knowing who I want to hire for the GM.

As instinctive as selecting what pair of shoes to wear.

As simple as talking to my mom.

I know what I want.

"I fell in love with Crosby," I confess, my throat catching, "and I think the timing is all wrong."

"But you think you'd be foolish not to try to make it work?"

A tear slides down my cheek. "I do. I want to have it all. And really, why be a fool?"

She lifts her mug and clinks it to my glass.

That night when I slide into my bed, two messages light up my phone.

One is a reply from my friend in Europe.

Scarlett: You should have it all. And if something is getting in the way, figure out how to get rid of it and go get your all.

Then a note from my brother.

Eric: Just landed. Anything interesting happen while I was in the Maldives?

.   .   .

I run my thumb over his message. Should I tell him? Well, not that I discovered I love when Crosby plays with my ass.

But rather that I'm in love with his best friend?

I flash back to the mantra that has served me well.

Don't be afraid to speak up.

I answer Eric with three words.

Nadia: Yes. Crosby happened.

31

CROSBY

I cut the engine in my mom's driveway, grateful that she stayed up for me. I head up the steps to her lemon-yellow Victorian house, lined up amid the painted ladies on Steiner Street, and the second I reach the top, she opens the door with a soft whoosh.

She lifts a finger to her lips, letting me know Kana's asleep. I nod and slip out of my shoes as I go inside. We pad quietly to the sunroom at the back of her house on the far side from the bedrooms.

Starlight streams through the windows, and I grab a seat on the rattan couch, tossing my keys on the table. Mom pats my leg. "Want some tea? Some sliced mango? Kale soup?"

Laughing quietly, I shake my head. "Nope. Just good old-fashioned advice."

"Ah, that's a piece of carrot cake," she says, then pats my leg again. "I assume this is about Nadia?"

"How did you know?" I ask, but truthfully, I'm not surprised.

"Like I said the other night, it's been years."

"Yeah, what did you mean by that?"

She licks her lips, a sign that she's thinking. "It means I always saw something between you two. But especially you. You were so . . . enchanted with her."

My heart warms like the sun. "Sounds about right."

"You loved listening to her tell stories, you loved talking to her, and you were nearly impossible to pull away from her when you were at their house," she adds.

I groan, dropping my head into my hand. "What am I going to do?"

Her soft laugh fills the room. "Stop being so superstitious, I presume?"

I look up. "Why do you assume I'm being superstitious?"

"Because I raised you. You always liked your routine, everything in order. Practice at a certain time. Putting in so much work. Wearing your lucky socks. If you had a bad game, you'd figure out what you'd done differently and try to undo it," she says, calm and knowing.

I push out a forced laugh. "Sounds like me."

She smiles like it's a fond memory. "And you'd analyze every game. See what you could learn from it. Do better. It's served you well in baseball, all the way to the major leagues." She squeezes my leg. "But I suspect you're not worried about baseball right now."

I slump back against the couch, heave a sigh, and scrub a hand over the back of my neck. "No. I'm here about the woman. The one who *enchants* me."

She chuckles knowingly. "Well then."

I cock my head, meeting her eyes. "Well then, what?"

She rolls her eyes, something she rarely does. "I feel as if your question has already been answered."

I frown, trying to unpack her meaning.

But then I stop.

I stop analyzing, and I listen to what she just said.

I can't apply baseball logic to women. I can't force superstitions on love. And I definitely can't expect lucky-sock reasoning to apply to my past.

Or my present.

Or the future I want to have.

"So what if I swore off women?" I say, straightening. "So what if I was taking a break?" I stand to pace the room. "Who cares if I *should* take things slow, or if the timing is wrong? None of that matters."

Mom simply grins.

I grab my keys from the table. "This isn't about being smart or measured or patient. This is about not being a dumbass who lets the woman who enchants me pass me by."

She stands, clasping my shoulders. "I couldn't have said it better myself."

I hug her hard, kiss her cheek, then get the hell out of there, dialing Eric from the car.

He starts speaking as soon as he picks up. "Well, I bet you—"

"Listen, I broke the pact. I don't care. I'm in love with your sister. Some people aren't meant to be just friends."

He coughs, sputters, then laughs. "I'm not in the least bit surprised."

Ten minutes later, I pull up to the curb outside

Nadia's house, turn off the car, and call her as soon as I hit the sidewalk.

She answers right away, sounding breathless. "Hi, what's going on?"

"Wait. Are you going somewhere?"

"I'm in the elevator. I was going to see you."

I grin like it's going out of style. "Talk about lucky socks. I'm right here, waiting for you to buzz me in."

Thirty seconds later, I see her through the glass door, coming through the small lobby, a wild smile on her face.

She lets me in, and I lift her in my arms, kiss her gorgeous mouth, and say what I should have said yesterday morning. "Screw adulting. I'm in love with you."

32

CROSBY

Nadia wraps around me like a koala, her legs around my hips, her ankles hooking over each other behind my back, her arms around my neck.

I couldn't be happier to have her go all marsupial on me.

Still, I tip her back so I can look her over. She's absolutely adorable in a peach hoodie, jeans, and Converse sneakers.

"Were you going to catch a Lyft or something?"

She nods, laughing and smiling. "Told you I was going to see you. And yes, I better cancel the Lyft. But first I just want to say, adulting sucks." She drops a kiss onto my lips. "And I am stupid in love with you. I don't care about timing or how things are supposed to happen. I don't care about dating in a certain way or certain order."

The beautiful admission spills out of her in a fantastic rush.

A rush that makes my heart thunder, and my happiness meter redlines, going off the charts. "You're taking the words right out of my mouth, sweetheart. I don't care either. I was so caught up in my old mistakes that I didn't realize till tonight that leaving things between us as just friends would've been the biggest mistake of all."

"I'm so glad you're here," she says, roping her arms even tighter around my neck. "I was going after you to tell you that too, because I'd be a fool to let you go without saying how I feel."

"Let's not be fools," I say softly.

She kisses the corner of my lips. "Let's not." She pulls back, a brow arching. "But I should cancel the Lyft."

I set her down, she grabs her phone from her back pocket, and a few taps later, she proclaims, "Done!" and slams her body against mine, snuggling up against me. Holy hell, I love this woman's affection. I love how she wants to get close.

"Do that again," I murmur.

"I want to do everything with you." She presses harder against me, then gazes up at me, her tone going all vulnerable and thoroughly sweet. "This is what I realized this weekend—I wanted a relationship like Eric and Mariana have, or Brooke and David, or my mom and dad. I thought we needed to do it that way. How they did." She pauses, takes a breath, and smiles once more. "But you and me, we can do things our own way."

"We sure can, sweetheart," I say, buzzing with possibility as I brush another kiss to her lips, savoring the moment, the contact, the connection. "We can do everything our way. And I just hope you'll forgive me for being so stupid yesterday," I say, sliding my hands up her back, never wanting to stop touching her.

"There's nothing to forgive. I agreed to be all adult about it too. What a ridiculous idea," she says with the most adorable eye roll.

I laugh. "So ridiculous."

My right hand slides into her hair. "God, I love your hair. It's so soft and fantastic, and I just want to touch it and touch you and kiss you and taste you and make love to you."

"Well, you went pretty quickly from 'so ridiculous' to wanting to bang me," she says, a little saucy. Or maybe a lot.

"That's the thing, Nadia," I say, squeezing her hips. "I want everything with you. I want all the things. And I can't believe I thought we had to stop. But I hope you know the reason was that I love you so damn much. So much that I was terrified of messing this up." I watch her, making sure she knows that, though we can have fun anytime, I'm dead serious now. "I let you go because I wanted to ensure we could have something someday. I didn't want to risk messing up the best thing that's ever happened to me." I lift a hand, stroking her cheek. "You're the best thing, and you have been happening to me for *years*."

This is the truth I've learned in the last week with her. I was drawn to bad girls, but only because I'd been missing a piece of my heart for the longest time.

I'd surrendered it when this gorgeous woman went

to prom with another man. When I felt the first inkling of jealousy over the mere possibility of something.

Ever since, I've been looking for that *something* in all the wrong places. But ever since Nadia gazed at me with those wide, vulnerable eyes, I've known that she's the lost treasure I've been searching for.

"It's been years for me too." She cups my face, sliding her thumb along my jaw. In those brown irises, I see my long search reflected back at me, all my hopes echoed. "It hit me at the rehearsal dinner—I've had a big crush on you for a long, long time." She sounds giddy with happiness. Her eyes glisten with it.

I lift my thumb, swiping away the hint of a tear. "Don't cry, sweetheart."

"It's because I'm happy. Because this is crazy and amazing and wonderful. That's what I realized at the dinner—how much I care for you, how much I feel for you. And I've kept realizing it over and over again. But it's not teenage you. It's who you are now, the man I've come to know in the last week. It's the way you talk to me and laugh with me and tease me and take care of me. It's the way you touch me and hold me and want me. It's the way you understand me."

I beam from deep within. "I love everything about you, Nadia. And I've loved getting to know the woman you are now. That's the woman I'm in love with. So the last thing I want to do is get on that plane tomorrow morning with us on hold. I don't care if I'm gone for a month. And I know I'm on the road a lot, but I want you to be mine and I want to be yours, no matter what."

Laughing, she presses another kiss to my lips.

"There's FaceTime, and sexting, and phone calls. And then when you come home from a week on the road, there's super-hot homecoming sex."

I growl, my eyes narrowing, lust tearing through my body. "I love your dirty plans for us."

"I've got dirty plans for us tonight too."

I thread my hands through her hair. "Ask me to spend the night, and I'll say yes."

"Spend the night."

It's more of an order than an ask, but I'll take it.

* * *

Even though we nixed the whole friends-with-benefits scheme, we're definitely friends still, and we're definitely enjoying the benefits.

For instance, my cock is benefiting right now from Nadia's eagerness to try a new position. She climbs over me in bed, having already stripped me to nothing in record time. Straddling me, she sets her hands on my chest. Then she slides her wet pussy against the hard ridge of my cock. Back and forth, silky and hot. Over and over. Closing my eyes, I groan in pleasure. "You better not tease me all night long, sweetheart."

"But what if I do?" she purrs.

And really, what if she does? "Fine, fine. Tease me all night. I'm yours."

She rocks her hips up and down along my shaft, her breasts swaying, her hair flowing. She's an eager vixen, ready to explore all this new terrain.

Electricity sparks along my neurons as heat builds and builds with each luxurious swivel.

But then she slows her moves and presses her hands harder against my chest, clearing her throat. "Do you have any tips for this position?"

I love that she's unafraid to ask questions. It does remind me, too, that sometimes I might need to teach her. Don't mind that at all.

"Go slow when you take me in," I tell her, running my thumb over her lower lip.

She nips my skin. "Okay, I can do that."

"Because it's new to you. That's all. And if you don't like it, just tell me. We'll adjust. I'll adjust."

With a relieved nod, she reaches for a condom on the nightstand. She scoots down me, opens the wrapper, then stares at it like it's a one-thousand-piece puzzle, one of those brain-breaking ones where every piece is the same color.

With a laugh, I take it from her. "We'll practice condom stuff another time. For now, I'll take care of wrapping it up," I say, rolling the protection down my shaft.

"Maybe next time we won't need it," she says in a sultry bedroom voice. "I'm going on birth control."

I jolt with pleasure at the prospect of fucking her bare. But fucking her covered is a gift too.

I hold the base of my dick, offering it to her. She moves over me, gripping my length at the same time then rubbing the head against her center.

Her eyes flutter closed, and a soft groan falls from

her lips. "Feels so good," she whispers as she takes me in the slightest bit.

Then more.

Inch by inch, she lowers onto me, her pussy like a tight glove.

My body shakes as she drops down.

We both gasp at how good this feels, how close we're connected, how much we want this.

Shuddering, she draws a deep breath, her hands gripping my chest, her fingers playing with my nipples. She's quiet at first, and still. Adjusting maybe.

Or possibly savoring, judging by how her eyes darken, float closed, then open again. How her breath stutters.

Then, she bends closer.

Moving and swaying, taking and giving.

As my body heats up, I let her set the pace, let her find the rhythm that she needs.

Because I've got everything I want right now. I've got her, on me, with me.

Soon enough, we're moving in tandem, gasping and grunting, sweat slicking between us, skin burning up. Her noises intensify, pitching up, lasting longer, her moans like a dirty song, like filthy music to my ears as she rides me.

My hands slide up and down her back, traveling along her soft skin, threading through her hair.

As we tangle together, I'm grateful, so damn grateful, that we're here tonight, before I leave, enjoying every second of loving and fucking, fucking and loving.

And coming as one. That's what we do, reaching the

edge, blasting off, a blur of heat and pleasure, of sounds and cries. Of bodies and hearts crashing into each other.

After we both gasp and laugh and pant, I let out a long, happy sigh. "Even though we're not doing the friends-with-benefits thing anymore, I want you to know I have never enjoyed the benefits as much as I do with you."

Her eyes twinkle with mischief. "Maybe that's because we're friends and lovers."

"Yeah, I'm pretty sure that's why. And there's nothing accidental about that."

A little later, she falls asleep in my arms, something I hope she'll do every night when I'm in town. That's how I want this to be with us. This new *us*. Every day, every night.

* * *

In the morning I wake at the crack of dawn, take a quick shower, and pull on my clothes. She's brushing her teeth as I zip up my jeans.

Seeing me dressed, she spits out the toothpaste. "So, I guess this is it?"

I look at my watch, my heart heavy because I have to go but full because, well, we're in love and it is fucking awesome. "I've got a plane to catch."

She turns off the faucet, sets down the toothpaste, and walks over to me, sliding her hands up my chest. "So, this is us? We're, like, a thing now?"

I grin, beyond confident when I tell her, "You're mine. Don't even try to get out of it. I'm going to call you and text you from Arizona every day. When I get back here, I am going to be so goddamn horny and wound up that I'm probably going to spend the entire night going down on you, fingering you, fucking you, making love to you."

She shimmies her hips. "It'll be more than a month, so I'll pretty much be like a virgin again."

I laugh, cup her cheek, and kiss her mouth. "I love you, Wild Woman."

"I love you too, All-Star."

* * *

Three hours later I'm at the airport, duffel checked. I walk to the gate where the team plane is parked.

Lily Whiting, the reporter from the Sports Network waits, press pass around her neck. She's here to interview some of the team before we head to spring training.

Good. I've got something I need to say on camera. When Lily strides over to me and asks if I'm ready, I say yes.

Her camera guy mics me up, then Lily asks me a few questions about the upcoming season. As Chance and Grant wait a few feet away, arms crossed, watching intently, I tell her the things I want to work on, what the team needs to do to win, what I'm most looking forward to. Then I make good on my promise.

"And mostly what I'm looking forward to, Lily, is working with Chance Ashford and Grant Blackwood," I say, gesturing to my teammates. "Have I mentioned that those guys are absolutely the most talented players in all of baseball? And so is Holden Kingsley of the San Francisco Dragons. They're the best. They're better than me," I say, since those were the terms of the pact. The one that I broke. The one I'm damn glad I broke.

Lily gives me a curious stare. "Those are things you don't hear very often from athletes about other players, especially their rivals."

I meet the eyes of my friends, who are slack-jawed but clearly amused.

"True. But sometimes when you know the truth, you've just got to say it aloud. And they are the absolute best." I grin, grateful to be giving this confession because of what it means. What I have because of it.

She turns to the camera. "And there you have it."

I thank her and head onto the team plane with my guys. Grant claps me on the back as we walk down the Jetway. "So, we're the best?"

Chance cuts in. "He said it. He must mean it."

"Of course I mean it," I say as we step into the galley.

Grant shoots me a skeptical look. "Or maybe you're just madly in love."

I toss a glance at my teammates, shrugging, smiling, owning it. "There's no 'maybe' about it. I absolutely am."

Soon the plane takes off. I glance at my feet and tense when I realize I forgot to pick out a pair of lucky socks for today. I'm wearing basic, ordinary dress socks with my suit pants.

But then I relax because that's okay. Because socks don't make the luck. You make your own by finding what you love and making sure you're not too superstitious to let it get away.

I send a text to the woman I adore.

Crosby: Just so you know, I'm not crediting the corgi butts for the way I feel for you. It's you. I am crazy in love with you. Also, your butt is cuter than any corgi's.

EPILOGUE

Nadia

About A Month Later

Here's the other issue I have with dating sites.

Nowhere do they mention that long-distance love affairs are worse than dental exams.

Okay, fine. There are a *few* benefits. The first time you have Skype sex is crazy hot.

And okay, the second, third, fourth, and fifth times are incendiary too. I have a family of little darlings and big darlings, and Crosby likes watching me use them all. Maybe I'm shameless, or maybe I just know what I like, but this show-and-tell does the trick for me along with his words as he urges me on, as he talks dirty to me and sends me over the bunny-hopping cliff.

Plus, in his hotel room on the other end of the

camera, my boyfriend looks smoking hot when he takes his thick cock in his hand, slides his fist up and down, and gets himself all the way off, telling me the things he wants to do to me when he returns to San Francisco.

I haven't visited him in Arizona. The timing hasn't lined up. My work schedule prepping for the next season has been insane, but Matthew and I hired the GM we wanted, and Kim is doing a fantastic job.

One evening over a late dinner, my English friend and I toast to how we're slowly but surely winning new fans before the season even starts, thanks in part to Kim's masterful chess play with athletes and the deals she's inked for a new rising star tight end and a fantastic defensive lineman, among others.

"Admit it, we're brilliant for hiring her," I say, lifting my wineglass.

"We are the most brilliant," Matthew quips.

"And we're going to deliver a Super Bowl win, and then just imagine—you won't have to take wine-and-painting classes to meet new women," I say, before taking a drink of the chardonnay. "They'll fling themselves at the Hawks CEO."

He cracks up, then sets down his glass of red, his expression suddenly serious. "Maybe I won't have to wait till then to meet someone new."

My eyes widen. "So, does that mean Phoebe's history officially?" I knew it was ending, winding down every day, it seemed. But I hadn't yet heard that his relationship was on the chopping block.

"Don't look so happy. But yes. Earlier this week she said she'd had enough, but truth be told, I had too. She hated my job. She wanted me to quit." He sounds matter-of-fact, but I know it's not easy.

I narrow my eyes, huffing. "I'll never let you go."

"You better not. Because I don't want to go."

"Good. I'll just have to make it my mission to find you a fantastic new woman in this city."

"You really think I should start dating again?" He sounds skeptical. "I was mostly joking about the wine-and-painting thing. I'd honestly just go for me."

"I get why you wouldn't want to date again. But I know you. You like being with someone. When it's right, that is."

"And how would I know if it's right?"

I smile, answering from the heart. "If it feels too good to be true, but it's completely true."

"Sounds like a movie."

"Yes, and sometimes stories like in the movies come true. If you put yourself back out there."

He takes a beat, perhaps considering it, then nods. "Maybe I will, then."

I clap once, glad for my friend. "Let's see. Where do I know a fun, chatty, bighearted single woman?"

He laughs. "Nowhere, because they don't exist."

"Hush." I hum thoughtfully. "Maybe Crosby knows someone."

Matthew laughs doubtfully, a twinkle in his green eyes. "I'm sure your baseball star beau knows loads of single women."

He has a fair point. Except wait a second. "I might know someone." I lean closer and whisper, "I'll find out if she likes wine and painting."

"You do that."

* * *

The day that spring training ends and my guy boards a flight back to the Bay Area, I'm a certifiable jackie-in-the-box, ready to spring with desire the second I see him. Just a few more hours now.

It's a Friday night, and I head out to dinner with my family. Eric and Mariana. Brooke and David. My mom and her new beau, Craig, who loves to chat about '70s music and is completely adorable.

Over apps and dinner at a restaurant near my place, we catch up on what everyone's been up to for the last few weeks. During dessert, Eric lifts his fork to take a bite of the tiramisu, then clears his throat, meeting my gaze. "I guess all you're waiting for is to see my best friend tonight?"

With a delicious grin, I nod. "I am indeed."

Brooke laughs. "Yeah, she's only been checking her phone the entire meal."

I shoot her a stern look. "I have not been doing that."

My mom purses her lips like she's holding in a smile. "You kind of have, Nadia."

I hold up my hands in surrender. "Do you blame me?"

"No. I completely understand," Brooke says, sliding her hand down her husband's arm.

David blushes then drops a kiss onto her cheek. "I don't blame you for wanting your hands on me."

My family is full of perverts, apparently.

Including yours truly.

At the end of the meal, I nearly jump out of my seat, that much closer to seeing Crosby. I make my goodbyes and walk the few blocks home, enjoying the night air, the hint of a warm breeze as March nears its end in San Francisco.

I relish being home. I thought I would miss Vegas, but I don't. This is where I was meant to be.

With family, with new friends, with a job I absolutely stinking love.

And with a guy I've known for so many years but am getting to understand in a new and incredibly wonderful way.

Maybe this is what the universe had in mind after all.

Or maybe, just maybe, I made sure I wasn't fool enough to miss my chance when it came.

An hour later, the blue-eyed, crooked-grin-sporting, steady-handed third baseman and all-around good guy strides through my door, cups my cheeks, and kisses the hell out of me.

I melt into his arms, kissing him back just as hard, just as hungry.

Just as desperately.

It feels so damn good to share this wild, wonderful want with him. I tug on his shirt, drag him to the bedroom, and rip off his clothes.

"I guess I know what you missed the most," he says, his voice a naughty rasp.

"Find out just how much," I say, my hands racing over his skin.

And oh, he does find out. He moves over me, sliding into me, and, for the first time ever, filling me with no barriers between us.

We're even closer like this, even more connected. It's electric bliss, it's supercharged lust, and it's mad, passionate love as we come together.

When we're done with round one, I drag a hand down his chest. "About your cousin Rachel," I say.

"What about her?" He tilts his head, curious.

"Well, you said she had a jerk of an ex and liked to keep herself busy by setting other people up."

"I did say that."

"I happen to have a very good friend who's newly single and is a great guy."

"You don't say," he says, catching my meaning.

"Maybe the matchmaker needs us to play matchmaker," I say, then I tell him more about Matthew and he tells me more about Rachel, and we decide they'd be perfect for each other.

He sends her a text, and I send one to Matthew, and a few minutes later, we've arranged a blind date for them.

"Now that we've accomplished that, I was thinking we might need some new rules for us," I say with a smile.

He kisses my shoulder, dragging his lips along my warm skin. "And what would those be?"

"That we have lots of sex," I say.

"Rule one," he says with a roll of his eyes.

"That we keep asking for what we want," I add.

"Rule two."

"And that maybe I buy your team," I say.

He cracks up. "You're joking?"

I laugh too. "I am."

"Okay, here's my rule, then," he says, his tone going serious.

I push up on my elbows, letting him know I'm paying attention. "Hit me up."

He strokes my hair then grazes his thumb over my jaw. "You let me keep on loving you."

I kiss his lips, whispering the only possible answer. "Yes."

Then, I get out of bed and grab a gift from the bureau. Sinking back onto the mattress, I give him a pair of chipmunk socks. "For the season. They'll be your new lucky socks. Just don't wear them during sex."

He cracks up. "Why would I wear lucky socks when I'm already getting lucky?"

Sounds like we have a deal.

EPILOGUE

Holden

It's a beautiful night in April when Crosby swings by and picks me up to head to an event at the Legion of Honor. Chance is with him too, so we make our way over to the cocktail party benefitting a number of local charities.

Along the way, my agent calls to let me know the Dragons finally hired a new manager.

"Perfect timing. Opening Day is only . . . tomorrow."

"Better late than never," he says, then gives me details on the guy. He has a good resumé, and I met him once. He made quite an impact.

Something that had been weighing on me just turned into something awesome. "Excellent choice," I say to Josh.

As I head into the Legion of Honor with my buds, I tell them all about the new manager.

"Sounds like the baseball buddha," Crosby says.

I'm grateful to have made good friends in town, and to be playing for a team that's looking up. I'm determined to do everything I can to keep up the hard work. Nothing can get in my way.

Except, once I head into the event, a familiar silhouette walks into my line of vision.

Blue eyes. Blonde hair. Full lips that I know so well. Lips I explored late one night nearly two years ago. Is it really her? My what-if woman? The one I haven't been able to stop thinking about. I take a step closer. She turns to me. Eyes lock. Skin tingles. It's her. In the flesh. In person. In the same damn town once again. This feels like the start of a second chance.

The woman I've never been able to get out of my head.

ANOTHER EPILOGUE

Crosby

A year later

It's been a hell of a year, and I can't complain.

I didn't even need lucky socks to make this fantastic season happen.

I still wear my chipmunks, only they're not the be-all and end-all anymore. They're just fun, something I enjoy.

Chipmunk socks, flamingo socks, donkey-wearing-glasses (aka the "smart-ass") socks . . . Nadia gives me a new pair every month. I give her gifts too.

Every time we go to an event, I give her a new wrap.

Other occasions call for lacy lingerie.

And sometimes she opens a box of shoes from me,

since I'm pretty damn good at picking out sexy-as-fuck heels for my woman to wear.

Like, say, when I bend her over the bed, the couch, or the table.

Life is good. We make ample use of her toys, her furniture, and all my tuxes—because we have lots of events to attend.

We're one of those *well-known couples*. The billionaire team owner and her all-star boyfriend. I don't mind playing second fiddle to this power broker. I happen to find power in a woman an aphrodisiac.

Other men might be intimidated by the size of her . . . wallet.

Other men are not me.

Besides, I know what I do to her in the bedroom—and out of it. She lets me take care of her in every way, and that's all I want.

Tonight, I don the chipmunks with my tux for the awards ceremony where Nadia's general manager will be honored. Nadia couldn't be prouder. Kim has accomplished a ton in the past year—logging a terrific season, snagging wonderful players, and winning back tons of old fans while gaining new ones.

I drop my phone into my jacket pocket and head to the front door of her place, picking up her purse for her as she scurries to join me.

I stop in the doorway, then smack my forehead, like I forgot something.

"We can't leave without me giving you the gift I picked up for you for the awards event," I tell her, all bossy.

She's frazzled, rushing, wanting to get out of here. "Okay. But can I open it in the car?"

I shake my head. "Nope. You've got to open it now because you're going to want to wear it to the event."

She laughs. "You're right," she says, glancing at her bare shoulders. "It's cold in San Francisco, and you always give me the best wraps."

"I do indeed."

But I don't have a wrap for her tonight.

Instead, in her doorway, the same place where I kissed her ravenously the night we set the rules, I drop down to one knee, take her hand in mine, and speak from the heart. "Nadia, do you remember that night a year ago when we went to the Sports Network Awards?"

She blinks, whispering, "I do." Her voice trembles, and I love that sound, love the way she wears her emotions so visibly.

"That was the night we really came together," I say, vulnerability in my tone. But certainty too. "That night we started to acknowledge everything that was happening between the two of us," I say, my chest filling with warmth, with clarity. "That was the night we admitted we felt something for each other, and we didn't stop. We didn't let things like rules or guidelines get in the way. We made our own rules every single day."

With a smile that could light up the city, she squeezes my hand. "We sure did make our own rules."

I draw a steadying breath. "I want to keep making up rules and breaking them with you. I want to keep loving

you and making you happy. I want you to be my plus-
one, my partner, my friend, my lover, and my wife. Will
you marry me?"

With tears already streaming down her gorgeous
face, she falls to her knees, wraps her arms around me,
and says, "Yes. I have been so ready to marry you for a
long, long time."

"Good," I say, glowing, joy filling every cell as I take
out the box from my pocket, flip it open, and enjoy the
hell out of the way she gawks.

It's quite a ring.

It's big, bright, and contains all kinds of carats.

It fits her.

She's a woman of the city. When she goes to meetings, to conferences, to dinners, doing her badass thing,
I want everyone to know she's taken in a big way.

The way I'm taken too.

With her.

I slide the ring on her finger, and she stares at it,
awestruck. "So now I'll be plus-oneing with my groom?
Is that the romantic comedy that Hollywood is going to
make about us?"

"They are," I say. "And spoiler alert—it has a happy
ending. Every day and every night, it has a very happy
ending."

Just like us.

THE END

Interested in the other guys? They all have passionate, sexy love stories too. Holden's story with the new coach's daughter bats next in *The Virgin Game Plan.* After that, Grant and Declan's epic love story spans five years in the "Men of Summer" duet—*Scoring with Him* and *Winning with Him.* And finally, Chance's romance with Grant's sister Sierra comes in *The Virgin Replay.*

But wait, there's more!
Here's a little something extra—a bonus scene featuring some supporting characters you might be wondering about.

Matthew's Epilogue

All couples seem to like to play the same game. The let's-set-up-our-single-friend one.

Nadia's been champing at the bit to play it ever since Phoebe and I split up. Tonight, I suspect she's going for the kill at the Spotted Zebra in a one-two punch.

One being her, two being her beau.

"So, Crosby and I have this idea," she begins, setting down her drink.

"Sweetheart, it's pretty much *your* idea," Crosby puts in.

"That's not true. It's definitely *our* idea," she says, chiding him.

"Nope. It's yours. I'm just going along with it," he says, stretching out on the striped couch, flashing a you-go-first grin at his woman.

I make a rolling gesture with my hand. "Serve it, Nadia. Clearly it's your idea and I've got a feeling I know what it is."

"You do?"

"I do," I say, smiling and waiting.

She rolls her eyes, then huffs out a "fine." She leans closer. "Crosby and I think you should go out with his cousin."

Crosby leans and kisses her cheek. "You do. You think he should."

"Are you saying you disagree?"

He shakes his head adamantly. "Nope. Not one bit. You're always right."

She kisses him back. "See?"

"I see he's been well-trained," I remark with a laugh.

Crosby lifts his glass. "Only way to be, man," he adds.

"In any case, I want to set you up with Rachel," she says, then tells me more about Crosby's cousin, and when Nadia's done, I have the perfect idea where to take her out on a date.

* * *

I'll admit it. I've developed quite an affinity for wine and painting. It's not simply because the classes are a great way to meet women.

I don't go there to meet women.

I go to Wine and Sip in the heart of Hayes Valley for two reasons.

One, dealmaking all day long requires some serious unwinding afterward, and any man who fails to recognize the need to say *fuck it all* to work for an hour or two will burn out.

I love my job, so I don't want to burn out. Ergo, wine and painting is necessary.

Two . . . hedgehogs.

I grew up with hedgehogs as pets.

They're literally adorable.

And all I wanted as a kid was to draw Daisy and Oliver, the hedgehogs.

Small goal, but it was mine. Unfortunately, I was total shit at drawing.

Like, literally my entire life. So I decided, why not actually try to engage the right side of my brain? All day I'm completely taxing the left side, analyzing, strategizing, inking contracts.

But once a week, the right side gets the attention.

Tonight, though, I'm not going to wine and painting alone, with my paintbrush and my deliberate but still pathetic attempts to craft a hedgehog, or an otter, or a penguin onto a canvas.

I'm going on a blind date.

It's been ages.

As I get ready, I know one thing for sure—it's time to ditch the three-piece suit.

I pull on a long-sleeve shirt and a pair of jeans, run my hand through my hair, and peruse my reflection.

Since I don't look the part of a sports executive, maybe she won't worry about the way my job can take up a ton of my life.

Maybe she won't even think about it.

"Right. Trick her. Good plan," I say to my reflection, shaking my head, trying to shake off Phoebe and the past. "Or maybe, just be yourself. Put yourself out there."

I repeat Nadia's words of advice. Reminding myself that Phoebe isn't every woman.

Phoebe was Phoebe, and Rachel is Rachel.

A writer.

A romance novelist at that. Apparently, that's why she was so fixated on setting up Crosby's cousin.

Well, let's see how this blind date goes with the romance novelist.

I leave my apartment, walk the ten minutes to Wine and Sip, and then wait outside.

I'm here early. I check my watch, then scan the street for her, though I don't entirely know who I'm looking for. All I know is she wears glasses.

I half expect her to show up all frazzled, like the stereotypical heroine in a chick flick. Wearing bright patterns or paisley and a knit cap, carrying a ton of bags, dropping papers on the pavement, her eyeglasses sliding off too.

She'll be late, and she'll apologize profusely while flashing a winning smile, and I'll pick up the papers and say it's not a big deal . . .

And holy fuck.

Is that her?

If so, she's nine minutes early, and she's . . . gorgeous.

With the fog rolling behind her, a brunette wearing electric-blue glasses click-clacks down the street in black boots, jeans, and a—who the hell knows—some kind of top.

I'm pretty sure my jaw comes unhinged.

I wasn't expecting her to be beautiful.

I didn't even ask to see her photo.

All I wanted to know was if she had a big heart and liked to talk.

Nadia said yes to both. So I said yes to the blind date.

Now here is the woman with blue glasses who is dressed simply, smiling, unfrazzled, early, and utterly lovely.

"You must be Matthew," she says when she reaches me.

"And you must be Rachel," I say, trying not to grin wildly. But failing completely.

"Last time I checked," she says. "But I could be pretending to be her. How would we know? We didn't even exchange photos. Was that a terrible idea?" she asks, all playful and endearing already.

"I guess we're just going to have to take a crazy chance that we're each other's blind dates. Though I did hear you paint a fantastic giraffe, so that'll be the proof, I suppose."

She narrows her chocolate-brown eyes. "Who's spilling all my secrets?"

"Can you believe it? But maybe you want to show me this terrific giraffe."

She mimes waggling a paintbrush. "I've got a paint-brush, and I'm not afraid to use it."

* * *

Thirty minutes later, we've finished our first glass of wine, and I'm admiring the neck on her animal, and she's admiring the spines on mine.

But not completely.

Actually, that's not admiration at all.

She's studying my painting like it doesn't add up. Pointing, she asks, "Do you think maybe your hedgehog looks more like a puddle?"

I pretend to be offended. "Are you kidding? That is a gorgeous hedgehog."

She sets a hand on my arm and laughs. *"Matthew."*

My gaze drifts down to her arm, then lingers there as she leaves her hand on me, like she's imprinting warmth through my shirt onto my skin.

I'd like her to leave her hands on me.

I'd like to get my hands on her too.

I'm equal opportunity handsy.

I point to her painting. "Well, I think your giraffe neck is more like a . . ." I trail off, still distracted by her hand on me.

"Like a what? Say it. You can't hurt me. I'm like a hedgehog with spikes that protect me."

I laugh, and this might be the most I've laughed on a date. Ever. "Fine. It really looks a lot like . . . well, a sausage."

Her lips part in an O. "You're the worst for not

complimenting my talent." Then she smiles at me and shrugs. "We're terrible at painting."

"That seems to be the case."

She lifts her glass. "But very good at wine?"

"I'm excellent at wine," I say, all confidence and deliberately sexy bravado.

"Well then. Want to go to a wine bar and just talk some more?"

I beam at her. "Let's ditch the giraffes and hedgehogs."

"It's so sexy when you talk about oddly shaped animals."

I lower my voice to a dirty rumble, playing up the phone sex voice. *"Penguins. Foxes. Squirrels."*

"Ooh, yes, tell me more, tell me more. It's all sexy in your accent."

* * *

Three hours later, we're still talking at the wine bar.

We talk about work, and the city, and music and family. "I'm glad you love your job," she says.

"Yeah? Why's that?"

"I love mine. I'd only want to be with someone who also loved his job. I think it's a great thing."

"I can't tell you how fantastic it is to hear that," I say, relieved, delighted, even.

"How fantastic?" she asks, all playful and flirty.

"Utterly, completely, thoroughly fantastic."

She smiles, sets her hand on my arm again, and says, "Good. Because it's all true."

And this might be one of those dates that's too good to be true.

At least I think it might be. I haven't had any dates like that.

Since we're getting on so well, I decide to go for it. To ask the important question. "Rachel, level with me. Is this date too good to be true?"

She narrows her brows. "Well, if I were writing a romance novel about this date, it would end with us discovering you're my boss, or I'm your boss, or you're secretly buying my business, or I'm secretly buying yours. Or maybe my brother doesn't want me to date you because you're a player, or perhaps I have amnesia and can't remember you tomorrow. Or the other option is I also own a tattoo shop and you just opened the competing one next door, and now we're mortal enemy rival ink shop owners."

I blink. Amazed. A little turned on, too, by how fast her brain works.

I'm more amazed at how quickly this connection between us is crackling with electricity.

With spark.

With desire.

I clear my throat. Adopt a serious expression. "Well, I suppose now is the time to tell you about my secret life as a tattoo shop owner. And my nefarious plans to buy your business. Thus, we clearly can't date."

She frowns. "I'm sad. First time I don't want my life to be like one of my novels."

My heart thumps harder. "So if this were your book, what would happen next?"

She leans in closer, the jasmine scent of her hair lingering near my nose. "We'd kiss."

Oh, do I ever like her creative mind. So I pick up the thread.

"But then I discover you're my long-lost . . . ah, fuck it."

I lift a hand to her face, cup her cheek, and lean in.

I pause when I'm inches away from her gorgeous pink lips, and continue the story in the only direction I want the night to go. "And the kiss wouldn't be too good to be true. It would just be so damn good."

I lock eyes with her, savoring the flickers of desire in her brown irises, enjoying the flush of her skin.

Her breath hitches. "It absolutely would."

I brush my lips to hers, gentle at first, a tease of a kiss.

She gasps, a sexy murmur that sends sparks racing across my skin and makes me wrap a hand more tightly in her hair, hauling her closer, kissing her a little harder, a little greedier.

I taste her lips and get to know the flavor of her kiss.

A little like wine and lip gloss, fantastic first dates and the possibility of even better second ones.

When I break the kiss, I make sure of the latter.

"Would you like to go out with me this weekend?"

"I would love to."

"But would that ruin the plot of your next novel?"

She shakes her head, grinning like she's as giddy as I am about seeing each other again. "In this case, I don't want life to imitate art. I just want to see you again, Matthew."

That's what we do that weekend, and a few days later, and the next one, and the next.

Because I'm learning that putting yourself out there again is worth it.

Some first dates aren't too good to be true.

They're true and real, and they become everything I could ever want.

Many months later, we go to Crosby and Nadia's wedding together, and as we dance, I have a feeling that we're going to be dancing together for a long time.

Maybe soon just like they are.

Just good and true.

ALSO BY LAUREN BLAKELY

FULL PACKAGE, the #1 New York Times Bestselling romantic comedy!

BIG ROCK, the hit New York Times Bestselling standalone romantic comedy!

THE SEXY ONE, a New York Times Bestselling standalone romance!

THE KNOCKED UP PLAN, a multi-week USA Today and Amazon Charts Bestselling standalone romance!

MOST VALUABLE PLAYBOY, a sexy multi-week USA Today Bestselling sports romance! And its companion sports romance, MOST LIKELY TO SCORE!

WANDERLUST, a USA Today Bestselling contemporary romance!

COME AS YOU ARE, a Wall Street Journal and multi-week USA Today Bestselling contemporary romance!

PART-TIME LOVER, a multi-week USA Today Bestselling contemporary romance!

UNBREAK MY HEART, an emotional second chance USA Today Bestselling contemporary romance!

BEST LAID PLANS, a sexy friends-to-lovers USA Today

Bestselling romance!

The Heartbreakers! The USA Today and WSJ Bestselling rock star series of standalone!

P.S. IT'S ALWAYS BEEN YOU, a sweeping, second chance romance!

MY ONE WEEK HUSBAND, a sexy standalone romance!

CONTACT

I love hearing from readers! You can find me on Twitter at LaurenBlakely3, Instagram at LaurenBlakelyBooks, Facebook at LaurenBlakelyBooks, or online at Lauren-Blakely.com. You can also email me at laurenblakelybooks@gmail.com